THE SCALES OF INJUSTICE

The Doctor Who *Monster Collection*

Prisoner of the Daleks
Trevor Baxendale

Touched by an Angel
Jonathan Morris

Illegal Alien
Mike Tucker and Robert Perry

Shakedown
Terrance Dicks

The Scales of Injustice
Gary Russell

Sting of the Zygons
Stephen Cole

Corpse Marker
Chris Boucher

The Sands of Time
Justin Richards

THE SCALES
OF INJUSTICE

GARY RUSSELL

BOOKS

3 5 7 9 10 8 6 4 2

First published in 1996 by Virgin Publishing Ltd
This edition published in 2014 by BBC Books, an imprint of Ebury Publishing
A Random House Group Company

Doctor Who is a BBC Wales production for BBC One.
Executive producers: Steven Moffat and Brian Minchin

Silurians originally created by Malcolm Hulke

The Random House Group Limited Reg. No. 954009
Addresses for companies within the Random House Group can be found at
www.randomhouse.co.uk

A CIP catalogue record for this book is available from the British Library.

ISBN 978 1 849 90780 4

Editorial director: Albert DePetrillo
Series consultant: Justin Richards
Project editor: Steve Tribe
Cover design: Two Associates © Woodlands Books Ltd, 2014
Production: Alex Goddard

Printed and bound in the USA

To buy books by your favourite authors and register for offers,
visit www.randomhouse.co.uk

INTRODUCTION

I clearly have a thing for reptiles. You see, I love all of Malcolm Hulke's stories unconditionally – between 1967 and 1974 he wrote some of the very best *Doctor Who* telly adventures of all time. Only two of these don't feature reptiles of some sort: *The War Games* (1969), which he co-wrote with Terrance Dicks, and *The Ambassadors of Death* (1970), which he reworked from David Whitaker's original scripts. OK, so *The Faceless Ones* doesn't either, but the villains are called Chameleons, so that'll do for me. But *Frontier in Space* has Draconians (and would have had a giant Ogron-eating lizard if the budget hadn't reduced it to an inflatable rubber duvet-monster). *Colony in Space* offers up a bizarre human-slicing robot that pretends to be a giant stock-footage lizard (come on, buy into this...) and of course *Invasion of the Dinosaurs* gives us the biggest lizards of the lot!! Huzzah for the reptiles.

But Mr Hulke's greatest contribution to *Doctor Who*, for me, was *Homo reptilia*, Earth Reptiles, the Eocenes, or – as we all really know and love them – the Silurians and Sea Devils. Huzzah for our three-eyed subterraneans and their fish-eyed marine cousins.

Viewers of the most recent breed of Silurians, as represented by the likes of Vastra, Alaya and Bleytal in modern *Doctor Who*, may be confused by the three-eyed Silurians in this book. Back in 1996 when *The Scales of Injustice* was originally published, the modern, humanoid-looking Silurians hadn't been imagined. But the story within makes it clear there are all sorts of variations in Silurian physiognomy, much as we humans have different skin colours, so it's quite possible to imagine scientists like Malohkeh running around in the background of the scenes with Icthar or Baal.

So, other than an overwhelming love of those cute ickle reptiles, why did I write this book? Was it a fascination with shady, undercover Government types represented here by their pre-Torchwood vault of alien tech? Was it my love of the Brigadier and, as a result of conversations with my late friend and fellow traveller Nicholas Courtney, a desire to fill in some background details of his home life and the pressures of running UNIT? Was it a determination to give Liz Shaw a (hopefully decent) send-off story? Or was it just my absurd obsession with tying up ludicrous threads of UNIT personnel, trying to give everyone possible a mention, however brief, amidst seeing Mike Yates win his promotion? Truth be told, it's all of those things mixed in with a lifelong passion for the Third Doctor's era, and my favourite season of *Doctor Who* – which was Jon Pertwee's first, broadcast in 1970.

It's also been pointed out that I seem to take a bizarre pleasure in killing people in this book in a variety of different, gruesome ways. Curiously, if I were to write this novel in 2013, sixteen years' practice and experience has shown me that I don't really like bumping people off. There are a good half a dozen characters herein that the 2013 Grussell would have left alive, because that's a far greater writing challenge. Killing characters is easy; justifying doing so is hard; using their experiences to change them rather than ending them, hardest of all, but definitely more rewarding. I'm not sure that this particular aspect of the novel is satisfactory. So yeah, apologies for the high body count. Put it down to youthful inexperience and an erroneous belief that that was what *Doctor Who* was about.

However, re-reading the story now, two things I am terribly happy with still make me proud. Firstly, the Vault, the pale-faced man and his two Irish Auton assistants (their stories continue in the currently out-of-print-but-maybe-one-day *Business Unusual* and *Instruments of Darkness*, both Sixth Doctor and Melanie Bush novels), a shameful example of a writer falling in love with his own characters, and yet I don't apologise for it because, well, I honestly think they're not half bad and interesting and justified their subsequent returns and expansions!

The other thing of course are the *Homo reptilia* (naturally I wouldn't dream of claiming it was me who reminded writer Chris Chibnall of the phrase when he was planning their 2010 return in *The Hungry Earth* but, um, it was). Drawing on everything Malcolm Hulke wrote, both in the TV stories *Doctor Who and the Silurians* and *The Sea Devils* (and the respective Target novelisations, which are glorious gems of books, possibly two of the greatest *Doctor Who* books ever published), I tried to weave an original story rather than a retread of what had gone before. Throwing in the development of both species' culture as seen in *Warriors of the Deep*, Johnny Byrne's 1984 sequel to both stories – a superb script maybe not realised on TV as successfully as it deserved to be – rounded off my research nicely. Everything I needed was there, I just had to put it all together. I'm incredibly proud of how the *Homo reptilia* function in this story, and if the reader gets a tenth of the feeling of civilisation, background and reality of these marvellous creatures, then I shall consider it successful.

And although mileage in your opinion of the Myrka on TV may differ, again I do hope you feel it deserves its place in this book, minus the less-than-successful prop seen on TV (by 'less than successful', I do of course mean 'laughably pants, frankly'). You see, I left nothing out!!

So let's sit back, and read on and if you really want to, you can start a tally of the outrageous (and irredeemable) continuity references that litter the book. At the time it was first published, reviewers uncharitably reckoned there were 'hundreds'. I reckon a mere ninety-nine, and a couple more…

Gary Russell
October 2013

This one's for Paul Neary and Mike Hobson.
It was fun while it lasted.

Memorandum

To: Professor Andrew Montrose
Research and Development
Department of Sciences
Cambridge University
Cambridgeshire

October 14th

Dear Professor Montrose,

Regarding the existing agreement between your Department and Department C19 of HM Government's Ministry of Defence, reference number JS/77546/cf.

As you know, C19 has, over the past few years, continued to subsidise a great number of individual projects and courses and co-sponsored a number of staff at your facility.

As per the above agreement, C19 requests four attachments to begin immediately at locations of our choosing. These simultaneous attachments are scheduled to run between twelve and twenty-four months.

The researchers we require are:

Richard Atkinson
Doctor James D. Griffin
Doctor Elizabeth Shaw
Cathryn Wildeman

Please inform the above that their attachments will be beginning on Monday 21st October. They will be collected by our representatives and taken to their place of work.

Please inform the attachees that to comply with the Civil Defence (Amended) Act (1964) they will be required to sign the Official Secrets Act (1963) before leaving Cambridge.

You can assure the attachees that they are not being seconded to work on any projects that they may find morally objectionable, including weapon-development programmes, military hardware design, or any related matters. Many thanks for your co-operation in this matter.

Yours faithfully,

Sir John Sudbury
Administrator
Department C19
Ministry of Defence

Sir Marmaduke Harrington-Smythe CBE
The Glasshouse

October 14th

Dear Sir Marmaduke,

Further to your requests stated in your letter of 23rd September, I write with two important points.

Firstly, the future of the private nursing facility known as the Glasshouse. We are pleased to confirm that we have extended your existing contract for a further eighteen months, effective October 31st this year. Our payments to you for this service have been increased by 2.3%, effective the same date.

You will, I'm sure, join with me in acknowledging that there have been teething problems; some while you were setting up this most essential service to our Ministry; others as we co-ordinated the necessary administration (specifically the use of the Official Secrets Act (1963)). However, the Minister now joins other members of C19, myself included, in feeling that we have reached a satisfactory standard of care and convalescence for our servicemen with injuries unsuitable for traditional hospital treatment, and with suitable respect for the total confidentiality required by this Department.

The second point is the one raised in your letter of September 27th, concerning the Glasshouse's requirement of better scientific staff to work on the materials we provide. To this end, we are subsidising your proposed redevelopment of the basement area into a laboratory, provided that only staff supplied by ourselves should be aware of its existence. In addition, four new members of staff will be supplied to you, paid for by this Department. The team will be headed by Doctor Peter Morley, with whom you may already be familiar through his work with the Department of Applied Sciences at Warwick University.

If you have any further questions, please contact me at your convenience.

Yours sincerely,

Sir John Sudbury
Administrator
Department C19
Ministry of Defence

Memorandum

FROM: Commander, British Branch, UNIT
TO: All Staff
REF: 3/0038/ALS/mh
SUBJECT: Scientific Adviser, arrival thereof
DATE: 24th October

I am pleased to announce the forthcoming arrival of Elizabeth Shaw to UNIT as our Scientific Adviser.

Doctor Shaw has been working with the highly regarded Montrose team at Cambridge for the last few years, and will be joining us on Monday 31st October. She will be answerable directly to myself and Captain Munro, and will be setting up our new scientific department. She will also work closely with Doctor Sweetman on medical matters.

I feel sure you will join me in welcoming Doctor Shaw to our organisation, and will give her all the help and support she needs during her period of adjustment. We all look forward to her becoming a valuable member of the team.

Brigadier A. Lethbridge-Stewart
Commander
British Branch, UNIT

Andrew Montrose
The Cupps House
Bridge Street
Cambridge

To: Richard Atkinson
        Doctor James D. Griffin
        Doctor Elizabeth Shaw
        Cathryn Wildeman

October 25th

Dear Colleague,

I enclose a copy of the letter I received today from C19. You've all known that this might happen, and it seems they finally want their pound of flesh.

All four of you will need a few days to sort out your lives and tie up your current projects. I don't know where any of you will end up, either as a group or not. Sorry. We're pretty much in C19's hands there. All I do know is that Sir John Sudbury is trustworthy. If he says the work's non-military, I accept that.

I'm sorry we probably won't work together again here at Cambridge. As you know I'm due to retire from here in May next year and I expect you'll be incommunicado for the next year or two. I'll keep a slice of cake for each of you.

Make the most of this opportunity. It may look a little Orwellian, but it won't be. Enjoy, my dears, enjoy!

Stay Hip and Cool.

Andrew

'Jesus,' coughed Grant Traynor into the darkness. The tunnel reeked of chloroform, condensation and antiseptic, plus a blend of amyls nitrite and nitrate, and urine. All combined together in a nauseous cocktail that represented something so horrible that he couldn't believe he was involved in it.

Why was he there? How could he have sunk so low that he had ever accepted all this? Over the last ten years or so Traynor had not only accepted but even taken part in events so abhorrent it had taken him until now to do something about it. At the time, it had just been part of the job. Now, he couldn't understand how he had ever participated in the operations without vomiting, or screaming, or raising a finger in protest.

Well, that didn't matter, now that he'd finally realised what had to be done. He had decided to blow it all wide open, blow it totally apart.

'Once I'm finished,' he grunted, as he tripped over another lump in the tunnel floor, 'they'll never be able to show their faces in public again.'

The papers. All he needed to do was to reach a telephone and tell the papers about the place. In three hours, he guessed, they would be there, swarming all over the laboratories, offices and, best of all, the cavern.

The cavern. That was the place he really wanted to see shut down. That was where all the horrors took place. Where some of the most evil acts ever had been performed, allegedly in the name of science, research and history.

'Yeah, right. Well, they'll be exposed soon. They'll—'

There was a noise in the dark. Where was it coming from? Behind him? In front? He had to strain to listen – the tiny amount of light in the tunnel was barely enough to enable him to see where he was treading, let alone yards ahead or behind. A snuffling sound, like an animal. Like a pig snorting out truffles. It sounded like the...

'Jesus, no! Not down here!' Grant moved a bit faster. 'They know I've gone. They've sent the Stalker down here! After me!'

The snuffling noise was nearer, and this time he could hear the growl too. A deep, slightly tortured growl that would send even the most ferocious Rottweiler scurrying for safety. And Traynor had helped to make it sound that way; he knew its limitations. Or rather, he knew that it didn't have any.

He must have got a good start on it. No matter how fast it could run, he reasoned, he had to be way ahead. But it could see far better than Grant Traynor could and it could see in the dark. It could track via scents; everything from the strongest garlic to the mildest sweat. He'd been responsible for introducing that particular augmentation, and he knew how effective it had been. Surely it had to know he was there. Surely –

But maybe not. Traynor stopped for a second and listened. Perhaps they were bluffing, hoping that hearing it in the tunnel with him would scare him, make him reconsider. To go back to them. Fat chance.

It was nearer now. That growl was getting louder. Much louder. Which meant it was definitely closing the gap between them. But how far behind was it, and did he have enough of a lead? He quickened his pace through the darkness, ignoring the intermittent pain when his outstretched hands cracked against the unseen stone walls.

'That's right, Traynor,' called a voice further back in the dark. 'We've sent the Stalker after you. Are you close by?'

Traynor stopped and pressed himself against the tunnel wall, as if the dark would protect him from the Stalker. They were murderers, all of them. What if someone else should come down here? Innocently? Mind you, Traynor considered, then he would have a hostage. They would never let the Stalker get an innocent.

Hell, *Traynor* was the innocent. He wasn't doing anything wrong. They were the ones doing something wrong.

'Traynor, come back to us.'

Stuff it, you lisping creep. As if I'd trust you. Maybe, Traynor thought, he should tell his pursuer what he thought of him and his bloody henchmen back in the Vault. Maybe – what was he thinking of? That would only serve to let the Stalker know where he was hiding.

It was definitely closer. But Traynor was positive that he couldn't be far from the gateway. And the chemical stench had to be confusing the Stalker to some extent. Surely…

'Traynor, please. This is so pointless. You knew when you signed on, when you signed the OSA, that you couldn't just walk away. We need you back, Traynor. Whatever your gripe, let's talk about it. You're too useful to us, to our boss, to lose you like this.'

Traynor smiled and let his head loll back against the damp wall. He smiled without humour. There was no way he was falling for that.

'Traynor?'

They were so close now. And that creep was down there, personally, with the Stalker. You're brave, I'll give you that, Traynor thought. Psychotic, twisted, malicious and evil. But brave.

But he wasn't going to let admiration stop him. He wouldn't let it hold him back. He simply couldn't. Getting out, spilling everything to the papers, was too important. It was too –

'Hello, Traynor.'

'Oh God.' Traynor could only see one thing in the dark – his own reflection caught in his pursuer's dark sunglasses. The same sunglasses his pursuer always wore whatever the weather, wherever he went, whoever he saw.

Traynor saw fear reflected back into his own eyes. The fear of a man caught by his immediate boss and the Stalker.

'I'm sorry, Traynor. You had your chance, but you blew it.'

Traynor was momentarily aware of a snuffling noise near his left foot, and then he was falling, and then the pain hit. He screamed, his mind filled with nothing but agony, as the Stalker bit cleanly through his lower leg. He fell, feeling himself hit the floor, his blood adding the scent of human suffering to the overpowering smells in the tunnel. Somewhere in the darkness, someone was chuckling. The last sensation to pass through Grant Traynor's mind was one of bitter irony as the Stalker bit deep into his side, tearing through flesh with genetically augmented fangs that he'd designed for precisely that purpose.

Liz Shaw stared around the laboratory at UNIT headquarters, gazing towards the jumble of test-tubes, burners and coiled wires. Then there were the less recognisable scientific artefacts, probably from other worlds, or alternate dimensions at the very least. Well, maybe. Whatever their origins and purpose, they were strewn in untidy and illogical designs all over the benches. Doing nothing except being there.

They annoyed her.

It was ten-thirty in the morning, her car had taken nearly thirty minutes to start, and it was raining. No, frankly she was not in the highest of spirits.

'The sun has got his hat on. Hip-hip-hip hooray! The sun has got his hat on and he's coming out to play!' The Doctor was singing out of tune, off-key and with little feeling for rhythm, tempo or accuracy but, Liz decided, it would just about pass a dictionary-definition test as 'singing'. Maybe.

She had been stuck in this large but rather drab UNIT laboratory for eight months now staring at the same grey-brick walls, the same six benches with the same scattered tubes, burners and Petri dishes for far too long. Liz told herself often that before her 'employer', Brigadier Lethbridge-Stewart, had whisked her down here she had been enjoying her life at Cambridge, researching new ways of breaking down non-biodegradable waste by environmental methods. It had been a challenge, one that looked set to keep her occupied for some years. Scientific advancement rarely moved fast.

Instead, she had fought a variety of all-out wars against Nestenes, strange ape-men, stranger reptile men, paranoid aliens and other assorted home-grown and extra-terrestrial menaces. Her initial and understandable cynicism about the *raison d'être* for UNIT had quickly given way to an almost enthusiastic appreciation for the unusual, unexplained and frequently unnatural phenomena that her new job had shown her. Her most recent assignment had pitted her against an alien foe not only far away the tropics but, via the Doctor's bizarre 'space-time visualiser', back and forth in time as well. UNIT had provided her with novel experiences if nothing else.

But as she twirled a pen between her fingers and left her subconscious trying to make some sense of the complex chemical formula the Doctor had scribbled on the blackboard during the night, three things were gnawing at her mind. How much longer she could cope with UNIT's sometimes amoral military solutions; how much longer she could cope with UNIT's cloak-and-dagger-Official-Secrets-Act-walls-have-ears mentality; and how much longer she could cope with UNIT's brilliant, sophisticated, charming, eloquent but downright aggravating, chauvinistic and moody scientific adviser.

Oh, the Doctor was without doubt the most inspiring and intellectual person (she couldn't say 'man' because that implied human origins, and she knew that to be wrong) she was ever likely to meet. He was also the most insufferable. And he needed Liz as an assistant about as much as he needed a bullet through the head.

Hmmm. Sometimes that analogy had a certain appeal…

'Are you in some sort of pain, Doctor?' asked the Brigadier, popping his head round the door of the UNIT laboratory, an unaccustomed broad grin on his face.

The singing stopped abruptly. Liz wanted to point out, as brusquely as she dared, that her employer had just said exactly the wrong thing. She did not get the chance. Instead, the Doctor stopped what he was doing with a sigh. Liz was none too sure exactly what he was doing, but it looked complicated and tedious, and she had decided ten minutes earlier not to enquire – the Doctor could be very patronising when he was irritable. And he was frequently irritable.

'Did you say something, Brigadier, or were you just releasing some of that pent-up hot air you keep in your breeches?'

The Brigadier crossed the lab, pointing with his favourite swagger-stick at the shell of the TARDIS, which was standing in the corner. 'Can't upset me today, Doctor. I've got my happy head on.'

The Doctor picked up his tools and turned back to the bench at which he was working. 'Oh, good.'

Liz decided some tact was called for. 'And why's that?'

The Brigadier turned to her and smiled. 'Because, Miss Shaw, today our C19 paymaster Sir John Sudbury is due here to tell us exactly how much money we're getting in this coming financial year.' He perched on the edge of a bench and leant forward conspiratorially. 'If we're really lucky, I might get a new captain out of it. Quite impressed with young Yates – fine officer material. Might even give you a pay rise.'

Liz laughed. 'Oh come on, I doubt the money gods are that kind.'

The Brigadier shrugged. 'Maybe not.' He nodded towards the Doctor, who was working feverishly as he quickly moved his equipment round, a soldering iron in one hand. 'And what exactly is he up to?'

Liz shook her head. 'I don't know. I came in this morning and he was seated exactly where I'd left him last night. I don't think he's slept a wink.'

The Doctor swivelled round, the hot soldering iron

pointing at them like some kind of alien weapon. 'My dear Liz, sleep, as a wise man once said, is for tortoises. And if you must know, Lethbridge-Stewart, I'm actually obeying your orders for once.' He got up, placed the soldering iron on its rest and let his jeweller's eye-glass drop into his hand. 'As usual, the two of you have been so absorbed in chit-chat that you've failed to notice an important omission from this lab.' He had crossed the room and was standing face to face with the Brigadier. Taking the military officer's swagger-stick, he twirled it like a magician's wand and tapped the side of his head. 'Worked it out yet?'

Liz stared around for a moment and gasped. 'That TARDIS console. It's gone!'

The Doctor smiled at her. 'Well done, Liz. Top of the class.' He shot a look back at the Brigadier. 'At least someone round here can use their eyes.'

The Brigadier shrugged. 'So where is it?'

'Back in the TARDIS?' ventured Liz.

'Right again.'

'Pah,' snorted the Brigadier. 'How'd you get something that big through those tiny doors?' He pointed at the TARDIS as the Doctor leant against it.

'Elementary, my dear Alistair, quite elementary. After our little sojourn in the Pacific Islands, and poor Amelia Grover's sacrifice to the future, you asked me to try and get the TARDIS working. Well, the console is back in there and I'm currently trying to restore functions to the dematerialisation circuit. Satisfied?' He walked back to the bench, took off his smoking jacket and laid it over a stool. 'Now, I have work to do.' He gave the Brigadier a last look. 'Goodbye, Brigadier.'

The Brigadier stood. 'Yes, well… I suppose I've got to make sure everything's ready for Sir John and old Scobie.'

Liz smiled. She had a soft spot for Major-General Scobie. 'When's the general going to be here?'

The Brigadier looked at his watch. 'Sergeant Benton's collecting him from his home about now. Will you join us for lunch? Cold buffet, I'm afraid, but the best I can offer.'

Liz nodded. 'I'd be delighted.' She threw a look at the Doctor's back. 'That's if there's nothing for me to do here?'

Without looking up the Doctor grunted something about idle hands, finger buffets and military officers admiring pretty legs.

'I'll take that as a "no" then, shall I?' She turned back to the Brigadier. 'Twelve thirty?'

'On the nose, Miss Shaw, on the nose.' He gave a last look at the TARDIS. 'Through those doors? Pah. One day I'm going in there to see exactly what he's spending UNIT funds on.' Picking up his swagger-stick and flicking it under his arm, the Brigadier marched out.

Liz crossed to one of the lab's huge arched windows and stared down onto the canal below. It had stopped raining and the sun was just breaking through the clouds. A colourful narrow-boat was navigating the lock, a tan shire horse waiting on the towpath, given a brief respite from providing the barge's horse-power. The morning seemed to be getting better. Liz smiled; she liked sunny days.

Behind her a low moan went up. Or singing, depending on whose definition one accepted:

'Raindrops keep falling on my head…'

Liz threw a clipboard at him and stormed out of the lab.

Daylight. Can't be done in daylight.

Night. It has to be night, or someone might see, might try no, *will* try and stop me. Can't let that happen.

So cold. Why is it so cold? The sun is up. Bright sun but it seems… further away? No, must be an illusion. But the sky. Look at the sky. A haze. Dust and dirt between us and the blue sky.

Air is dirty. This world is polluted. Probably irreversibly. Why couldn't they look after it better?

Ridiculous fools. Pathetic idiotic primitives. Cretinous Apes!

Once upon a time Jossey O'Grahame had been an actor. Once upon a time he had been Justin Grayson, star of stage, screen and radio. He had been there in the golden days of Ealing comedies, Lime Grove dramas and Riverside support features. He'd worked with Guinness, Richardson and Olivier in films during the fifties. He'd had to shoot a young Johnny Mills in *Policeman's Lot*, marry Jane Wyman in *The Game's Up* and assault Trevithick in *They Came from the Depths*. The sixties had been good to him, radio and television making the most of his talents.

'There's no higher responsibility than great potential,' his agent had once said. But then there'd been that scandal with the silly young model – he couldn't possibly think of her as an actress after he'd worked with the likes of Dors, Ashcroft and Neagle in that aborted comedy film about the power crisis, *Carry on Digging*. He'd been thrown off the Pinewood lot, his contract and reputation in tatters, and the production company had sued him for compensation over the scrapping of the film. And all because the little tart had written a stupid letter and taken too many sleeping pills.

The papers had proved to be fair-weather friends. Their coverage of the story had been relentless and unforgiving.

Eventually Jossey had 'retired' to the south coast and

had spent eighteen months touring the holiday camps, bingo halls and small clubs, rehashing old Galton and Simpson comedy material, until finally he couldn't take it any more, and his bank manager couldn't take any more of him. He was bankrupted, washed up for good.

So here he was, living in the cheapest bed-and-breakfast he could find, leeching off charity and the public purse. With no future, every day became the same. He spent his few waking hours watching the waves spray against the rocks at the foot of the local lovers' leap, clutching a bottle of cheap whisky, and wondering over and over again whether he should take the plunge himself.

As he stared once again at the endless ebb and flow below, and listened to the screeching of the seagulls as they circled over the small town below the cliff, Jossey knew that he lacked the courage to jump. Besides, this place was a lovers' leap, and no one had ever loved him, nor him them, so what was the point? He tugged his worn overcoat around his thin frame; it was cold for late March, and the wind across the cliff top was brisk and bitter. The half-empty bottle of whisky glinted at him, and he took another dram to keep out the cold, keep his spirits up. Something would happen to change all this, he was sure. His brief moment in the public eye wasn't over yet. One day, his name would be in the papers again.

There was a strange hissing sound. Had it been there a while, and he hadn't noticed it? It crossed his mind that there must be a car or motorbike parked behind him on the cliff top, and one of the tyres had sprung a leak. Hefting himself around, he was intrigued to see nothing. No car, no bike, nothing hissing. The wind whipped through the thin grass around his bench, but this was a different sort of noise.

'Who's there?' he muttered.

No reply. He peered down towards the edge of the cliff. Nothing. Maybe it was something to do with the old cottage a few hundred feet away, the one the hippies had taken over for midsummer a few years ago, when they released those pretty doves. Love, peace and harmony. Ha. No chance –

There it was again. Not really a hissing. It was more regular this time, like breathing. Perhaps someone else up from the town, then, come for a drink and a chat. The breathing of someone with a bronchial infection, too much smoking and drinking. He should know.

'Larry? Larry, is that you? Stop mucking about, would you?'

Then he saw it. And wanted to scream, but couldn't. All he could manage was a whimper as something caught all the noises in his throat and held them back. His eyes tried to take it in, tell his brain that it wasn't real. He gripped the bottle of whisky tighter, and something old and forgotten crawled into his mind.

Devilback! Run, run for my life. The Devilback is after me, they're all after me, yelling and screeching. Hissing and spitting, I can hear them… A net. I'm in a net, dragged backwards. Screaming. Mother. Father. Help me. No! No, don't let them touch me… don't let them take me back to the pen! I can't stand the pen. Left in the sun for days, no food or water, with my fur getting drier and mangier as the insects crawl all over it, in my eyes, ears and mouth. Can't get clean enough. No family. No friends. Just the growling of the Devilbacks. Must struggle, must get away from them, must scream…

Jossey O'Grahame saw the vision of half-remembered terror bend towards him, wobbling its… its head?

PAIN! Overwhelming pain and heat swept over him as

he felt his skin contract suddenly, growing too tight for his body. His mouth dried up, stalling a scream in his throat. His eyes hurt. His ears wanted to pop. The bottle in his hand grew hot suddenly, the whisky inside bubbling and steaming. He tried to let it drop but his hand seemed to be melted to it. With a frightening calmness, he knew that the pain in his chest meant that his heart had stopped working. He saw the face of his mother smiling. The bottle shattered, shredding his hand, spilling its boiling contents over his smouldering coat. He didn't notice.

And for a final flickering moment, Jossey knew for certain he'd never play Lear.

No! It can't be dead.

Only wanted to stop it making that awful noise Apes always made. This one had that look in its eye – millions of years later and still they fear us. An adult, this one, surely, so why did it try to make a noise? Young hatchlings, yes, but adults? Pathetic creatures. Maybe Baal is right, the best way to deal with vermin is to destroy. But Sula doesn't agree, says we need their DNA to help us. Who's right?

Curse Sula. Curse Baal, too – he wants a hatchling, he should get it himself. Instead, this Ape sees things it shouldn't and dies. The Apes always mourned their dead, so there will probably be a family of them here soon. Their telepathy is basic, mostly instinctive and empathic, but functional.

Nothing yet. Strange. Still, better hide. Yes, shelter there.

I sense nothing alive in it. Safe. Now to wait until nightfall.

*

Liz's day was getting better.

First off, she'd gone hunting for some spares for the electron microscope she was trying to improve. If there was one thing she'd learned from working with the Doctor over the last few months, it was how to cannibalise various 'primitive' scientific devices and rebuild, modify and generally improve them.

Mister Campbell, the stores-manager, had been more than happy to delve into his darkest drawers and cupboards to find what she wanted and load it all into a cardboard box for her.

'Always willing to help a fellow inmate,' he laughed.

Liz smiled back, thanked him for his time and left with her box, trying to ignore the slight crawling of her skin that she always felt when talking to the Scotsman. His predilection for what he thought to be harmless flirting with the few female UNIT officers and staff was renowned throughout the building. Carol Bell had been the first to warn her about Campbell's 'charms'.

'He's all right if you just grit your teeth and smile. Anything more than that and he'll take it the wrong way.'

Maisie Hawke, UNIT's chief radio operator, had concurred. 'There's so few of us that he's starved for attention. We tried complaining to Jimmy Munro once but he said he couldn't do anything about it.'

That, Liz decided, was typical of Captain Munro, who was now back in the regular army. Nice enough chap, but never one for confrontations or discipline.

It was on the way back from the stores that she'd thudded into a new young private, Boyle, who'd offered to take her box up to the lab.

'It's on the second floor,' she explained. 'Can you find it?'

Boyle had saluted in the way that all newcomers to

UNIT did a – combination of eagerness to please anyone who might be an officer even if they weren't in uniform, and pleasure at seeing a young woman about the place – and marched off with the box, muttering that he couldn't wait to introduce himself to the Doctor, about whom he'd heard so much.

For a top-secret organisation, Liz thought wryly, there's a lot of gossip about UNIT going on in the regular army. Still, UNIT probably wasn't considered the greatest of postings, and the rumours of danger and high casualty rates must far outweigh the truth.

On the other hand, UNIT's mortality rate was the highest of any section of the British Army, and some information about that was definitely in circulation – Liz knew of at least three privates who had requested duty in Northern Ireland rather than serve in UNIT. And Liz had to acknowledge that, to Lethbridge-Stewart's credit, he never attempted to strong-arm any of the soldiers who had made that decision; he simply accepted their refusal and moved on to the next potential recruit.

And now UNIT was being investigated financially. Liz had been aware from the day she had joined that UNIT was not as well funded as it ought to be. Special weaponry and the latest electronic gadgets, most classified as top secret, were the staple diet of Mister Campbell and his stores. Designing and prototyping these items cost what UNIT's opposite numbers in the CIA referred to as 'the big bucks'. The British branch of UNIT didn't have big bucks or even medium bucks, and while its equipment might be decades ahead of state-of-the-art commercial technology, it was lagging behind its rivals.

'Good morning, Miss Shaw,' said Mike Yates, carrying an armful of rifles.

She nodded back at the handsome sergeant, thinking not for the first time how his rather public-school good looks reminded her of some hero of a boy's comic from the fifties, or an Eileen Soper illustration of one of Enid Blyton's intrepid child adventurers. Mike and Liz had shared a couple of tense situations, and while Liz would never claim they were close friends, she did feel a certain bond with the young sergeant.

She remembered that the Brigadier had already asked for her opinion on Yates as possible captain material. If honesty, integrity and reliability were essential requirements for a military promotion, then Mike Yates fitted the bill perfectly.

'Where are you off to with that lot?' she asked, nodding at the armaments.

'Stores. Being put away for a rainy day.'

Liz frowned.

'Well.' Mike shrugged his shoulders. 'If we're on an economy drive to get more funding for UNIT, it struck Benton and me that the less hardware there is lying around and looking surplus to requirements, the better our chances of more dosh.'

'Hmmm. As a taxpayer, I'm not sure I approve.' Liz tapped his hand playfully. 'But as a poor overworked and underpaid lab rat, I appreciate it enormously.'

Smiling, Mike wandered off in the general direction of the Armoury. Liz watched him go for a moment and then continued on her own tour of the building, making her way to the Brigadier's office. She wanted a quick natter with him about the correct protocol in dealing with Sir John Sudbury – she'd never met the man, and a few pointers on what she should or shouldn't say to him could be useful.

After all, it was always best to keep on the right side of C19.

March 27th

I am so bored. This place is about the dumpiest dump Dad could find. I've been here two days now, and they've been two of the crappiest days I've known.

It's been a while since I wrote anything in this diary and I really ought to as my early memoirs are going to be a best-seller when I'm a famous politician and world statesman.

At least, that's what Dad always says. I'd rather be a singer or an actor or something exciting, but he says there's no money in it. Isn't there more to life than money? Mum always says that I shouldn't be asking things like that at my age, whatever that's supposed to mean. Mrs Petter says we're never too young to think about money and the good and evil it causes. Dad says she must be a 'bloody commie', but I think she's making sense. It's all very well to be loaded like Dad and the others in Parliament, but there are lots of people who aren't and Dad doesn't know what to do with half of his cash. Just before they sent me here, he bought a boat. I know he'll never use it. Steve Merrett called it a status symbol. I asked Dad on the phone last night what that meant, and he said Steve and his father were just jealous, and that next-door neighbours were scum. Which means Steve was obviously right.

'The Memoirs of Sir Marc Marshall OBE. Volume 2: Formative Years of Teenage Angst'. I wouldn't bet on it. But I've got going now, and there's nothing else to do here, so…

Why am I here? Bloody good question, Marc, I must say. Officially 'the sea air will do you good and Aunty Eve has been wanting you to visit ever since you were old enough to be on your own.' Yeah. Right. Truth is, Mum and Dad are having a month of be-nice-to-the-constituents, and every night it's barbecues, folding newsletters and postings, or endless meetings with various local groups. And I, of course, would get in the way.

Mrs Petter said that I should be proud that my Dad does something for the community but I think she was being sarcastic. Maybe that's what a bloody commie is – a teacher who thinks parents are one thing but tells their children the opposite. I'll ask Aunty Eve.

Anyway, this place is called Smallmarshes and it's in Kent. Apparently it's not far from Hastings, which Aunty Eve says is good for shopping, and Dungeness, which Aunty Eve says is good for nuclear radiation. I don't think she likes it. Come to think of it, I remember her and Dad arguing about nuclear reactors once. She's Mum's sister, and he's never liked her. He doesn't like me much either. Probably explains why he sent me here for the school holidays.

Steve Merrett's dad runs a newsagents down on Deansgate. His mum works in that big office block above the car park next to the Arndale Centre. She's a secretary or something. Why can't my parents be normal? Why does Dad have to be an MP? Why doesn't Mum go to work like everyone else's mum?

This afternoon I'm going to Dungeness to stand next to that nuclear reactor and get radiation poisoning and then all my hair will fall out and my skin will go green and I'll die and it'll be in all the papers.

Why?

Because it'll really freak Dad out. Yeah.

All right, working on the assumption that the average

14-year-old doesn't die from standing next to nuclear reactors – Aunty Eve's still alive and she said she tied herself to the gates of Dungeness once – I'll write about it later. Let's face it, there's nothing else to do here.

'Marcus?'

Don't call me Marcus. It's Marc. 'Yes, Aunty Eve?'

'Lunch is ready.'

Toad in the hole? Fish Fingers? Not Spaghetti Hoops on brown toast, please? Something with a bit of meat in it, or I'll die.

'You'll like this. Potato skins filled with cream cheese and red kidney beans. Get it while it's hot.'

Oh. Fab. Just what I wanted.

'Doctor Shaw, always a pleasure to see you, m'dear. How are things? Stewart looking after you properly, is he?'

Liz smiled at Major-General Scobie. 'Everything is fine, thank you, General.' She adored the way that the weasel-featured old general always called the Brigadier 'Stewart', as if refusing to acknowledge the UNIT CO's English heritage, purely because he knew it annoyed the younger man.

Scobie, Liz had decided on her first meeting with him some months before, possessed all the looks that casting directors would kill for whenever they wanted an ageing military officer. A tiny snow-white moustache gripped his upper lip, beneath a beaky nose that protruded from a thin face with cheekbones upon which you could rest teacups. Excursions to Burma during the war and a long posting with his late wife in Singapore during the fifties had left him with a permanent suntan that unfortunately looked as if it had come straight out of a bottle. But the best thing about him, Liz thought, was his steel-grey eyes that could reduce a new private to jelly with one glance. Experience would teach them that beneath the gruff exterior lived a virtual pussycat of a man; yet one who was fiercely loyal and dependable. A top-rate commander, Jimmy Munro had once called him, and Liz had learnt how right that assessment was.

Scobie and the Brigadier had some sort of love/hate relationship. Being a regular army liaison officer, it was Scobie's job to challenge and investigate Lethbridge-Stewart's every move, but Liz frequently felt sorry for the Brigadier. Old Scobie often seemed to play devil's advocate to the point of ridiculousness. Still, if it made UNIT more efficient and saved a few lives now and again, it was worth it. Deep down, Liz knew, the Brigadier agreed. But such was his character that he'd never let anyone know that – least of all Scobie.

Army men, Liz had decided long ago, were just overgrown schoolboys who had exchanged their catapults and stink bombs for mortars and guided missiles.

As she popped a cheese vol-au-vent into her mouth, she spared a glance at a newcomer, who was escorted in by Private Boyle. This was obviously Sir John Sudbury, a rather chubby man who had 'Minister for reducing cashflow' written all over him. Almost bald, except for tufts of hair around his ears, he had the ruddy complexion of a man whose liver wasn't likely to last another five years. His dull, red-rimmed eyes suggested long exposure to too much cigar smoke, probably wafting around whatever ridiculous gentlemen's club he and his friends frequented near St James's Street, SW1.

This rather grim impression was offset by a beaming smile that creased his heavily jowled face into something

Liz could only picture as the face of a drunken sea lion. He almost hopped across the Brigadier's office, arm outstretched, and gripped Scobie's hand. He began to pump it furiously.

'Scobie, old man, how the ruddy devil are you, eh? And Lethbridge-Stewart,' he continued without a pause, leaving Scobie silently mouthing a riposte. 'Good to see you again, old chap.' He swivelled around, waving to Boyle as he left, shutting the door. 'Splendid young man that, Brigadier. Polite, pleasant, chatty. Good to see your troops are up to their usual standards.' He swiped a vol-au-vent off the desk and swallowed it whole, pausing only to take a proffered glass of mineral water from Carol Bell as she offered it to him. 'Thank you, Corporal,' he mumbled, nodding at her as she smiled back. 'Splendid set-up, Brigadier, quite splendid.' His eyes rested on Liz. 'Ah, and who is this young charmer, eh? Didn't tell me you had even more young ladies around the place. Corporal Bell not enough for you, what?'

Liz knew she would normally be steaming at such sexism, but Sir John's manner was so buffoonish and inoffensive that she knew getting annoyed would be pointless. The old man hadn't a clue how sexist he was being. From the corner of her eye, however, she could see the Brigadier beginning to panic. Good, Liz decided. At least she'd got *him* trained.

'Sir John Sudbury, I presume?' Liz shook his hand firmly. 'My name is Elizabeth Shaw. I'm one of UNIT's scientific corps.'

'Of course you are, m'dear. Doctor Shaw isn't it, from Cambridge? Doctorates in chemistry and medicine, honorary doctorate in metaphysics and humanities. Plus assorted qualifications in economics, history and Latin.

Have I missed anything?'

'Apart from my sixteen-plus in metalwork, probably not. I'm flattered.' Liz found herself blushing. She coughed, trying to hide her embarrassment. 'That, and my research work into the paranormal.'

Sir John looked surprised. 'Really? I must have missed that. Been studying your file recently, have to confess. I've had to get genned up on all this space defence stuff ever since Jim Quinlan's death meant I had to take on his workload as well. Sorry, but it takes time.'

Liz nodded. 'Of course. Well, that last interest has only started since I began working here. I found I needed to… broaden my horizons somewhat.'

Sir John Sudbury scooped up another vol-au-vent and flopped into a convenient swivel chair. It creaked dangerously under his weight as he swivelled to face her. 'The Doctor's influence, no doubt. Marvellous chap.'

The Brigadier looked astonished. He shot a puzzled look at Liz but she had to shrug back – she had no idea that the Doctor had met Sir John.

'At the Pemburton club, Brigadier. Lord Rowlands' Gang of Four, you know. Excellent bridge player, your Doctor. We partner-up a lot.'

The Brigadier nodded dumbly while Liz tried to picture the Doctor, the great anti-establishment provocateur, sitting in a gentlemen's club in London, playing cards. The image was too horrible to cope with, so she just smiled at Sir John. 'Does he cheat?'

Sir John stared back in mock horror. 'Cheat? Young lady, are you suggesting that an honorary member of the Pemburton, and a guest of Lord Rowlands to boot, would cheat? Heaven forbid, he'd be expelled on the spot if anything like that occurred.' He finished off his mineral water with a grimace. 'Foul new stuff. Bloody French rubbish.' He looked back at Liz. 'D'you like it, Doctor Shaw?'

'Call me Liz, please.'

'Thank you, Liz. Can you drink this imported donkey's—?'

The Brigadier harrumphed loudly. 'Gentlemen, to business?'

'Of course, Stewart,' concurred Scobie, pulling his tie a bit tighter. 'We should be discussing UNIT's funding. That is, after all, why we're here.'

'Hence the mineral water rather than a decent Bolly, eh, Brigadier?' Sir John winked at Corporal Bell, who nodded discreetly and left. Liz smiled, knowing exactly what Bell was up to. She waited a few seconds herself and then quietly exited the room, shutting the door behind her. The three men had already sat around the Brigadier's desk and were shuffling their papers, eager to start the meeting. She wondered if they'd even noticed her leaving.

Standing in the outer office, Liz paused for a moment. She'd been hoping to talk to Major-General Scobie for a while longer. Since the Doctor did not seem to need her at the moment, there seemed no harm in waiting here until the meeting finished, and having another few words with the Brigadier's visitors. She settled herself into a large and well-worn armchair upholstered in red-leather, which sat beside the secretary's desk.

The low rumble of the three men discussing their financial business permeated the door. Liz found herself hypnotised by the rise and fall of the conversation, punctuated every so often by Lethbridge-Stewart's outraged expletives as yet another proposal for an additional truck or sergeant was denied by a government intent on cutting taxes in its next budget. She let her head lie back on the soft armchair and lifted her legs until they rested on the edge of the desk. She closed her eyes and let the drone of the voices carry her away.

God, she was tired. She realised that ever since joining UNIT's never-ending crusade against everything unusual she'd had no time to herself, her friends and even her family had all been ignored. When was the last time she'd phoned her parents? Or seen Jeff Johnson since he'd gone back to the regular army after his stretch in UNIT had ended? She'd not kept in touch with Justin and Laura at Cambridge despite all her promises to them; and no matter how many times she told herself it was all because of the Official Secrets Act, she didn't believe that any more than she knew they would.

Was she happy? Jeff had asked her that on their last night out. Was a role in UNIT, as nothing more than the Doctor's assistant, really what she wanted? Seriously, Jeff had been so furious at her. She had more brains than most of the UNIT team put together, he had said. And she couldn't give him an answer. Just why was she languishing in this backwater, tucked just outside London on the A40, when she could be heading research teams at Cambridge, getting recognition for her work, and doing something worthwhile for people? She could be discovering cures, learning the secrets of the world, pushing forward the frontiers of science.

And yet, she'd argued, wasn't that what her work at UNIT was all about? Mankind would have fallen to the Nestenes, or the terrible liquid gases that Stahlman had discovered, if UNIT hadn't intervened. And hell, even if the Doctor did most of the work, it was Liz who had eventually found the cure to the reptile-men's disease.

Not many people could have understood the Doctor's notes and made the same intuitive leap that he had. Nevertheless, Liz knew that deep down, she did agree that she was wasting her time at UNIT. Jeff was right. It was time for something to change.

The trimphone on Lethbridge-Stewart's desk trilled. She opened one eye, reached out and plucked it off its rest, nestling it under her chin.

'Yes?'

The Brigadier appeared at the door to his office, summoned by the ringing. He harrumphed and held out his hand, but Liz closed her eye and pretended not to have seen him.

'I see.'

The Brigadier harrumphed again.

Liz sighed and opened her eyes. 'If it was for you, Brigadier, I would have passed it to you the first time you grunted.' She shifted in her seat, turning to face away from him, unwilling to see the reaction on his face and wishing that she had thought before speaking to him so rudely. She spoke back into the phone: 'Sorry. Go on, Doctor.'

The phone tucked under his chin, the Doctor was wandering around the laboratory, staring through the window at the canal one moment, facing the huge green arched doors the next, then squatting on the spiral staircase that led to the little roof garden he kept above the lab.

'Liz, I cannot begin to explain to you how important this is. I've managed to reconnect the stabilising dio-nodes and the transceiving telo-circuits. All I need to do is feed in the directional memory wafers and weld the dematerialisation casing back into the artron filaments.

Then a few months of steady-state micro-welding and it'll be completely finished. Where would you like to go?'

'Cambridge,' came the reply.

The Doctor stared at the phone, screwing his face up in puzzlement. 'But Liz, what about Florana? Or the wonderful waters on Majus Seventeen?'

'Cambridge has wonderful waterways, Doctor,' came the reply. 'It'll be May Week soon. You'd like that. Lots of toffs on punts sipping champagne and playing bridge.'

'Liz it's June.'

'May Week's in June.'

The Doctor frowned. 'I'm confused. But all right, maybe Cambridge soon. But surely you'd like a spin off-planet. Somewhere out there?' He pointed toward the ceiling, knowing that, although she couldn't see him, Liz would imagine the gesture.

'No thank you, Doctor. I prefer to keep my feet on terra firma, you know.'

The Doctor shrugged. 'Oh well, suit yourself. I'm going back to work.'

He stared at the receiver for a moment, then put it down. Instantly the phone rang again. He snatched it towards his ear.

'Changed your mind, have you?' he asked.

'Hello?' came a man's voice; quiet, sibilant and clearly quite aged.

'Who is this?'

'Is Elizabeth Shaw there, please?'

The Doctor paused. 'Who's asking?'

'Hello? Is Doctor Shaw available, please?'

'I asked who is calling for her? Is that her father?'

'Is she there, please?'

'Look, who are you? How did you bypass the

switchboard? In fact how did you get this number?'

There was a faint click from the phone, and nothing more.

'Hello? Hello?' The Doctor replaced the receiver. It was unusual enough for him to get phone calls – very few people outside UNIT knew him but in all the time he'd been exiled on Earth and working in this lab, he couldn't remember anyone ever phoning for Liz before. Come to think of it, she didn't seem to have friends or family; none that she ever talked about, at least. Maybe a trip to Cambridge would do them both good – he'd offer to drive them up there in Bessie and try to meet some of her friends. 'I really don't know anything about you, do I, Miss Shaw?' he murmured to himself. 'Then again, I've never asked.'

He resolved to change that and, in doing so, put the memory of the strange phone call to the back of his mind.

From her vantage point overlooking the bay, Jana Kristen stared down at the policemen as they swarmed across the grass and sand dunes like flies around a corpse. Which, she decided, was roughly what they were. As a journalist it was her job to show an interest in anything unusual and, to be frank, in the sleepy backwater of Smallmarshes, a dead tramp was about as much news as you could hope for.

Like all good journalists, she had her notebook, micro-recorder and point-and-shoot Nikon camera with her. Right now they were lying behind her, on the uncomfortably hard bed in Room 9 of the Bayview Guest House. She was one of only three guests in the three-storey converted house; and the other two were out shopping. They were a young couple, obviously here without either parents' permission, who had told her they were looking for a week of romance and excitement. Hah! Like hell. They were here because they fancied each other rotten.

Pathetic.

Jana herself had once had what she thought were feelings for a man. She'd met him at home in Amsterdam, and they had spent a couple of weeks cycling around the countryside. She'd soon realised that, while anatomically well-developed, he'd been mentally stunted and she'd had to dispose of him. Witless innocent.

Pathetic.

She sat on the bed and stared at the painted wall opposite. Brilliant White (she could picture the Dulux tin now) over dirty wallpaper, with a hint of damp. Every room painted the same by the owners, a charmless couple called Sheila and John Lawson. Sheila was always going on about whatever faded television personality was working the fleapits in Hastings; John would nod and go back to reading his tedious newsletter of the Rollercoaster Passengers Club of Great Britain (inc. Eire). 'I'm trying to get them to set up a theme park in Smallmarshes,' he had enthused to her. Jana hadn't enthused back.

Pathetic.

'Better get some work done,' she muttered as she picked up her camera, slung it over her shoulder and popped her notebook into her bag, then left her room and jogged downstairs, hoping not to meet her hosts along the way. There was no sign of them, so she made her way to the coin-operated phone. Dumping a pile of change beside it, she dialled a London number and waited.

March 27th (still)

I'm on my way back to Aunty Eve's now. God, this train is

bumpy, which explains why my writing's so crappy.

So that was Dungeness. What a creepy place. You come out of the station near the seaside and walk down this long road that eventually vanishes. It's like one of those roads on an airfield, made in concrete segments. I thought I'd gone wrong until I found a row of small houses. Horrible things that looked like they'd blow over in a harsh wind. All grey and dreary, with a few clothes on lines in front. A few kids were playing with a dog, but that was it as far as life went. Then I found a lighthouse and a small café/shop.

And there was the Nuclear Power Station, blocked off with this massive metal fence. No one was friendly there at all, especially the guard. I asked if I could look around and he just said 'No' and that was it. There were more houses to the right of the power station. They looked like they'd been picked up from Salford or somewhere and dumped there. Terraces, made from ugly red bricks and in bad repair. More washing lines and dogs. No kids though. I grabbed a hot dog from the shop, went to look at the lighthouse couldn't get in there either and wandered down to the beach. Stones. No sand at all. It looked so desolate that all I felt like doing was throwing stones back into the sea, stone after stone after stone. Mrs Petter once told me that was undoing millions of years of evolution or something. It'd taken millions of years for those stones to get to that beach, and I threw them back in. If Aunty Eve's right, we'll all be radioactive cinders by the time the stones get back to the beach, so it doesn't matter anyway.

Now I'm nearly back in Smallmarshes. It's ten past three. I'll stop off at Casey's and see if Aunty Eve's magazines have arrived like she asked. No doubt she'll tell me what a good boy I am. I want to go home. Home home. Manchester. I want to see Steve and Matt and Alex and Jacqui and Ozmonde and the rest of the gang. I want my own bed, my own room, my own sheets and pillows and everything. I HATE THIS PLACE.

Pulling into Hell now, so I'll write more tonight.

Marc Marshall closed his diary as the train drew into Smallmarshes station, brakes squealing. He put the pencil into the leather tube attached to the book's cover, then dropped the diary into his green duffle-bag with its Sylvester and Tweety Pie stickers. He slung the bag over his shoulder and got off the train.

He stood outside the station and stared down the long road that ran down to the seafront, with its guest houses and shops. Aunty Eve's road was the third on the right. He could see Casey's newsagents just on the far corner, beside the Highcliffe Guest House. Down to the right, the south, the town fell away into streets of depressing houses, all the same, inhabited by old people who couldn't afford a house in Brighton or Bournemouth. The cliff was to the north, a green hill with the town at its feet, as if the buildings were too lazy to attempt the climb. From here he couldn't see the white chalk of the cliff face, but he could make out the single-track cliff road that led from the town up to the highest point, from which it was possible to see France on a good day, and then onwards up the coast. Halfway up it was the abandoned old cottage which Aunty Eve had said ought to be demolished. 'A death-trap,' she'd called it. Probably the only interesting place in the whole of Smallmarshes, Marc decided.

As he began wandering towards it, he saw vehicles and figures on the cliff top and on the road going down. He squinted against the late afternoon sun. Police.

Excitement at last, he thought. Something had happened if the police had been called in. Smallmarshes itself only seemed to warrant a couple of panda cars and a bicycle, yet there were more than a dozen men and women, several cars and a van up there. Best leave them to it, he decided. They wouldn't want some strange Northern kid in the way. Besides, Aunty Eve would know what was going on.

Marc had all but put the abandoned house out of his mind when something caught his eye. Something had moved in there. A curtain had been flicked by someone. He didn't know who, but it wasn't a policeman, he was sure.

He looked at Casey's, then at Aunty Eve's road, and set off up the cliff road. It was steeper and further than it looked, and after ten minutes he was almost out of breath. He put his duffle-bag on the ground and as he did so, decided he'd finally have something interesting to put in his diary tonight. He mopped his brow with his sleeve, and carried on. He'd pick up his bag on the way back. Who was going to steal it with so many police around?

As he wandered away, the bag toppled over and the diary flopped out, nesting in the grass.

Written across the front in flaking correction fluid was the name 'Marc Marshall'.

WPC Barbara Redworth, on assignment to Smallmarshes from Hill Vale station in Hastings, found the duffle-bag. She hadn't noticed anyone around, but she guessed that its owner had to be in the ramshackle building – if they were anywhere else, they would have been seen by her or her colleagues.

She left the bag where it was and walked into the building. Considering it was the middle of the afternoon, the place was astonishingly dark. WPC Redworth didn't have a torch with her and she cursed quietly, then called out. No one replied.

She was dimly aware that she was in a two-storey building – a flight of stairs with a moth-eaten carpet was set near the front door. She was standing in what must have been a living room, and to the back she could see a doorway leading to an equally dark kitchenette. It wasn't until she fumbled towards the doorway that she noticed the sofa and seats – mildewed and rotten, but undoubtedly recently disturbed. The coverings had been ripped away, revealing bright yellow foam, without a hint of dirt or mould upon it.

She glanced up at the darkened windows: there were no curtains, but the seat coverings had been hung over them. Stumbling over unseen debris on the floor, she tried tugging at the makeshift drapes, but they wouldn't come away. As her eyes finally adjusted to the light, she realised that the seat coverings were not held up by nails, or pegs or even string. They had been melted onto the walls at all four sides. It looked as if a blow-torch had been fired against them, from the scorch-marks on the walls. Soot came off on her fingers as she stroked one edge.

She heard a creak, the sound made when someone moves on weak floorboards, trying to be quiet.

Someone was upstairs.

'Hello?' No reply, and no more noise. She reached the foot of the stairs.

'Hello? My name is Barbara Redworth. I'm a police officer. Is anyone there? Are you hurt?'

No reply.

'I found a bag outside. A green duffle-bag. Is it yours?' Still nothing. 'I only want to help. I'm coming up.'

It briefly occurred to WPC Redworth that she could use her radio to call for back-up; a bit of support, in case something awful was upstairs. She'd seen a few corpses in her time: pensioners who had been left unattended at Christmas; a young homosexual, his head pulped by queer-bashers. Even a suicide, who'd deliberately driven his car into a petrol pump. But somehow she felt, perhaps by instinct, that whatever was in the cottage, it was still alive. There wasn't that awful smell of death – although over the rank dampness of the rotted furniture, she couldn't smell much at all. She began to climb the stairs, wary of their stability.

And there he was. A boy, about thirteen or fourteen, hunched up against the wall of the bathroom. He was huddling against a filthy toiletbowl, staring at her. No, through her, as if he couldn't focus on anything. To the left, partially hidden behind the bathroom wall, was an old white enamel bath. The toilet was against the other wall, next to a cracked basin. On the floor was a small heap of mud-caked rags.

Gradually WPC Redworth's sense of smell kicked back in. If the boy had been wanting to use the toilet, he'd not got there in time, and as she stared at his trousers, she could see tell-tale marks that confirmed this.

Drug addict, she decided. Out of his head on something. It was shocking at his age – he'd probably be dead in a couple of years. Poor kid. WPC Redworth had a brother of fourteen; how easily it could have been him.

The boy was shaking very slightly. The bathroom window had again been covered by something – a towel, she guessed. It had fallen away at one corner, letting some light in, and she could see he was dark-haired, with a reasonable complexion – unusual for a drug-addict. He was wearing a white T-shirt, a name in blue stencilled letters ironed across the top: M.A.R.C. His pale jeans were soiled, as she had guessed, but his white plimsolls were still very clean, despite the muck on the floor.

'Marc? Hello, I'm Barbara. Someone carried you up here, didn't they? Your shoes are too clean for you to have walked through this. Are you all right now? Who brought you here?'

She wasn't expecting a reply, so she jumped when the boy pointed at the bath, his hand shaking uncontrollably. WPC Redworth walked slowly into the bathroom, her hand on her truncheon, and turned to look at the bath. It was full of dirty brown water, and stank of stagnation. Without taking her eyes off the bath, she reached out and tugged the towel away from the window, puffing lumps of plaster with it. It flashed through her mind that whatever had melted the towel to the wall had done a thorough job.

Sunlight filtered in through the salt-encrusted broken window, and she could see everything more clearly now. The water in the bath was more than just dirty, it was positively opaque but she could just make out a body beneath the yellowish scum on the surface. Had Marc murdered his abductor? Dropped him into the bath and drowned him?

As WPC Redworth leant over the bath, the surface erupted into a fountain of dirty water, scum and slime. She couldn't scream, her mind wouldn't let her. Some previously unused, dormant portion of her brain simply took over, forcing her to realise that to make such a noise would be a sign of weakness. All she saw was a human-shaped green/yellow something. A flash of three eyes, scales, a puckered leathery mouth and, most stupid of all, a garment like a long string vest.

And then WPC Redworth realised that she had recognised something she could never have seen before. And yet she remembered...

Must get away, run for my life. The Devilbacks, yelling and hissing. Spitting. I have to protect the family even if they catch me the family must be saved. I won't let them touch me... won't let them trick me into leading them to the others. Those eyes, staring from every angle, every tree and bush. Every path. I'm being watched. The Devilbacks think they'll trick me, but I know not to be fooled, not to let my kin go to their filthy camps to be killed... They'll never catch me, I know how to swing off that branch, over the river and they'll lose my scent. Not even the Devilbacks can track me through water.

Nothing will stop me –

No!

No, there weren't that many just now. Blocked, I'm blocked at every turn.

Filthy vile reptiles. Disgusting evil –

No! Not the eye! Not the middle eye! Please. Oh, it hurts... hurts so much... pain, I can't take the pain... no –

Something heavy and damp slapped into the side of Barbara Redworth's head, sending her sliding in the muck on the floor, back towards the doorway. All she could do was stare at the damp-ridden wall, aware that two figures were walking over her. Who were they? Why where they there? Where was there? Who was she? What was she?

Three eyes. She remembered.

She dipped her fingers in the thin layer of slime and mud that covered the floor and began making patterns on the wall with it.

If anyone had seen her, they would have said she was insane, drawing meaningless pictograms. But what was left of WPC Redworth's shattered mind knew that drawing the pictures was very important, for some reason she could not understand or explain.

'Drawing pictures? Of what exactly?'

The Doctor was clearly excited as he read the report Corporal Hawke had handed him.

'I'm not sure, Doctor, but Sergeant Yates said I should tell you immediately.'

'Thank you, my dear. And Mike was right to do so. Liz, have you seen this?'

'Obviously not, as Maisie's given the only copy to you.' With an exasperated shake of the head, Liz took the report from the Doctor. As she did so, she caught sight of a sympathetic grin from Hawke. She returned it.

'Well?' the Doctor asked. 'What do you think?'

'I haven't read it yet. Give me a chance.'

She scanned through the pages, vaguely aware that Maisie Hawke was still standing awkwardly in the laboratory, as if waiting for something. The Doctor paced for a second, deep in thought, then turned to the corporal.

'The Brigadier hasn't seen this yet?' he asked.

'No, Doctor.'

'Good. I'll take the copy through to him myself, so I can discuss the implications with him immediately.'

'Are you sure, Doctor?'

'Yes, absolutely. It's no trouble, and I'm sure you've better things to do than deliver messages.'

Liz, still deep in the report, was aware of Maisie leaving the room. A few moments later, she looked up. The Doctor looked down at her, expectantly.

'What are you going to tell the Brigadier?' she asked.

'Nothing,' the Doctor snorted. 'Knowing him, he'll try and blow them up again.'

'That's not entirely fair, Doctor,' Liz said, 'but I take your point.' She pulled up one of the lab stools, sat on it, and withdrew her pipe from her handbag. Without speaking, she filled it and lit it, puffing slowly to get it going. All the time, her eyes never left the report, reading and re-reading every paragraph.

'So,' she said between puffs, 'so, what we've got here is a burnt corpse, a missing boy and a disturbed policewoman, linked by a bag found near a house. And the woman drawing primitive pictures of bison, woolly mammoths, sabre-toothed tigers and tall, man-sized bipedal reptiles with three eyes.'

'They're back, Liz. They're back.'

Liz looked at the Doctor, noting that he could barely conceal his excitement as he threw his cape over his shoulders.

'Keys,' he muttered. "Where are the keys?' He scrabbled around various benches until he suddenly stopped and looked at Liz. 'You've got them. I gave them to you yesterday.'

Liz nodded. 'Uh-huh. And before I give them to you, just confirm something.'

'What?'

'That you're going to drive off down to Sussex and play Hunt-theSilurian without informing the Brigadier.'

'No.'

'What?'

'No. You're wrong.'

Liz was surprised, but pleased. 'Oh. Right. What then?'

'We're going to jump into Bessie and drive to Sussex without telling the Brigadier.'

Liz held up her hands, but already knew that there was nothing she could say to stop the Doctor from going.

'Now Doctor, we both work for him and although I don't like it very much, I do regard him as a friend. I'm not going to just disappear without him knowing. He has a right, you know?'

The Doctor suddenly sat opposite her. 'To what, Liz? A right to what? To destroy them? To get his clod-hopping soldiers down there, tearing up the seaside trying to find something new to shoot?' He stuffed his hands into his voluminous cape pockets and shook his head slowly. 'No, Liz, don't you see? I can't let him. Not yet. This time I've got to try and communicate properly. To make both sides see sense before we have a repeat of Derbyshire. Before the Brigadier wipes out yet another colony of intelligent, decent, amazing beings simply because he and the likes of Sir John Sudbury are afraid.'

'I thought Sir John was a bosom buddy.'

'Listen, Liz,' the Doctor continued. 'The Brigadier is a brave man. He's not stupid, his mind is quite open and receptive, but first and foremost, he's a soldier. Queen and country and all that. But us, we're scientists, aren't we? We see a wider, global picture. Universal, if you like.' He got up and held his hands out for the keys. 'Please, Doctor Shaw? We have to find the Silurians and help them.'

Liz stared at him and then gave him the key. 'I don't know where you're going Doctor, because when I came back to the lab you had gone, taking Corporal Hawke's report with you.' She shoved the papers back into the internal OHMS envelope and placed it in his cape pocket. 'You only want me there to navigate, anyway. I'm not spending two hours in Bessie getting cold and irritable while you ignore my directions and claim you know a quicker way.'

The Doctor beamed. 'I'll see you tomorrow then.'

'Yes, I'm sure.' Liz tapped the contents of her pipe into a sink and washed away the dark ashes. When she turned back, the Doctor had gone. Now, she thought, all she had to do was tell Maisie Hawke to say that only the Doctor had seen the report. Subterfuge, that was all she needed.

The Doctor's sprightly yellow roadster, Bessie, cut along the A40 through London, whizzing down the Euston Road, then along Farringdon Road and over Blackfriars Bridge. Having rounded Elephant and Castle and passed along the Old Kent Road, the car then took the A2 out of London, heading towards Kent.

Wrapped up in the excitement of discovering more Silurians, the Doctor failed to notice that he was being followed by a grey Ford Cortina, matching his route and speed but always hovering three or four cars behind.

Inside the car were three people. A bearded Nigerian drove, dressed in a chauffeur's uniform. He sat silent and unsmiling.

In the back seat were two other men. One was young and very pale, as if he hadn't seen sunlight for a few years. He was smartly dressed, with short black hair and dark glasses. Emerging from under his glasses and running down his left cheek was a livid scar which connected with a slightly mutilated top lip.

The other was slightly older, blond and tanned, wearing casual slacks and a blue sports coat. Cradled in his lap was a large pistol, fitted with a large suppressor and with a set of marksman's sights mounted on its barrel.

The pale man passed his companion an envelope. Inside was a copy of the report that Hawke had given the Doctor, appended with two 10" x 8" black-and-white photographs. One was of the run-down cottage on the cliff, a duffle-bag abandoned in the foreground; the other showed a young woman in police officer's clothing being dragged, evidently with some resistance, away from the house and into an ambulance.

'No survivors,' said the pale young man, his voice soft and lisping. 'Especially not the Doctor.'

EPISODE
TWO

Traynor didn't come. He hadn't made it.

Damn.

Traynor supplied all the evidence he could, but is it going to be enough? Probably not, but the man did his best. Now it is my job to continue the exposé. Reveal the truth. Bend the rules and let the British public know what exactly their taxes are spent on. And how so-called 'defence budgets' are being spliced off into less traditional resources.

Enclosed with this letter are documents which prove that the worst fears Traynor and I had about C19 were entirely accurate. Poor old Sudbury has no idea. Fool. At the time of writing this, dear Elizabeth, I have no idea if it will be you who receives it. I hope it is. Forgive my necessary deviousness but all tracks have to be covered, all prints wiped and tapes erased, as they say. Naturally, you have no idea who I am and that is for the best. Once you have all this information, you are equipped to deal with C19, or at least ensure someone will. Maybe UNIT, if they're not too far involved themselves. Trust few people, dear Elizabeth, for

treachery thrives upon further treachery.
I, meanwhile, will hopefully pass back into
the faceless anonymity whence I crawled.

Poor Grant Traynor. He so craved medals
and accolades for serving the public good.
I told him he'd never get them. I'm quite
sure this will all be swept away eventually,
but as long as C19 has been stopped, his
sacrifice will have been worth it.

In my next and final report, I will try
to supply you with exact names, dates and
faces. I'm off now to track them down.

Au revoir.

A friend

Liver-spotted hands yanked the paper from the dilapidated SmithCorona typewriter. Arthritic fingers slowly creased it and slid it into a plain OHMS manila envelope.

The old man strained to rise from his chair, cursing quietly as the muscles in his back moved a fraction later than all the others. He paused for a second, letting his body adjust to the new posture.

'Now,' he murmured. 'Who? And where? And, for that matter, why?' He pulled the green curtain away from the window and daylight illuminated the small, sparsely furnished office. He flicked off the greenshaded brass desk lamp and nodded briefly at the portrait of the Queen that stared down from a fake wood-panelled wall opposite.

The telephone rang, and for a second he looked around, confused, trying to work out where the annoying sound originated. Of course, he recalled, it was under the cushion he'd thrown over it last time it rang. 'Extension sixty-four. Yes?' he snapped in a tired voice. 'I'm busy.'

'Too busy for an old friend?'

He paled, grateful that his caller couldn't see his face. 'Hello. What can I do for you?'

'I understand that you have a meeting tonight. I'd like you to miss it. I'd like you to travel down to the South Coast.' As always, the younger man's lisp caused the 's' sounds to become soft 'th'es.

The old man shivered. It was an order, not a request. As always. 'All right. Where?'

Directions (or rather, instructions) followed and, after he had received a curt farewell, the line went dead.

The liver-spotted hands rolled another sheet of paper into the SmithCorona, in anticipation of another missive tomorrow.

Elsewhere in the building, people carried on with their jobs, ignorant of exactly what was going on in Room 64. Outside, Big Ben chimed three o'clock and the siren of a police patrol boat echoed up the Thames towards Vauxhall.

The receptionist sat behind her chrome and glass desk. Her immaculately creased white outfit, and the tiny white cap on her head announced her role as a nurse as well as telephonist, book-keeper and information desk attendant. She nibbled at the top of her pen as she stared across the hallway and through the polarised glass doors opposite. Outside, two people waited and watched as a car drove up. She strained hard to listen for any traces of conversation, but gave up. It did not really concern her anyway, and she had her own work to do.

'Good morning Sir Marmaduke. Always a pleasure to see you.' A short dark-haired girl, also in a crisp white uniform, almost curtsied as the rotund figure heaved himself out of his chauffeur-driven car. Nodding breathlessly in reply, Sir Marmaduke Harrington-Smythe CBE, psychologist and analyst, walked slowly up the five steps of the five-storey white building, known to the few aware of its existence as the Glasshouse.

He knew that someone would have watered the flowers in honour of his arrival, as well as those crawling plants that seeped over the tops of the balconies above the main doors. The staff would have polished the windows, which were white and barred in keeping with the thirties architecture, with its squat design and rounded corners.

He stopped at the top of the steps for a moment to stare up at the rich blue panoply of the afternoon sky, which contrasted sharply against the stark white of the building as it caught and reflected the sunlight.

The young dark-haired girl glanced at her companion, an equally dark-haired young man, his hair trimmed to the same page-boy style as hers. He wore an equally pristine white outfit, but with trousers instead of a knee-length skirt. That was the only real difference between them. Well, thought Sir Marmaduke, that and the fact that he'd never heard the boy speak a word, nor had ever met anyone who had heard him speak.

In unison the girl and boy leant back, pushing open the double glass doors for him to enter the Glasshouse.

The receptionist looked up as Sir Marmaduke entered, and smiled a greeting at him, which was returned. She turned to watch the odd couple as they followed Sir Marmaduke down a long sterile white corridor. They walked a few paces behind him, perfectly in step, every gesture performed in complete unison. Neither was ever an inch or a second out of place.

The Irish Twins they were called; although the receptionist was aware that no one in the building really knew if they were twins, Irish or otherwise. She lost sight of them as Sir Marmaduke led the way down into the patient area. Underground.

Doctor Peter Morley tried to stop his hand shaking as he placed the plastic cup under the cold tap. He desperately wanted to relax, to take a deep breath and sigh loudly. Anything was better than letting his nerves overcome him.

He stared at himself in the bathroom mirror, seeing his thinning hair tinged with grey streaks that had not been there before his arrival. Dark rings surrounded his already sunken eyes. At school they had nicknamed him 'The Skull', rather unfairly, he had always thought. His hair had been receding and his features pinched since he was about ten but 'The Skull' had been going a bit far. Now, as he regarded a face that had been cooped up in this place for eight long months, he began to think it wasn't so much wrong as premature. He noticed a slight tic in his left eye – a sure sign of tiredness.

'I need sleep, you know,' he said to the security camera just above the cubicle door. 'Some privacy wouldn't go amiss, either. I might want to pee.'

His only reply was the continuous slow blink of the tiny red light atop the camera, reminding him that every conversation and action was being monitored and recorded all day, every day. Eight months he'd been here at the Glasshouse, stuck in the basement and hidden away from the world, and still he felt nervous about peeing in front of the camera. He wouldn't mind, but the urinal was side-on to the door so the camera saw… well, everything.

'And I thought using the gents in the King's Head was embarrassing.' He washed his hands, refilled his plastic cup and swigged down some deliciously cold water. Best thing about the place; the food and drink were always first class.

He threw the cup into a blue disposal sack, knowing it would be incinerated at the end of the hour, regardless of whether it contained one cup or fifty documents marked 'Top Secret'. He turned, sighed, ran a hand through his few strands of hair, pushed the door open and stepped back into the bustle of the basement.

He was standing in the general work area, his three assistants milling around. They appeared to be oblivious, as ever, to his mood and even his presence, but Morley suspected that they just chose to ignore him. Or was he just letting his paranoia get to him? And when had he become so paranoid, anyway?

Determined to stop being so morbid, Morley watched his team at work. Jim Griffin, the analyst, was running some experiments on a massive array of computers, speaking every result into a tape-recorder as it appeared on the small screen in front of him, and occasionally scratching at his nose with a biro. His dark hair spiked as if five thousand volts had been run through him. On a bench on the other side of the room, Dick Atkinson, the chemist of the team, was heating something porridge-like in a microwave and inserting metal rods into it, reflecting the microwaves back into something that might once have been a leg of lamb.

Near the double doors was Cathryn Wildeman, the short, dark-haired American zoologist, fiddling with an electron microscope and looking hard at something

Morley couldn't begin to imagine.

All three of them stopped their work suddenly and stared at the doors as the reason for Morley's earlier nerves could be heard thundering at the Irish Twins as it approached:

'Absolutely not, Ciara. We don't have time for such trivialities. I want her processed and passed to D Wing ASAP, is that understood?'

'Of course, Sir Marmaduke,' came the predictable response.

Morley allowed a quick smile to cross his face – anything that meant the gruesome twosome got a dressing down had to be good news. Sir Marmaduke's unwelcome face quickly dispelled any pleasure from his mind as the obese figure pushed the doors open and strode into the laboratory as if he owned the place.

Which he did, Morley reminded himself.

'Peter!' Sir Marmaduke bellowed. 'Peter, a word. Now!' He pointed towards Morley's tiny office at the far end of the lab. Accurately sensing the various moods of the newcomers, Morley's three staff quickly turned back to their work as if no interruption had taken place, while Morley himself meekly followed Sir Marmaduke to the indicated office. He swallowed hard, trying to force the knot of anxiety out of his throat. Whatever had brought Sir Marmaduke down here had put him in a foul mood, and Morley seemed to be the cause of it. Morley didn't even register the annoyance of having the Irish Twins follow – someone else in the room, even them, had to be of some benefit. A glance at them, and their matching ear-to-ear grins, failed to reassure him.

Sir Marmaduke pushed the door open and pulled on the light cord, showering the little room with flickering fluorescent light for a few seconds before the tube settled and bathed them in a harsh unnatural white glow. It gave the pristine white of the Irish Twins and their uniforms a faint electric lilac look.

'Sir Marmaduke, how are you?'

Sir Marmaduke sat at Morley's desk and stared at a white cup half-filled with cold Bovril. 'Waste, Peter, I cannot condone waste.' He gingerly picked up the cup, nodding at the Irish Twins. They both moved immediately, but in different directions for once. The female took the cup and dropped it into a blue disposal bag hanging on the side of a filing cabinet. The male turned to the security camera over the door and produced a slim black box from a pocket. He aimed the control at the camera and pressed a button. The red light blinked off.

'I didn't know you could do that.' Morley stared at the Irish Twins.

'Well, of course you didn't. You're not that important, y'know.' Sir Marmaduke clearly had no qualms about offending Morley, and the doctor was so used to his rudeness that he barely noticed it any more. 'You work here on a need-to-know basis, Peter, and that's how it's going to stay. Rest assured that Ciara and Cellian here are far more my eyes and ears than any number of governmental security cameras.' He waved Morley to a small, uncomfortable seat in the corner of the room. It was, the doctor found himself musing, the one where he normally threw his newspapers – the ones sent via the internal mail. Heaven forbid that he might venture outside and buy his own. Oh no, totally forbidden. Someone might see him and that would never do. Imagine the reaction –

His reverie was broken by the Irish Twins leaving the

office. A thought flashed through Morley's mind as he watched Ciara. She was beautiful. Her walk, her poise, her face and her figure were all perfect. What he would give… No, forget that. Mind you, he had to acknowledge that the male twin was just as handsome, with his square jaw, sparkling blue eyes, and jet-black hair in a fashionable cut. Cellian had one of those figures that Morley was jealous of – slim but sculptured. A clothes designer's idea of heaven. Probably.

The twins pulled the blinds down in unison, covering the glass partitions on either side of the door as they left the room. Morley knew from experience that they would be waiting just outside, like faithful lap-dogs for their master.

'Got a new one for you. A policewoman from down south. Look at this.' Sir Marmaduke produced an envelope from under his jacket. Morley ripped it open, then stopped before he got any further. It had a UNIT seal on it.

'Er, Sir Marmaduke, I'm not sure I'm cleared for this level of documentation.'

Sir Marmaduke shrugged. 'So? I gave it to you, ergo you're cleared for it. Now read it.'

Morley flicked through the file, seeing various UNIT memorandums signed by a Brigadier Lethbridge-Stewart, plus a couple 'dictated, but not read' by someone who was referred to only as 'the Doctor'.

'UNIT's Scientific Adviser. Your equivalent.' Sir Marmaduke indicated that he should carry on.

Morley started to flick through some photographs, each with a name stapled to it. BAKER, (Major) NORMAN (dscd RD1); LAWRENCE, (Doctor) CHARLES (dscd RD1); SQUIRE, (Mrs) DORIS (G/H RS1); MASTERS, (Rt Hon) EDWARD (dscd RD1); DAWSON, (Miss) PHYLLIS (G/H

RS1)... He put the file back on the table. 'Yes, I recognise the two women. The Dawson woman was a research assistant to old Scotty. I mean John Quinn, at Wenley Moor Atomic Centre. And Mrs Squire was a farmer's wife. He died, I think.'

'And where was Mrs Squire from?'

'Derbyshire, if I remember rightly.'

Sir Marmaduke nodded. 'And the connection is?'

Morley thought. 'Wenley Moor. It's in Derbyshire. Quite close in fact. Charles Lawrence was the director?'

Sir Marmaduke tapped the file. 'And Baker was his security officer, retired from the regular army after a little... mishap in Northern Ireland at the back end of the last decade. The other parliamentary chappie was assigned to "kill or cure" the place. Got killed himself, from a rather nasty plague that was eventually cured by this mysterious Doctor person at UNIT.

'Now, there's one other interesting thing about our two ladies from Derbyshire. What d'you know of their symptoms?'

Morley shook his head slowly. 'I'm very sorry, Sir Marmaduke, but I was down here. I don't know that I ever saw them more than two or three times. I didn't even realise they were connected.'

'No, I suppose not, Just a couple of civvies caught up in something top secret and needing the special ministrations of this place, eh?' Sir Marmaduke tapped his nose. 'But things do change, Peter. We now have a third connection. Look at this doctor's report; some northern chap called Meredith. He was the local GP up there. Both Squire and Dawson had to be restrained, claiming they'd seen monsters.'

Morley shrugged. 'Nothing unusual in that. After all,

the Glasshouse was set up for people like that. And UNIT, for one, keeps us in customers.'

'But few of them come to you, eh? Well, that's going to change. Our ladies from Derbyshire suddenly became accomplished amateur artists overnight. Began drawing pictures on walls, doors, anything else they could get hold of.'

'Formal, abstract or symbolist?'

Sir Marmaduke chuckled. 'Oh, very symbolist. Ever been to Lascaux? No, neither have these two. But they've been doing passable imitations of those French cave-pictures ever since they had their "experiences". And –' Sir Marmaduke leant forward – 'you've just gained your first one this year. Our policewoman from Sussex is scribbling mammoths, sabre-toothed tigers and something far more interesting all over the inside of her secure unit in Hastings Hospital.' He withdrew one last envelope from his jacket and opened it, placing two photographs side by side. One was of a man-like figure, but reptilian, scaled and ridged. On its head were a series of bumps, and a third eye. Clawed hands and a large, round, stubby nostril were the other striking features. 'Seen one of these before?'

Morley shook his head.

'That's what was in the caves at Wenley Moor. That's what drove our ladies round the bend. That's what released a previously unknown plague into Britain, killing thirty-eight people. And –' Sir Marmaduke tapped the UNIT file – 'that's what cost the Research Centre and UNIT a combined total of twenty-nine lives.'

'What is it?'

Sir Marmaduke shrugged. 'A reptile-man. In his report, UNIT's SA referred to them as "homo reptilia", or "Silurians". Frankly, they're bug-eyed monsters as far as I'm concerned. UNIT did their job right for once and blew them all up. Or so we thought, until WPC Barbara Redworth began sketching this.' He tapped the second photo, which showed a scrappily drawn but recognisable illustration of a similar creature.

'They're back, Peter, and this time we don't want them blown up. This time we want them alive, and WPC Barbara Redworth is going to lead us to them. You, my boy, and your team are stopping whatever you're doing and taking this on right now. I want this woman probed, analysed, debriefed and pumped with truth-serum until she tells us everything we need to know. I want one of these creatures alive. Alive and well and prepared to blow this government and its cover-ups, top-secret UNITs and covert military missions apart.' Sir Marmaduke leant forward and tapped the photograph of the reptile-man. 'And if I can discredit that pompous ass Lethbridge-Stewart and the rest of his C19 cronies, so much the better.'

The 'pompous ass' at whom Sir Marmaduke Harrington-Smythe's invective had been directed was at that moment steering his Daimler into the drive of a box-shaped, two storey house: 6 Moor Drive, Gerrards Cross, Buckinghamshire.

Built about eight years previously in dark red brick transported down from the Lancashire hills, the home of Brigadier Alistair Gordon Lethbridge-Stewart stood alongside four identical houses in a cul-de-sac; the small entrance from the main Slough-to-Amersham road was concealed between large evergreen trees.

Number Two housed the Pike family: all Alistair knew about them was that he was some sort of quantity surveyor with an American accent, and they had three boys who yelled a lot.

Number Four was occupied by the Pryses; a couple in their late fifties who lived alone. They had a voluminous family who descended upon the cul-de-sac every Sunday lunchtime and blocked everyone else's drives with their cars. Mr Prys was an advertising executive, while Mrs Prys was heavily involved with the local Women's Institute. Both were fond of rugby. Alistair could remember with a chill the day Mrs Prys presented their neighbours to the entire Welsh team on her patio, its pink and blue stone slabs clashing hideously with the players' red and white strip.

On the other side, at Number Eight, lived the retired Ince family who seemed to have come down from Southport alongside the red bricks used to build the five houses. A jolly couple, also retired, they were frequent hosts to bridge, backgammon and mah-jong evenings, some of which Alistair attended with his wife Fiona. Unlike the other three families, the Inces' garage was not full of motor vehicles; instead it seemed to be some sort of shrine to deceased greenery. No matter how often Mrs Ince planted and potted her shrubs and flowers, they withered up and died quicker than she could buy replacements from the Cadmore End Common nurseries.

As he stopped his engine, Alistair glanced towards Number Two, and noticed the addition of a basketball net over the garage door. How long had that been there? In any normal family he could have sauntered into the kitchen and asked his wife or daughter.

His family was anything but normal. 'Failing to communicate' was the current parlance. 'Falling apart at the seams' was his preferred description. Gritting his teeth in anticipation of the welcome that awaited him – he had no idea what form it would take, but he was sure it would leave him feeling drained and unhappy – he slid out of his seat, picked up his briefcase and scooped up the dark blue blazer which lay across the passenger seat.

Dropping the car keys into the pocket of his grey slacks, he dug inside the blazer for his house keys. He need not have bothered. The front door swung open and, with a delighted cry of 'Daddy's home!', Alistair's main reason for living rushed towards him, arms outstretched, an ecstatic grin across her 5-year-old face.

Slipping into 'hard-working father home from the office' mode and mood, Alistair dropped onto one knee and hugged Kate, his daughter. She hugged him back with the fierce joy that adults so rarely achieve. He stood up, swinging her around and she responded by gripping tighter and letting out a delighted whoop that momentarily deafened him.

'You, Tiger, are getting heavier every day. Or I'm getting older.'

'No, Daddy. Mummy says it's because you don't spend any of your time with us and I change and you never see it!' said Kate with a loud gurgle of pleasure.

Alistair remembered a magazine article he'd read once on child-rearing. 'Beware what you say around the young,' it had warned. 'Children will imitate and repeat all manner of things, often at inappropriate moments.'

How true. And to whom had Fiona offered that particular comment about his absence? Virginia? Doreen? Mrs Anderson the cleaner? Most likely she'd remarked it to her father – the interfering old fool who made mother-in-law jokes seem very wide of the mark.

Kate turned, her attention drawn away for a second, and Alistair looked up to see that Mrs Lethbridge-Stewart was standing in the front doorway, a towel in her hands. No welcoming smile there. No hug. No giggle of joy at seeing her husband for the first time in seventy-two hours.

Not unusual.

With a sigh born from eight years of sad familiarity, Alistair disentangled himself from Kate and walked resignedly towards his waiting wife. He knew that, for the sake of the neighbours and his daughter, there would be a pretence of happy families; a peck on the cheek and a token enquiry about the day's work.

He was wrong. Fiona Lethbridge-Stewart just turned and went back inside the house without saying a word.

As he stepped into the warm hallway, suppressing an urge to adjust the thermostat on the wall, he saw a flash of pastel-green nylon trousers as Fiona went back into the kitchen. The door closed behind her with a soft but definite thud.

'Daddy, look what Miss Marshall showed us how to make today.' Kate was waving a small cardboard sunflower at him, her eyes bright with joy at her father's return.

Pausing only to glance back at the kitchen door, Alistair dropped almost effortlessly into 'good father' mode again and knelt down, commenting on the brightly coloured fake flower. He pointed at the yellow petals, brown face and bright green stem. Kate nodded at his every word, smiling beautifully. Every inch a mirror image of her mother, he thought.

'I tried showing it to Mummy,' said Kate, staring for a moment at the closed kitchen door, 'but she said to show it to you. She said that if I did, you might remember we were here. Or something.' Kate pouted suddenly. 'What did she mean?'

Alistair rose and started to climb the stairs. 'Did she

indeed? Listen, Tiger, I'm going to go upstairs to get changed out of my office clothes. Why don't you help Mummy get the dinner?'

'We had dinner.'

'Oh. When?'

'Ages ago.'

Alistair considered that, in the light of his daughter's ability to judge time, 'Ages ago' could be any time within the last hour, otherwise she'd be hungry again by now. It seemed that Fiona had given up even bothering to wait for his return.

He was aware that Kate was staring at him. Even behind her excitement over his return and that flower thing, he knew she could sense something was wrong between her parents. What could he say? Army life didn't teach you how to deal with 5-year-old girls asking awkward questions. Hell, army life didn't teach you how to cope with 35-year-old wives who didn't even know anything about your job. Not for the first time, he cursed the Official Secrets Act.

No wonder Fiona was getting edgy. It was something of a miracle she hadn't left him already. How many other wives had the problems she faced? He would bet Doreen Prys was able to phone her husband at work, got invited to office parties, and knew the names and wives of other people in her husband's social circle. Poor Fiona had to content herself with the neighbours, her parents and a few local women who ran Tupperware parties.

What kind of life had he offered her all those years ago? And what kind of life had he subsequently provided for her?

'Daddy? Daddy, are you all right?'

Alistair refocused his attention on his daughter at the foot of the stairs, half-smiling at her. 'Tell you what, Tiger.

D'you remember that bear we won the other week at the Christmas fair?' The other week? Three, nearly four months ago at least.

'Aloysius?'

'That's the chap. How about you go and get him and we'll see if we can find some biscuits for him, eh?'

Without replying, Kate dashed past him up the stairs, and went into her bedroom.

'Give me five minutes, Tiger, and I'll come and find you both, all right?' he called after her.

There was no reply, which he took to be an affirmative, and returned to his own thoughts as he pushed open the bedroom door. Instantly, his UNIT-trained reflexes told him that something was wrong. It was nothing he could immediately put his finger on and yet...

There was no ticking. The alarm clock was gone. He looked down at his bedside cabinet. No clock. No moustache-trimmer. No creased paperback. Not even a box of tissues.

He put his bag down and walked slowly to the wardrobe nearest his side of the bed. It was empty. He stood silently for a second, looking around him, then left the room and opened the next door along the hall, into the spare room which doubled as a guest bedroom.

The room was dark, with its curtains drawn, but even in the dim light he could tell that the bed had no linen on it. From the temperature, the radiators were not switched on either. He flicked the light switch and opened up the solitary cupboard. Sure enough, his suit jackets were hanging there, along with his trousers and his shirts. Underwear, socks and vests had been crammed into two small drawers, and a box of tissues lay on the floor next to a couple of pairs of casual shoes.

The alarm clock lay face down on an uncovered pillow, unwound and silent. Rather like his marriage.

'Daddy, are you sleeping in here tonight?'

Alistair Lethbridge-Stewart, the Brigadier, could face Cybermen, Yetis and Autons. He could send soldiers to their deaths and he could shoot someone without a second's thought. He could chastise and manipulate staff and lead a top-secret paramilitary organisation attached to a Government ministry.

What Alistair Lethbridge-Stewart, the father, suddenly and sinkingly realised he couldn't do was to provide a stable home for his 5-year-old daughter. He couldn't answer her questions. He couldn't tell her what he did for a living. He couldn't be around when she needed him. And as that thought sank in, he understood too that his wife must have realised the same thing, many times over. He would try harder to be a better father and husband. He would.

He was still hugging Kate tightly, desperate to hold back his more dramatic emotions when Fiona marched up the stairs to tell him frostily that someone called Mrs Hawke from the office was on the telephone.

Jana Kristan was already at Hastings General Hospital, pacing up and down in the reception area of the casualty department, when the two nurses – one male, one female – walked in.

It was the precision of their step, and the way they looked in unison at everyone and everything, that alerted her. Jana was aware of the receptionist and various patients staring after them as they wordlessly marched down the corridor leading to the hospital wards, having not said a word to anyone; not even each other. The receptionist shot a look at the security officer (probably hired from some local firm, paid by the hour and only waiting for his shift to end – pathetic) but he just shrugged and carried on inspecting his copy of the *Daily Sketch*.

As the receptionist returned to her papers and forms, Jana gave everyone in the area a final cursory glance and followed the mysterious nurses. There had been something compelling and almost unnatural about them. It had reminded her of over-wrought dancers, incapable of casual movement. A brother-and-sister double act, perhaps? Or twins?

Jana glanced at the various doors as she walked down the off-white corridor, seeing names of doctors and specialists. Cupboards, medical examination areas and even the occasional small toilet broke the monotony of wooden doors embedded in the sterile, flat walls. There were a couple of dimly lit sub-corridors which didn't seem to go anywhere interesting, two sets of lifts, and a fire escape from the basement area.

Before long, Jana realised that not only had she no idea where she was going, but that there was no sign of the mysterious nurses. She wasn't worried that someone might ask her why she was there; she had learnt long ago that if you walked around quietly but with just enough nonchalance, people assumed you had the same right to be there as they did, and they left you alone. Just in case you were more important than they were.

But for security, to complete her camouflage, as Jana passed an open door and saw a couple of white coveralls hanging there, she grabbed one, ducked into a side-corridor and quickly slipped it on, glancing at the name-tag and photo card. Hopefully no one would look too hard and see that as a six-foot blonde, Jana was hardly suited to the role of a hospital janitor, and could not really be Tommy Taftitti, presumably of Caribbean origin.

Continuing her search, Jana found herself in a ward, the curtained-off beds telling her nothing she needed to know. She considered 'accidentally blundering' into each cubicle but decided that, before long, someone would challenge her and break her disguise.

'Hey, you there.' Jana turned at the sound of a voice. A young doctor, his hair untidy and his eyes heavy with weariness, had emerged from one of the curtained booths, and was pointing angrily at a distant cupboard. 'Yes, you. Cleaner. Get me some disinfectant and a mop, there's a mess in here.'

For a moment she was tempted to ignore him, but then she thought better of it. Exaggerating her Dutch accent, she apologised and shuffled towards the cupboard. As she opened it and leant down to get the liquid, a door at the far end of the ward swung open.

It was the two nurses. She ducked down, pretending to search through the cleaning fluids as she watched them go into one of the curtained-off areas and emerge pushing a trolley with a patient on it, seemingly on their way to an operating theatre. A few overheard words exchanged between them and the young doctor confirmed this.

Ah well, so much for instinct – there was hardly anything sinister about that, Jana decided. Shaking her head at her own stupidity – pathetic, she admonished herself – she lifted the disinfectant and straightened up, facing the door they had just left through.

'TO WARDS 3, 4, 5' declared the hoarding above the door.

It took a moment to sink in. Then: 'Damn!' as her brain registered the problem. All the signs for the operating theatres she had seen on her way up the corridor had indicated forward. The odd couple and their patient were going in totally the wrong direction. Wherever the strange nurses were taking their patient, it wasn't to an operating theatre.

Dropping the disinfectant, she yanked her white coat off and dashed back the way she'd come. Valuable seconds had passed – enough for the two creepy nurses to have gone in any door, down any stairwell or into either lift.

'*Gaweg!*' she snarled as she slammed her fist against a door. How could she have been so stupid? What were they up to? Why was she spending so much energy chasing them – unless…

She dashed back down towards the reception area. The place had cleared a lot since she was last there, and there was no queue at the desk. She stopped, breathless, in front of the receptionist.

'Hi.' She tried to smile politely. 'You know those two nurses you saw earlier?'

'I see lots of nurses,' muttered the receptionist without taking her eyes from the pile of admission forms in front of her.

'Yes, well, let's try not to be obtuse, shall we? You know which nurses I'm talking about. We both thought they looked odd.'

The receptionist slowly raised her face and Jana realised it was a different woman from the one she'd seen earlier. She swore again, under her breath this time, and turned away to look at the security guard. Who had vanished. In fact, the reception area was totally empty.

'You cleared your patients quickly, didn't you? Ten minutes ago, this place was swarming.'

The receptionist leant forward, offering a pen and one

of her pieces of paper. 'You were here a few minutes back, were you? Did you fill in an admission form?'

'I am not a patient,' snapped Jana, stepping back. 'I am a… a visitor. Jana Kristan. Seeing a patient.'

'Oh. And which patient would that be?' The receptionist smiled insincerely.

Jana paused, swallowed and, despite her instincts – which she'd ignored too often today as it was – screaming for her to keep quiet, she jumped in with both feet. She opted to play the role of ignorant foreigner; it had served her well in the past. 'I am flying over from Holland. I am here to visiting my cousin, a policewoman. She was hurted in Smallmarshes.'

'And her name?' The receptionist's smile took on the falsehood of a pantomime villain's grin.

It didn't seem to be working. In a fairly blatant attempt to see if she could read the policewoman's name upside down, Jana leant towards and over the desk. The receptionist, caught by surprise, pushed her chair back to get away from the reporter.

In an instant Jana understood everything. She was trapped. The receptionist she'd seen earlier was lying face-down under the desk, a trickle of blood oozing around her ear. Whether the woman was dead or alive, Jana couldn't tell, but she immediately guessed that a similar fate had befallen the security guard and any unfortunate patients and associated relatives or friends who had been seated there ten minutes ago.

Aware that her cover had been blown, the fake receptionist tried to stand, groping across the desk for something that lay unseen under a pile of paperwork. Jana lashed out with her handbag, catching the impostor across the temple with its weight. As the nurse staggered back,

Jana yanked the bag open, puffing out a small, compact blue-grey pistol with silencer out of a side-pocket.

'In case of emergencies,' Jana said, and aimed.

The fake receptionist feinted back and then dived forward, catching Jana under the chin with a swift right hook. Surprised, Jana let herself drop to the floor but twisted sideways as she fell. Coming out of the roll, she slammed into a chair and sent it skittering noisily across the waiting area. She was up on one knee, the pistol aimed and firing in less than a second.

The bullet took the fake receptionist in the forehead. She flopped down hard on her chair, a look of complete amazement etched onto her face. Jana kept the gun on her for a second, just to be on the safe side, then scattered the papers from the desk across the floor. Under the admission forms lay a small blue-grey pistol, the same model as her own. Jana stared at it, then quickly swapped her gun for the duplicate after hurriedly wiping it clear of fingerprints. The impostor, it would now seem, had been shot with her own gun.

Without waiting to check on the real receptionist or trying to find the others, Jana scooped up her discarded handbag and plopped the new pistol inside. Pausing only to catch her breath and run a hand through her hair to straighten it, she walked out of the hospital. She kept one hand inside the bag, grasping the pistol in case anyone else came towards her.

There was no one around in the car park. She began to walk purposefully towards her red Mini, then stopped almost immediately. Everything in her training told her that something was wrong.

She darted across the car park, dodging behind and between cars, heading for her Mini. When she was still ten yards from it, she heard the first two shots from behind her, audible although fired from a silenced weapon, and she dived into cover between two cars. As she cautiously looked out, two more shots followed. They weren't meant for her.

The red Mini exploded in a ball of flame which scorched her face and sucked the breath from her lungs. The door and front wheels were flung forty feet into the air before bouncing down onto the blackened gravel. Hospital windows exploded inwards and a smart MG beyond her Mini was enveloped in flames, its petrol tank erupting seconds later, shattering more windows in the surrounding area.

Amidst the confusion, screams and fire alarms, Jana nodded to herself. 'Very good. A professional job.' They knew who she was, because they knew which of the cars was hers. And she knew what sort of people normally carried those blue-grey pistols, and how formidable their resources were. It was, she thought, time to disappear again. Right now.

It was a short sprint away from the carnage and through the hospital gates, out into the rapidly filling street. No shots followed her this time. Think fast. Blend in. If you behave as if your clothes aren't singed and your face isn't burnt, nobody will notice. Past on-lookers gathering to gawp at the carnage, stunned shoppers and halted cars, she walked swiftly but unobtrusively in the direction of Hastings railway station.

Although strictly speaking it was UNIT Headquarters' laboratory, Mike Yates, like everyone else, had come to think of it as the Doctor's laboratory. It had a sense of personality and purpose when he thought of it in that way. The Doctor belonged at UNIT, in his lab, and his presence made everyone feel safer.

Although he had not long been seconded to UNIT, Mike had come to respect and trust the Doctor's judgement in most matters.

'Weird, but good,' was Jimmy Munro's one comment on the subject, when Mike asked him about his future scientific adviser at a cricket match, shortly before joining UNIT. 'I didn't get to interact with him much because I gathered from the Brigadier that he was quite ill.' Mike remembered Jimmy Munro's cryptic smile. 'Apparently he'd gone grey and grown six inches, because James Turner had known him a couple of years back, and he said the Doctor was quite small and dark.'

On the strength of that, Mike had sought out Major Turner just before he and his dolly wife had flown out to his new posting in Ceylon – or Sri Lanka, as they now had to say.

'Oh, he was just divine,' had been Mrs Turner's main comment. 'I got some smashing pictures of him in the heat of battle.'

Major Turner had coughed suddenly. 'Isobel is something of a photography student,' he explained. 'But alas, everything she took during my time as a captain with the Brigadier is covered under the Official Secrets Act. Once you're fully ensconced in UNIT's happy bosom, I'll get Isobel to send 'em on.'

Mike Yates had arrived at UNIT, wondering which former captain had perceived the Doctor correctly. Now, after having worked closely with the Doctor during their recent sojourn in the Pacific Islands, he felt that neither of the opinions he had received really began to do the man justice. He liked the Doctor, although he'd never admit it out loud, and he liked the man's rarefied form of anarchy. He enjoyed the way the Doctor could out-do the Brigadier without actually humiliating him. And he liked the Doctor's assistant, Doctor Shaw, enormously.

Maybe he could ask her out for a date.

No. Perhaps not. She seemed a bit fierce and, while Mike guessed that was mostly a professional attitude – and probably used as a defence against the Doctor's irresponsibility – he seriously doubted he had the necessary experience or patience to break her resolve.

Nice legs, though.

Mike coughed as he prepared to enter the Doctor's lab. He was aware that he could be interrupting a vastly important experiment requiring non-moving air molecules (the cause of Corporal Nutting's most recent telling off) or a heated discussion between the Doctor and Doctor Shaw. On the occasions this had happened, the debate had been so far beyond Mike's sixteen-plus in General Science that he'd had no idea whether he'd intruded on the start, middle or end of the conversation.

Taking a deep breath, he knocked lightly on the green double doors and pushed them open.

'Sorry to interrupt, Doctor, but—'

He found himself alone in the laboratory. The windows were shut, the hatchway above the spiral steps seemed to be bolted from the inside, and the benches were free of any signs of ongoing experiments. The Doctor's cape was gone from the hat-stand near the window overlooking the canal. The window through which Mike had often found the scientist staring, miles away from anything or anyone.

'Oh,' he said aloud, feeling rather foolish.

The telephone rang, on the desk near the window, next to the funny police box that the Doctor kept there. It rang again as he considered whether he should answer it, and he reached for the receiver.

'Hello, UNIT laboratory, can I help you?'

'Is Liz Shaw there, please?' The voice was distant, polite and well educated.

'Not at the moment,' Mike replied. 'May I take a message for her?'

The phone went dead. 'Oh,' Mike said again. He replaced the receiver, shrugged his shoulders and turned to head back to the Duty Office where John Benton was setting out the Scrabble set. 'Must remember to tell Doctor Shaw that her father, or someone, rang for her.'

Marc Marshall was not sure what happened after the policewoman hit the wall. Not really.

He had a strange feeling of light-headedness, almost like floating. It reminded him of when he'd been ill about two years previously, with glandular fever. Drifting in and out of deep sleep, his mother's face fading in and out of focus. Everything feeling heavy, slurred and sepia-toned.

That's how he felt in the bathroom of the old house. That's how he felt when the three-eyed creature had placed him over its shoulder and carried him past the still woman. Was she dead? He didn't know. Marc tried to focus on what that meant. Dead. Someone was dead? He'd never seen anyone dead before but, despite the novelty, somehow he couldn't hold on to the thought. Couldn't concentrate on anything. He was drifting –

He was jolted into complete wakefulness by the sea. More specifically, by being dropped face-first into it. Coughing and spluttering as the salt water rushed into his mouth, he tried to get up, to stagger away. But it was dark now, and the seashore was deserted apart from him and his captor, who was holding him down. All he could see was a pair of dark shoes.

No, not shoes. Feet. But strange feet. Mud-brown over green leather… with three toes.

And claws.

Not leather – scales. Like fish. Or snakes.

Marc panicked, splashing backwards as far as he could go, and wriggled enough that the weight on his back was eased. As he felt the pressure relax, he pushed himself up, flipping back and landing on his backside.

And then he saw it. It. Whatever it was, it certainly was not a human – no fancy-dress costume could be that good. Besides, there was something about it that he was sure he remembered seeing before – somewhere, a long time ago…

Mamma! Where is Mamma? Have the Devilbacks got her? What about the others? Was everyone caught except him? Trapped in the strange cages with wood-that-isn't-wood that moves by itself barring the exit. The Devilbacks stare hard, stare with their red eye and the wood-that-isn't-wood entraps them all. That must be what happened to Mamma and the others.

Mamma!

'Mum! Help!' Marc stared up at the creature, trembling in terror. Somehow he knew it would hurt him. The third eye, there in the centre of its forehead he knew it, he'd seen it before.

And the mouth, where was its mouth? Was that hole with the flap a mouth or nose? How did it hear without ears? It had fins that flicked back, stretching out behind its head. Why was he even thinking about this? It had to be a dream? It had to be –

Marc tried rationalising it – what he saw simply could not be real. So why did he recognise it?

The scaly green reptile moved towards him. It was wrapped in a strange vest that hung to its knees. And then Marc realised he, too, was wearing a long vest. His normal clothes were beside him, wrapped in something that looked like plastic. Why wasn't he cold? Or very wet, for that matter?

'Where are my clothes? Who are you?' Marc had read stories in the papers. Young boys and girls abducted and sexually assaulted. Mum and Dad always told him to be careful of strange people. Was this reptile thing going to sexually assault him? Marc was not naive when it came to sex but nevertheless he didn't know exactly what a sexual assault was. Steve Merrett once said it was a kick in the goolies but Marc thought it had to be far worse than that. Sexually assaulted kids usually ended up dead.

'Please. I don't want to die.'

Please don't kill me. Take me back to Mamma. Back to the place with wood-that-isn't-wood. Please don't hurt me. Please don't stare at me and burn me. Please? Mamma!

Marc shuddered, but not with cold. It was something else. Something about the sight of this monster. It made him more frightened than he ever thought anything could. He wanted to ask it to let him go. To let him go home to Salford, to Mum and Dad and their awful society parties. To let him ring Aunty Eve, at least.

'Please don't hurt me.'

The thing held out a three-clawed hand. In it was a tiny box. For a split second Marc thought he saw the extra eye in the thing's head glow red but he was distracted by a sound from the box. Three chimes, in descending pitch. Over and over again. He became transfixed by the sound, and it seemed to fill his mind. His eyes blotted out everything else except the box. His ears stopped hearing the waves, the wind, even the heavy breathing of the thing. Just those three notes, like a flute.

That sound, from the noise-box that awful sound. No! It meant they were calling it. The King Monster. Mamma said it would eat anyone who went near it, even the Devilbacks.

King Monster would eat other Monsters, including the ones the Devilbacks used. The Pair-Hunters were the only ones who could fight back.

The noise-box called the Pair-Hunters, too. Mamma said they were worse than King Monster because they were cleverer. Mamma said they got Papa. One tracked him down and, though he was safe in the bushes, it saw him and stared at him. Mamma said he forgot the most evil thing about the Pair-Hunters while he watched the one in front, the one he didn't see went around behind. Mamma said Papa never saw it. The tribe tried to save him but the Pair-Hunters were too fast and Papa was gone.

Then the Devilbacks used the noise-box to call the Pair-Hunters back to their camp. Mamma said that if I ever heard the noisebox, I should run away as fast as I could. Hide in the trees, or under the bushes, but get away from whatever was being called. I can hear the noise-box now but there's nowhere to run and I can hear King Monster growling and…

Marc screamed, and held his hand to his head, and tried to get up. He had to stop the noise. Had to stop… stop whatever was being summoned from coming. He had to stop the noise.

It is screaming, making the noise their hairy ancestors made whenever the calling devices were activated. Chukk said they were advanced now, almost to our levels. So why is this hatchling screaming? I must stop it, but how? Last time I tried, the older male on the cliff top died. I must use less force.

Concentrate. Stop screaming! Concentrate.

It has stopped. The hatchling is quiet now. It is staring at me. I managed – at last I managed to turn its brain off without killing it.

Now, where is Sula?

Police Sergeant Robert Lines was known to his colleagues as Quiet Man Bob. Right now he was aware that they were staring at him aghast, waiting for him to ruin his reputation by exploding in frustration at the over-dressed man standing at the front desk.

Smallmarshes Police Station was not a particularly large building. It housed two interview rooms, a tiny mess and a shared resource area which doubled as Bob's administrative office, where messages were relayed from the Hastings CID Room.

The station also possessed a rather small and antiquated reception area, decorated with anti-crime posters, and anti-rabies adverts. To one side was a hatchway built into the wall, through which he was currently leaning, his knuckles whitening as they gripped the edge of the hatch. On the wall was a white clock which informed Bob that it was ten past eleven, and time he sent his officers home to their wives and children. They'd all had a hell of a day, and the last thing any of them needed was this.

'Look, I am very sorry, sir, but it is a police matter and not one for civilians, no matter how well-intentioned.' He forced himself to smile at the tall, white-haired gentleman facing him. He was a weird one, Bob was sure. Well over six feet tall, with straw hair rapidly giving way to pure white; probably in his early fifties. He had a lined face, its most prominent features a long beaky nose and a pair of piercing blue eyes that seemed about to pop out of his head. His clothes were astonishing, and very eccentric. Almost Edwardian in appearance, he wore a white frilly shirt and a royal-blue velvet smoking-jacket under a long black cape with red silk lining.

The eccentric smiled back at him. 'If we could talk privately, Sergeant, I'm sure I could persuade—'

'We are talking in private, Mister…?'

'Doctor, actually.' The tall man, pointed at one of the interview rooms visible behind the hatchway. 'Just the two of us?'

Sergeant Lines sighed and relaxed his grip on the sill of the hatch, wriggling his fingers to get the circulation flowing again. If only his goodwill could flow as easily. He nodded at the doorway to the left of the hatch.

The Doctor thanked him and opened the door, marching past the sergeant and straight into the small interview room.

Before Sergeant Lines had a chance to speak, the Doctor thrust an identity card into his hand. He stared at it, but apart from a recognisable photograph of the Doctor, the wording meant nothing.

'I'm sorry, Doctor, but I've never heard of this UNIT. What exactly do they do?'

The Doctor flopped into one of the hard wooden chairs. 'Save lives, mostly.'

'Sort of medical, then?' Sergeant Lines decided that since it looked like he was in for a long session, he ought to try and pretend to be hospitable. He picked up the internal phone on the table and pressed a switch. The faint buzz from his own office came through the receiver and the door behind him. After a second it was answered. 'Bob Lines here, Pat,' he said unnecessarily. 'I know it's late, but could you pop a pot of tea for two into IR2 please?

Thanks, love.'

The Doctor got up. 'I really don't have time for tea, Sergeant. There are things going on in Smallmarshes that need investigating.'

Bob Lines nodded slowly, sat in the opposite chair and motioned for the Doctor to sit again.

'Indeed there are, Doctor. But right now, you say you've driven all the way from London, with some information about what happened to WPC Redworth.' There was a knock on the door and WPC Patricia Haggard came in with a tray of teacups, milk and sugar along with a large black teapot. Thanking her, he shoved the door shut and poured two cups.

'Milk and sugar?'

'Three, please.'

Bob raised an eyebrow. 'Now, Doctor, let's start at the beginning. Who exactly are you, why are you here, what do you know about what's happened, and why should I be interested in this UNIT set-up?'

The Doctor swung his long legs up onto the table. With a flick of his shoulders his cape fell off, draping itself over the back of his seat. He began massaging the back of his neck. 'Well, that's a little difficult to explain, Sergeant. UNIT is attached to the Government and, as such, comes under the Official Secrets Act. However, I can tell you I am here because of the circumstances of WPC Redworth's injuries. We received a report that made me believe a visit was necessary.' He smiled widely. 'What was your other question?'

Sergeant Lines shrugged. 'Just "who are you?" However, I've no doubt that the answer to that is shrouded by the Official Secrets Act as well.'

The Doctor nodded apologetically. 'You'll just have to

trust me, Sergeant. I'm on the side of the angels.'

Sergeant Lines sighed and swigged his tea. 'All right, Doctor, but this is against my better judgement. Barbara Redworth was last seen healthy at fifteen forty-five this afternoon. We had been sent, along with the Hastings division where she was based, to investigate the death of a DAO on the cliff top.'

The Doctor held up a hand. 'DOA? Dead on Arrival?'

'No,' Bob Lines said. 'DAO is vernacular for Down and Out. We knew the deceased as Jossey but it turns out he was once a film star called Justin Grayson. His cause of death has not been certified yet.' He finished off his tea and offered the Doctor a top-up, which was declined.

Bob paused, drank some more, and continued: 'WPC Redworth was seen by one of my colleagues entering the derelict Seaview Cottage. She didn't come out, a couple of my lads raised the alarm, and she was found hunched upstairs, drawing pictures on the wall. No one could get any sense out of her. I understand from the ambulance crew that she became quite aggressive when they took her out of the house.'

'Had she been attacked? Was she injured in any way?'

Bob Lines held his hands up. 'I can't answer that, Doctor. I'm not a, er, doctor.'

The Doctor rubbed his neck again. 'All right, that's the official line. What's your opinion?'

The sergeant considered that for a moment. It seemed fair enough. In a strange way, he'd begun to trust this strange man. 'This is off the record, Doctor. I must ask you not to use my opinions as facts in any way. In fact, I'd rather you forgot I ever gave them.'

The Doctor concurred and Sergeant Lines continued: 'She may have been attacked. I'm confident Redworth wasn't sexually assaulted. When I saw her in the ambulance, her clothes were dirty and wet—'

'Wet?'

'Yes, wet. She was found huddled in a filthy bathroom, next to a bath full of murky stale water. A lot of it had got splashed onto her as well as the floor. To be frank…' Lines chewed his bottom lip for a moment before carrying on: 'To be frank, I wondered if she caught something contagious from the water.'

The Doctor shrugged. 'That would be a very fast reaction if she did. No water-borne disease could cause such an immediate effect, to my knowledge.'

Sergeant Lines drank more tea. 'The ambulance men agree with you, as it happens. Anyway, after that, she was shipped off to Hastings General Hospital, and we'll hear more in the morning.'

The Doctor stood up. 'Right, let's go, then.'

Sergeant Lines stared up at him in puzzlement. 'Where? The hospital? It's far too late in the evening.'

The Doctor shook his head. 'Good grief, I don't need to go to the hospital. No, I want you to take me to this Seaview Cottage. I presume you are sure that her assailant, if there is one, has gone.'

Sergeant Lines nodded. 'We searched the place from top to bottom. No one there at all. If it wasn't for the bruising on her face, which the ambulance men were adamant had come from a heavy blow, we'd have assumed she'd had, well, a breakdown of sorts.' The Doctor began pacing to and fro across the small room. 'The bag she picked up. Where is it?'

Sergeant Lines shrugged. 'Hastings, I presume. Shall I get it sent over?'

'Yes, please. Now, about this cottage.'

'Hold on, Doctor,' said Lines, holding his hands up again. 'It's nearly midnight. Now, I'm happy to help you, but not tonight. It's dark, we're all tired, and that building is so dilapidated, it's a death trap. There's no light, heating or even power lines to jury-rig anything onto. First thing tomorrow, I'll meet you here and we'll go up there with a couple of the boys.' He stared at the Doctor, anticipating a heated reply. 'But not tonight.'

'You are absolutely correct, Sergeant. I'll see you here at seven thirty?'

Sergeant Lines thought of a warm bed, a warm wife, and warm tea and toast. He also thought of his usual eight o'clock shower. Then he thought about Barbara Redworth. 'Seven thirty it is. Can I ask one question, Doctor?'

'Be my guest.'

'How did you, or the mysterious UNIT, find out about this?'

As the Doctor threw his cape back over his shoulders, he took a large manila envelope from an inside pocket. 'Your police photographer, I presume. Someone had the good sense to pass them to a higher authority, who passed them on to UNIT. And me.'

Sergeant Lines frowned as he glanced through the photographs. 'These weren't taken by a police photographer. Joe from Hastings photographed the corpse, but he'd gone by the time Redworth was found.'

The Doctor stared at him, then opened the door and walked out into the corridor, nodding a greeting at Pat, who nipped in behind him to collect the tea things. 'I'm sure it doesn't matter. I'll see you tomorrow morning, Sergeant. Thank you for your help.'

Sergeant Lines and Pat, tea things in hand, watched him go back into the reception area and then out into the warm night. The door closed and they were alone in the station. It seemed unnaturally quiet and peaceful after the day's chaos.

'Who was that exactly, Sarge?'

Bob Lines smiled grimly. 'I've no idea, Pat. But I'll tell you this: I've had some nutters come into this nick with wild improbable stories in my time, but no one's ever been as convincing or direct as him. I've no clue who he is, but I'm going to help him because I think he knows more than we do about what's going on.'

Pat slid the hatchway shut. 'You mean he's got the answers?'

Sergeant Lines turned the lights off. 'Yeah. He just hasn't got the questions.'

The Sandybeach Hotel was not exactly the height of luxury or haute cuisine, but the Doctor had already investigated the quality of the cheese and wine it stocked and, for an out-of-season seaside bed-and-breakfast, it stood up to his scrutiny remarkably well.

When he had checked in, a surly landlord had taken his crisp new notes obtained from the UNIT accounts' office and had offered him the 'customary welcoming glass of vino'. Despite the dinginess of the bar area, with flowered wallpaper and newspaper cuttings about local theatres pinned to a cork board, the two men were soon engaged in a long and hard discussion about the best wines, where to obtain them and how best to store them. The landlord had looked bewildered when the Doctor had described 'a pleasant little vinegar he'd picked up on Elbyon' but had chosen to ignore it, and pour another glass of the palatable house red instead.

The Doctor now stood outside the darkened hotel,

staring up at the window of his room-with-a-view. He felt for the front-door key in one of his cape pockets and, as his fingers felt the contours of it, something made him turn back towards the cliff-side.

Further up the long cliff path, he could just make out the shape of the lonely cottage on the cliff-edge, where Barbara Redworth had obviously seen something. Whatever it was, it had caused her to start drawing pictures similar to the ones he had seen during the incident at Wenley Moor a few months earlier.

And the Doctor knew he could not wait until seven thirty in the morning to find out. As the town clock chimed midnight, he gathered his cape tightly around him to keep out the cold sea wind and walked up towards Bessie. It took him a few minutes to reach the car, which was parked in a small lay-by at the foot of the cliff road, and opened the boot to extract a powerful torch. He tested it, sending a strong beam of white light into the dark skies above. Without the glow from orange city lights to obscure them, the stars flickered back in their incalculable numbers.

Using the light of the torch to guide him, he made his way along the narrow road, out of the town and up towards the remote cottage. As soon as the penumbra of the last street-light had faded, he turned back and scanned the street behind him. The man who had been following him since he left the hotel was no longer in sight. Perhaps it had been someone out late, catching a last breath of sea air before retiring. But the man hadn't looked or dressed like a local, and something at the edge of the Doctor's mind told him he was still being watched.

Not that it mattered, he thought. With his impeccable taste in clothes, it wouldn't be the first time that he had been followed by someone overcome with sartorial curiosity and awe. Given the way the seventies seemed to be going, he expected it to happen a lot more often in the next few years. The important thing for him at this stage was to investigate the cottage. He turned and strode off up the slope.

As he approached the building, he saw the blue-and-white striped tape cordoning off the whole area. His torch picked out a crude sign attached to the tape, politely informing the public that this was a police investigation area, it was unsafe, and they should stay well away.

Ignoring the warning, he ducked underneath and walked to the front door. His sonic screwdriver made quick work of dismantling the simple padlock, and he pushed the door open.

Like WPC Redworth, the Doctor quickly noted the fabric of the sofa-covering which had been melted into the window frames. He ran a finger along the join.

Definitely Silurian.

He made straight for the upstairs bathroom, but there was little to see there. Some of the bath-water had clearly evaporated. More material had been fused to the window, but a corner of it had been pulled away, revealing deep gouges in the plaster-work.

After a further ten minutes of searching, he had discovered very little. It was not until he was back downstairs, preparing to leave, that he saw the cellar entrance. It would have been easy to miss; a hatchway set into the stone floor of the ruined kitchenette, looking exactly like one of the flagstones except for two small recessed handles, made of rusted metal.

The Doctor slipped his fingers under the handles at either end and pulled up with a sharp tug. The trapdoor did not budge, but the corroded metal at one end gave way and he fell backwards, landing heavily on his backside, the cellar door unmoved.

He knelt over it, running his finger over the grooves around the edge. The police had clearly noticed it – there was fingerprint dust near the handles, revealing nothing – but, like him, they had failed to open it. Sergeant Lines would probably claim that as it had been unopened for so long, it would probably stay shut for ever.

The Doctor stared at it. The flagstone floor was much older than the rest of the cottage, so there must have been a building here long before the present one was built. A cellar in such an old building in a place like this would have been a passage or hideaway for smugglers or their wares, probably during the seventeenth century. In which case, there would be a bolt or lock on the underside, to foil the Customs men.

Setting his sonic screwdriver to a pulse, he passed it around the four sides until there was a bleep, like sonar, registering something beneath. Resetting the device, he concentrated on that area over the bolt, a thin cutting beam quickly severing the unseen bolt in two.

Seconds later the hatch was up and the Doctor was descending the damp wooden steps. At the bottom, dry sand formed a path leading into the gloom. The Doctor suspected that it would eventually lead to a concealed cave on the beach, hidden from the sight of any observers on the cliff top such as Customs men.

Checking his torch's power levels, he set off. Whatever had been in the house had clearly used this route. His suspicions were soon confirmed when he found two distinctive three-clawed footprints in the increasingly damp sand.

He was dealing with another colony of Silurians. Would they be hostile or relaxed? Would they allow him to mediate with the humans, as he'd tried to once before?

Before any of these questions could begin to be answered, he heard a cry, unmistakably a young boy or girl in trouble. He ran out of the tunnel and onto the blustery seashore.

The first thing he registered was the familiar sound from a three-note Silunan calling-box, carried on the wind. Flashing his torch in the right direction, he caught a glimpse of a Silurian talking to what appeared to be a half-naked human. A teenaged boy.

He switched his torch off. Something was stirring in the sea. He watched, fascinated, as another Silurian, also in a long mesh-like garment, rose from the waves. The Doctor noted that like the dry Silurian, this one had features slightly different from the ones he had encountered in Wenley, most notably two fins instead of ears, growing out and backwards.

'Hello?' he called. 'Hello, I want to help. I know who you are and—'

The Silurian from the sea was the only one that heard him. With a shriek, it turned and pointed at him. Its third eye began to glow red, its head moving rhythmically from side to side.

The Doctor saw the first Silurian stop talking to the boy and begin to run towards him. A second later, as the full effect of the Silurian eyeblast hit, he fell gasping to his knees.

'I want to help you all,' he gasped and then, with a small choking gurgle, fell face-down into the wet sand.

The damp Silurian walked over and kicked at the Doctor's prostrate body.

'Ape vermin. You will all be wiped out.'

Again, the Silurian aimed its third eye. The Doctor, gasping in hard and shallow breaths, began to writhe under the onslaught.

THREE

It was a tiny island, with a surface of rocks and lichen. A few low bushes and hardy flowers struggled to survive on its bleak surface, but most of the plants that tried to sprout rapidly died as the small amount of available earth was quickly used up, or washed away by the spray from the waves that crashed against and over the island's surface.

Once upon a time it had been attached to the continent that mankind referred to as Europe – southern France to be precise – but the movement of tectonic plates many millions of years ago had caused a cluster of rocky outcroppings to break away from the mainland. Violently dragged away by nature, and eroded by the lashings of the English Channel, they settled some way away and eventually became known as the Channel Islands by the French and British, who would spend centuries arguing over their ownership.

The average Briton or Frenchman asked about the islands can name Jersey, Guernsey, Alderney and Sark. The handful of smaller rocks that surround them are usually ignored. Most people are not even aware that they exist.

Of them all, the southernmost island, thirty-five minutes by motorboat from its nearest neighbour, is the least known and least visited. Less than half a mile across, it is known to the locals as L'Ithe. A couple of ornithologists once stayed overnight and, in 1969, a small group of hippies wanting to explore free love further than the Isle of Wight pop festival would allow hired a boat and sailed to L'Ithe to set up a commune.

They returned home within a week, claiming the island was haunted. The few papers that mentioned the story put it down to experiments with LSD, but a popular medium called Psychic Shirl travelled to the island with a reporter and photographer from the *Daily Mirror* to see if they could summon up any unearthly apparitions. They failed, and after a few weeks most interest in the island faded. This came as a relief to the inhabitants of the Channel Islands – it was one less potential attraction that would bring tourists to tramp all over their unspoiled countryside.

Only Tom Renault complained. Originally hailing from Rotherham (and christened Thomas Reynold), he considered himself the Channel Islands' only true entrepreneur and saw the potential of the 'Haunted Isle' as a tourist attraction. With his fake French accent and self-created heritage, Tom advertised his cheap holidays on the island as far away as the *Winchester Gazette* and *Portsmouth Herald*.

No one was interested. Worse, the other islanders began to shun him, notably after the Dame of Sark wrote to him personally and asked him to drop the idea. Writing back, he acknowledged her worries but explained that, as a businessman, he had every right to exploit whatever he could to make his livelihood. There had been no response. Having offended the islands' most revered figure, he was speedily ostracised.

Things became so bad that one day Tom announced he was leaving Jersey to build a house on 'his' island, where he would live. Deciding that being rid of Tom was preferable to trying to stop him, no one raised an eyebrow when he loaded up his rowing boat with wood and departed for L'Ithe.

Four days later, Tom's boat was found drifting near the Port of Guernsey. Sitting in it was Tom, or what was assumed to be Tom. The dead body was horrifically burnt, as was the bottom of the boat. It was suggested that he had knocked over an oil lamp, or that an ember from a cigarette had caught a leaking petrol can. The wood he was carrying must have combusted in seconds, and Tom would have been caught in the flames. No oil lamp or petrol can was found in the boat, but Tom might have knocked it overboard as he struggled.

A doctor from Southampton confirmed Tom's identity from his dental records and his remains were flown back to Rotherham, where two distant cousins and an old school friend witnessed his cheap burial in a local cemetery.

Only one fact of the case might have raised suspicion, but the Guernsey police never commented on it, although PC Stuart Halton had mentioned it in his report. PC Halton had been called to the scene when the boat was sighted; he was responsible for physically dragging the craft into the dock, and checking Tom's body. Later, he had the boat taken back to the station for safekeeping. Five months later, after an inquest recorded a verdict of accidental death, the boat was smashed up and used as firewood. What PC Halton had observed, and what everyone seemed to have ignored, was that the burning seemed to have continued underwater: the keel of the boat was scorched and charred. Moreover, the tiny hole that was leaking water into the boat seemed to have been burnt through from underneath.

Halton's report was filed away when the case was closed and never seen again. After a few months, Tom

Renault was almost forgotten, and not missed. As far as PC Halton and his colleagues were concerned, copies of the files were passed to the Police Records Department of the Central Office of Information. And forgotten.

Until they were read by a six-foot blonde Dutch woman called Jana Kristan, who had gained access to the Central Office of Information using her National Union of Journalists: Foreign Correspondents Chapel card.

She had photocopied PC Halton's report, ringed his comments about the direction of the burning in red, and returned the original file. As she had handed it back, and signed the COI waiver form stapled to the inside of the file, she had noted that three days previously, someone else had been reading it. Jana had tried to read the signature, turning it on its side and even upside down, but no matter what she did, there had been no way of deciphering the spider-like scrawl.

Then she had gone to London Bridge station and caught a train to Tunbndge Wells, where she had changed for the local service via Hastings to Smallmarshes.

'I am an Earth Reptile. It is what I always have been. It is what I shall be until the day I die. And beyond. Any works left behind bearing my name, the name Baal D'jo, will acknowledge to the future that whilst I lived, I was an Earth Reptile.

'I am an Earth Reptile. My heritage is the Earth. Not to cower below it. Not to cast it aside. My heritage is to walk freely upon the surface of my world. This world I, and my forebears, shaped. It is a world that, I acknowledge, may have forgotten me, but a world which will soon remember. It is a world that shall welcome me back with open arms and I shall wallow in its glory.

'I am an Earth Reptile. My future belongs to Earth, to my forebears and my ascendants. My future, brothers and sisters, kith and kin, is your future. Together we shall unbind the chains that hold us in the past, the misdemeanours of the old, ignorant and afraid. Together we shall reclaim Earth for ourselves. If the Apes will not accept our supremacy, they will be eradicated.

'I am an Earth Reptile. You are all Earth Reptiles. Today begins the dawn of our future.'

'Tautology, Baal.' Auggi punched a button on the console. 'Correct final paragraph,' she said to the computer screen. The last paragraph was immediately outlined in red. 'You'll need to rewrite that piece.'

Baal dragged a claw across the sensor pad. 'What about the whole thing, Mother? Is it what Chukk would call inflammatory?'

'Oh, I imagine so, Baal. In fact, I certainly hope it is. He could do with a shock. Your recital of this at Chamber tomorrow night will certainly give him that.' She stepped away from the computer. 'I shall leave you to rewrite the last part. "Beginning" and "dawn" mean the same thing in the sense you're using them.'

Baal stared at the text and then nodded his understanding. 'Thank you, Mother.' He looked her in the eye and held up his right hand, claws retracted, palm facing forward. She placed her palm flat against his and they bowed to each other.

'Good night, my dear.' With another slight bow, Auggi left the room and set off into the depths of the Shelter.

As she walked down the rough passageway to her quarters, she smiled. Everything was going to plan. Sula and Tahni should be returning from whatever task Baal had sent them on, while he was preparing his speech.

And she was, well, waiting. Waiting for her moment, her triumph. After all these years... she stopped. 'After all these years'. Interesting phrase. To her and the others in the Shelter, it had only seemed about ten years. In reality, it had been many millions.

Millions of years during which their civilisation had vanished without trace. The whole world had changed. Continents and land masses had moved and split, and where once there had been only a few land masses, now there were many. Icthar and the Triad had told her and Chukk that thousands of their fellows had died, oblivious to their fate, as tectonic plates and continental drift had pulverised their Shelters, killing them while they hibernated.

Icthar and his Shelter had awoken around forty years previously, and through the Triad's researches, much had been learnt of the 'new' occupiers of Earth. The tiny planetoid that the Science Division had spotted had not swept past Earth. It had not sucked the atmosphere away with it, but had fallen into orbit around the Earth. Having failed to leave their solar system, it had not triggered the machines that would awaken the Earth Reptiles from their hibernation. And so, the Earth Reptiles had continued sleeping for millennia until the Apes had unwittingly awoken them.

Auggi recalled the most exciting communication she and Chukk had received from Icthar, sent from the Triad's base on the other side of the world.

'We have thrilling news, Chukk,' Icthar had said. 'The Triad has received salutations from two Shelters, both within your immediate vicinity.'

Chukk had immediately punched up the unfamiliar map of the world as it was now. 'Are they on this land mass, or this?' he had asked, pointing wildly at green blotches of Ape-infested land.

Icthar had indicated the uppermost one. 'About a third of the way up, in the centre. And Chukk?'

Chukk had twitched his fingers eagerly, exposing and retracting his claws in that annoying nervous habit that he had. 'Yes?'

It had been Scibus, Icthar's second, who spoke. 'It is your brother's Shelter. Okdel lives!'

Chukk had been overjoyed, and it had fallen to Auggi, as always, to return normality to the conversation. 'Let us not forget, Nobel Icthar, that it was Okdel L'da, Bokka K'to and their associates who consigned us to this prison in the first place. I am… gratified that they have survived these millennia, but I will not share any elation about the personnel that Shelter contains.'

Scibus leant forward, as if he'd only just seen Auggi on his screen. 'Is that you, Auggi D'jo? We have news for your spouse. Is he there?'

Auggi stared at the figure before her. 'My apologies, Scibus. I assumed that you had taken note of Chukk's plentiful messages, relayed to your Shelter at great expense to our power resources. My beloved Daurrix did not survive the hibernation. Only my son and daughters remain to welcome me into aged wisdom.'

Icthar took centre stage once again. 'Enough, Auggi. Of course we were grieved to hear of Daurrix's death. Scibus had momentarily forgotten.' He seemed to stare through the monitor directly and for a fleeting moment even Auggi felt his presence in the room, as if his wisdom and benevolence really did touch all of them. With an involuntary shiver, she disposed of that thought. 'Remember, in the years to come, all Earth Reptiles are as one family again.'

Auggi had punched her hand onto the sensor, cutting the sound. Icthar was clearly still talking, but his well-meaning pearls of wisdom were lost to posterity.

Chukk had looked appalled. 'Auggi, that was rude. No, more than rude, it was a flagrant abuse of the privilege you have been granted.'

Auggi had been livid. 'Privilege? Just remember, Chukk, you are only leader of this Shelter because Daurrix is dead and your blatant fawning to Icthar in the old days made you something of a favourite with him. But know this –' she jabbed a claw towards the screen, where the Triad had realised they could not be heard and were peering at their monitors, trying to see what was going on '– know this, it is my son and daughters prepared to risk all to save us, while the Triad sit and debate. My family is prepared to die if there is any chance for the rest of the young here to survive.' Auggi flicked the visual contact off. 'Don't you dare try to revoke any "privileges" you believe you have honoured me with. I am here to stay, Chukk. Here to ensure you do not betray the principles for which this unique Shelter stands, rather than ingratiating yourself with our "fellow" Reptiles who, a few million years ago, sought to exterminate us all.'

Auggi was still staring at him, daring him to respond, as visual and aural contact was renewed by the Triad.

'Come in Shelter 429, this is the Triad Encampment. Can you see or hear us?'

The angry mother punched the sensor again and stared directly into the monitor. 'Yes, Tarpok, we can hear you quite well. We had a power fluctuation, leading to a communications breakdown.' She shot a glare towards Chukk. 'Chukk believes it is now sorted out satisfactorily.'

She stood up. 'I will leave you with him.'

Scibus spoke again. 'Before you leave, do not forget the news I had for you, Auggi. Your late partner's original colony has been awoken by Ape ships in the area, and has sent us a message. They are delighted that you are all alive and hope to speak to you shortly. They are located just below the central southern point on the same land mass as Okdel's Shelter. If there are three surviving Shelters in such a small area, there must be more. Finding them must become a priority.'

Auggi nodded. 'If my beloved's family has any true honour, they will find a way to eradicate the Apes and return our planet to us.' She tugged her webbed robe tightly around her and strode out of the communications room.

Now she stood there again, six months later. Okdel was dead, along with everyone in his Shelter. The Apes had discovered them and destroyed them. According to one of young Morka's final reports to Icthar, Okdel had betrayed them to the Apes and been removed from power. Morka had announced that they had used Bokka K'to's famous vermin virus on the Apes, but his last message said that the Apes had found a cure.

They never heard from the Shelter again. Icthar wanted to mount a rescue but, in an unusually sensible moment, Chukk pointed out that if neither his dishonoured brother nor Morka could have saved the Shelter, there was no point in risking discovery by travelling such a great distance on what would almost certainly be a fruitless mission.

Auggi thought it amusing that once again Icthar had suggested using Reptiles outside the Triad to investigate. And that when they refused, the idea of investigation was dropped. The Triad might be noble, all-powerful leaders of great quality and brilliance, but as far as she was concerned they were foolish cowards whose survival of the hibernation was nothing less than a tragedy for the rest of the Earth Reptile species. At a time like this, with the planet overrun by vermin, leadership would be better placed in the hands of one of the other Shelters – in fact, in the hands of anyone other than the Triad – or the aquatic military caste: the legendary Sea Devil Warriors.

Auggi's mind returned to Daurrix and his excommunication from the Sea Devil Warriors. Here they were, after all that disgrace, all that humiliation, expected to welcome the Sea Devils back as their brethren, as if nothing had happened.

Again, none of the Triad had ventured out of their Shelter to communicate with the Sea Devils themselves. That was hardly surprising. Icthar and the others were just as wary of the Sea Devil Warriors as everyone else. All those years of underwater inactivity had clearly addled their brains. Daurrix's uncle, an adviser to the Chief Sea Devil, had told her that they were planning an attack on the Apes using their traditional aquatic method: underside burning. Much as it pained Auggi to think along such lines, there was no getting away from the fact that Ape scientific progress had begun to mirror theirs. Another three or four hundred years and the Apes would be at the level Reptile society had reached before the Great Hibernation.

'I thought you had retired to rest, Auggi.'

She turned at the voice, and a chill went through her body. 'Good evening, Krugga. What brings you to this level so late at night?'

'Night? Day? Do we really think about such things, Auggi? Your greeting – so antiquated, so unreal.' Krugga strode in. Auggi stared up at him – even by reptile standards, he was huge, seemingly composed entirely of vast muscle. He wore a breastplate, like those worn by the Triad. No matter how hard the armourers had looked, they had been unable to find one entirely large enough for him, and the plate was ridiculously small against his bulk. He crossed the communications room in three strides, and began to check the equipment. Despite her sudden chill, Auggi was outraged.

'Are you checking up on me, Krugga?' She pointed at the communicator and console monitor. 'Who do you believe I was talking to? The Sea Devils? The Triad?'

Krugga shrugged, his breastplate creaking with the movement. 'I never suggested anything, Auggi. I am merely doing my job, as requested by Baal. The experiments are approaching an important peak and I need to ensure that your daughters can contact us when they are ready. Feel free to leave now, I am preparing to await their messages.'

Feeling dismissed, but also aware that arguing with Krugga was pointless, Auggi bowed. With a sarcastic bow back, Krugga raised his right palm, claws retracted, in the traditional gesture of friendship.

Auggi stared at him for a moment, her third eye glowing red in anger. Seeing a slight jerk in Krugga's form, she left the room, satisfied that she might have pushed him back down a peg or two.

Ten minutes later she was in the elevator returning her to the hibernation level, where the Earth Reptiles still kept their personal quarters. A few minutes after that, she was on her damp bed of seaweed and lichen, curled up and fast asleep.

The blond man with the suntan was not a very nice

person to know. His wife would have confirmed that, if he had not beaten her to death. If he had not been knifed in a gangland killing, watched by his then 21-year-old son, his father might have agreed.

Very few people had a good word to say about the blond man, which suited him fine because he had very little good to say about anyone else. The only people that mattered to him were his targets. Seeing them die at his more than capable hands was not just his job, but his hobby. His vocation.

His obsession with death had begun when he was a teenager, down at the local flea-pit cinema where he could watch cheap American movies heavy with gratuitous carnage and emotionless sex. The sex had never interested him; he felt almost embarrassed by watching it, and by the similar noises coming from the seats behind him. He went there for the violence. The power that came from aiming a gun at someone, pulling the trigger and ending a life so abruptly and succinctly. Who needed sexual gratification when there was death to be dealt out? Front row, centre seat, with every shot, every gun, every death in close-up. He revelled in it.

With the money from his first job, he began to buy every book and magazine he could find about weapons and death. Within a year, he had emptied his bedsit of anything that did not relate to weapons: knives, swords, explosives and firearms. Firearms were his favourites, and they became his true love.

He married a local girl he had met at a fairground. She had been impressed with his marksmanship at the shooting range, despite the misaligned sights on the air rifle. He gave her the fluffy elephant he won that night; she took his virginity. Two months later they got married. It had seemed like the thing to do, and for about six weeks it was a satisfactory arrangement. Then she began nagging him about getting a proper job and so he found one through his father, running errands for the underworld characters who ruled a majority of London's East End in the fifties. He liked the work, and his bosses liked him. The first person he killed was an accident; the second wasn't. The morning after, they gave him a gun and a photograph. He came back that afternoon with blood on his shirt, a smile on his face, and an extra two hundred pounds in his bank account.

Execution after execution followed: sometimes a bullet in the back of the head for disobedience or arrogance, sometimes straight assassinations in bars and clubs, cars and parks. He became known for his discretion and professionalism. The police knew he was the culprit but could not pin so much as a parking ticket on him.

He only ever made one mistake. He had returned home one night after disposing of two particularly unreliable police informants. His wife had been angry over something simple. Was it food for the dog? Was it that his dinner was cold? Had he forgotten her birthday or their anniversary? He could not really remember. It all seemed so insignificant at the time. She had yelled, screamed and thrown things. He had followed her up to the bedroom, pushed her onto the bed and pistol-whipped her around the head.

Dazed, confused and in a great deal of pain, she had begged forgiveness. Wrong. He'd thought she was strong, he'd respected her for that. Now he knew she was weak. She should have fought back. He shot her cleanly, up through the chin, spreading her brain all over the bed-sheets.

He grabbed a few clothes, threw them into a bag and left. He never went back.

He found out that a neighbour, alerted a day later by the whining of their Alsatian, had called the police. Finding her body with his bloodsoaked fingerprints all over her had given them all the evidence they needed; and the riffing on the bullet connected him to a dozen more murders. But by that time he was already in Brazil, and he kept moving.

The blond man stayed abroad for six or seven years, shifting from country to country, selling his services to anyone who could pay. Rich gangsters, South American governments, and even the American intelligence forces utilised his talents at times. He took their money and their equipment, and honed his skills until he believed there was no one better than him.

It had been one of his contacts in the CIA who had told him that if he returned to Britain, instead of the arrest he anticipated, the blond man would be welcomed by various parties. His safety would be guaranteed. The money offered was excellent. But it was the guns he was promised, the range and capabilities of them, that clinched the offer.

Taking as few risks as possible, the blond man flew into Manchester airport with black hair and a false passport. As promised, he was greeted by a man whose name he had never asked. He accepted jobs as and when they were offered, comfortable in the knowledge that the police were unable to touch him.

Now, he had been given the task of killing the man known as the Doctor, somewhere in or around Smallmarshes. It had looked like a simple job: trail the target, kill him in a remote spot, weight the body and dump it at sea. What had gone wrong, he never understood. The Doctor had gone into the deserted cottage just after midnight, and never came out. The blond man had waited half an hour before following him in, but there was no sign, trail or trace of the target. The blond man had watched the cottage all night, but when a police car arrived early the following morning he gave up and returned to London. He had been denied a kill, and he was puzzled and seething.

His nameless contact, a scarred, pale young man who always wore a suit and dark glasses, met him at London Bridge station. The car that had dropped him in Smallmarshes was waiting for them outside the station, the silent Nigerian in the driver's seat, and they drove over the bridge, then westwards through London. As they headed along the Embankment, the pale young man passed him a photograph.

'This man is your next target. He's not a villain. Well, within reason; he is a member of Her Majesty's Government. So security's going to be tight on this one.' The pale young man shifted slightly, leaning over the blond man's shoulder. 'We need him dead because someone is on our tail, trying to do our work for us and getting everything in a right old tizzy as a result.'

'I don't need to know that.' The blond man studied the corpulent figure in the photograph, memorising every detail of face and build. His pale companion appeared not to have heard him, and continued.

'With this poor man dead, we can heap the blame wholly onto Sir Marmaduke Harrington-Smythe CB bloody E, close down his little entourage and make life better for everyone. Plus the Glasshouse got hold of our policewoman before we could. Made quite a kerfuffle, I understand, at Hastings General. We need to expose them for that as well.'

As they turned right, then left into Parliament Square, the blond man stared up at the House of Commons. 'In there?'

'In there,' his companion confirmed.

'When?'

'Three o'clock this afternoon.'

'That's cutting it tight. Not much time for preparation.'

The pale man turned to him, his expression implacable. 'Can you do it?'

'No problem.' He patted his case.

The chauffeur pulled over in front of Westminster Abbey and the blond man got out. His strange employer unwound the car window.

'By the way. The Doctor?'

The blond man did not even pause. 'Job done. UNIT will be needing a new scientific adviser.' He picked his bag up, and walked down past the Methodist Central Hall and left into Petty France. He was soon just a part of the crowd, along with the tourists and visitors to the passport office. He entered St James's Park underground station and headed back to his tiny bed-sit in Notting Hill, preparing mentally and physically for his next job.

The moment Liz put the key into the front door of her flat, she felt a chill. As if someone had just walked over her grave, as the saying went.

She pushed the door open – something was blocking it. Letters. Circulars. A massive clothing catalogue of the sort that the previous tenant obviously thrived upon, because a different one seemed to appear every week. No matter how many times Liz rang or wrote to the companies, the catalogues kept coming.

She added it to the pile next to the phone and scooped up the rest of the post. Obviously Mrs Longhurst, her landlady who lived in the flat below, had not been in here for some time.

The Doctor, Liz recalled, had once offered Liz the use of a flat he owned in Soho, but central London didn't appeal to her. Born and bred in the Home Counties, Liz preferred the outskirts of the city to being in its heart. Besides which, the Dean Street flat was far too noisy and cramped, and she could never have kept a pet there.

She wandered into her living room, flicking through the various letters, tossing the circulars into the round waste-paper basket without a second glance, and following them with a couple of postcards of foreign climes, with trite clichés scrawled on the back. Liz abhorred clutter and saw no purpose in pinning up colourful photographs, twenty years out of date, from Rhodes or Egypt in her kitchenette.

Beside a rarely used black-and-white television that Mrs Longhurst had supplied, rattled a cage with a guinea-pig in it. Regularly fed and watered, more by Mrs Longhurst than by Liz, she was ashamed to say, John-Paul clearly wanted some attention. Liz wasn't an animal person at heart, but when she had first moved to London, a well-meaning Cambridge friend had bought her the two guinea-pigs as a house-warming gift.

One, Ringo-George, died soon after the move, and Liz found herself needing to keep the other more as a reminder of life at Cambridge and her friends up there, than out of any real liking for it as a companion.

Yet as it stared up at her now, Liz felt a rush of affection flood over her and she bent over, lifted the lid off the cage and scooped up the little bundle of fur, feeling it squirm and kick in her hand. She raised it to eye level and blew a kiss at it, adding a few silly noises for good measure. 'Aren't you the most beautiful guinea-pig in the world, then?'

People had told her that keeping a pet was a good way of relieving stress. She'd never taken it seriously until, as she flopped onto the sofa, she let John-Paul wriggle on her lap for a second, as he got comfortable.

'No, don't get settled,' she said. 'I want a cup of tea, if you don't mind.'

It was too late: John-Paul was breathing deeply, fast asleep, and she could not bring herself to disturb him. He looked so tranquil that she could feel his simple happiness spreading into her too.

She was definitely getting soft in her old age. Reaching across to the coffee table, careful not to up-end the animal, she used her fingertips to slowly drag the letters towards her. When they were close enough, she grabbed them and leant back, flicking through the pile. The first had a typed address, and a look at the back told her it was from her bank. 'Later.' The next was in the familiar handwriting of Jeff Johnson. 'Sorry, but a long lecture about my life, ruts, and lack of direction I don't need right now,' she said, putting it to the back. The third envelope was also hand-written but she didn't recognise the writing, and she was about to open it when she saw another, addressed in the same writing further down the pile. She compared them and opened the one that had come three days before the other.

```
Dear Doctor Shaw,
    I shall keep this brief. My friend
Grant Traynor and I are very worried
about  the  activities  of  C19.  You
```

probably know them as the liaison between the British Government, your UNIT group and the United Nations. But there is far more to C19 than you, Brigadier Lethbridge-Stewart, Commodore Gilmore, Major-General Scobie, and certainly Sir John Sudbury are aware.

We, Traynor and I, elected to try and contact you. Your non-military background makes you seem far more, shall we say, open-minded to the possibility of corruption and deceit at the highest levels. We feel that you have much less invested in the establishment than a military person, and less to lose except your personal honour. No one can demote you or cut off your pension if you disagree with them.

Traynor is currently based up at C19's north-eastern research station, attempting to find some concrete evidence to bring to your attention. Naturally, you don't know anything about C19's activities up north, do you? And why should you?

Well, we believe that you and every citizen of Britain, if not the whole UN, ought to know. What is going on there has terrifying implications for us all.

I am sure you know what the Glasshouse

is. You may assume (because we doubt anyone will have thought to tell you differently) that it is connected with C19, and therefore the Government, UNIT in Geneva and so on.

You would be wrong, I'm afraid. My dear Elizabeth, be prepared to discover the truth about many things you've taken for granted while at UNIT. You are the only civilian employed by UNIT and, despite your signature on the OSA form (I have the document in front of me), you are the only person within the operation who could uncover the truth.

You will have help. A journalist from Amsterdam is in the country. She is looking for a big story, and frankly we are inclined to help her get it. Breaking C19 wide open can only be beneficial for all concerned.

If you would like to know more, or meet up with the journalist, Miss Kristan, please let us know by leaving a light on in your living room window at 4am any night after the 23rd of this month. We will contact you soon.

I hope we can help each other and, ultimately our fellow mankind, by exposing the truth.

Yours,

A friend

There was no other name or signature.

Liz stared at the letter for a few moments, re-read it, and shook her head. What was going on? Why her? Was this a joke? Was Jeff trying to add some spice to her life? She tore open the subsequent letter:

```
Traynor  didn't  come.  He  hadn't  made
it.
   Damn.
   Traynor supplied all the evidence he
could, but is it going to be enough?
Probably  not,  but  the  man  did  his
best. Now it is my job to continue the
exposé.
```

Liz read the rest of it. The name 'Grant Traynor' rang a bell. Why? And why, if Traynor's identity was revealed, was her mysterious correspondent hiding his own identity?

She really wanted to disregard it as crank mail. But if that was the case, how had they discovered her connection to UNIT, and then found her home address? Even Maisie at UNIT didn't know it. Liz wasn't entirely sure if the Doctor had it either. As far as she knew, only the Brigadier knew where she lived. And Jeff and other friends. But UNIT-wise, she could only think of the Brigadier. Everyone else had the Cambridge flat's address and phone number.

Could Mrs Longhurst have told anyone? Unlikely. She thought Liz was only a civil servant who worked away from home a lot.

The phone rang and Liz jumped. John-Paul squeaked and raised a sleepy head. Liz was sure he had an annoyed glare on his face. 'Sorry,' she mouthed at him, picked him up and, with a quick kiss, replaced him in the cage, grabbing the phone on the way. 'Hold on a sec, please,' she said and threw the receiver onto the sofa.

With John-Paul locked away, she grabbed the phone and sat back down. 'Sony about that.'

'Hello. Doctor Shaw?' A woman's voice, with some kind of European accent. Liz was going to ask who it was, but the letter caught her eye and she decided to make a stab in the dark.

'Yes, this is Liz. Is that Miss Kristan?'

There was a pause and then the stranger spoke again: 'Yeah. Yes, I am. How did you know?'

Liz could not really answer that. 'A guess.'

'Well, I'm impressed. Did you get a couple of letters from a friend who didn't give you his name?'

Liz said that she had but, having not been at home on the night of the 23rd, she had failed to light the lamp.

'Light the lamp? Jesus, how melodramatic. The British sense of humour is well known, but that's almost medieval.'

Liz laughed. 'Well, Chicago in the thirties, at least. Look, do you understand any of this?'

The woman on the phone said she did not. 'My editor in Amsterdam gave me a message a few days ago, telling me to go to the Central Office of Information in London, where I was told to look up a particular file about a fire in the Channel Islands. When I got there and showed them my identification, there was a letter waiting for me, telling me to go to a place called Smallmarshes and watch.'

'And did you?'

The woman laughed. Quite a nice laugh, Liz thought. 'Yeah, I went. Pathetic place, full of pathetic people, but very... well, English I suppose. But I certainly saw some interesting things and I think we should discuss them.'

Liz felt torn. On the one hand, it sounded as though something of genuine importance and interest might be going on. On the other, she wasn't sure that she wanted to be involved. Still, she reasoned, one meeting would not commit her to anything. They agreed a time and place, and Miss Kristan hung up.

A few moments later, the telephone rang again.

'Hello. Is that Doctor Shaw?' It was the voice of an old man, with a rich, upper-class accent.

'Who are you?'

'Unimportant, Elizabeth, quite unimportant.'

Elizabeth. No one called her Elizabeth, apart from her mother and father when they were tetchy. The man on the phone was certainly not her father. The letter once again caught her eye. Its anonymous author had called her Elizabeth.

The voice carried on: 'I tried to reach you at UNIT. Spoke to the Doctor, I think, and some army clod later, but I'd obviously missed you. I'm glad you're home. Please don't bother asking how I got your number or address. I watched your flat, but there was no light. I can only assume that you have not been back lately.'

'No. No, I've… Now look, who are you?'

'Traynor's dead, poor chap.' There was a short silence. 'If you want further proof that we, or rather I, am telling the truth, watch the news tonight. I'm going to tell Jana Kristan to do the same, now I know you've spoken. Au revoir.'

The phone went dead. Liz stared at the silent receiver in her hands, her mind trying to sift through, sort out and make some sense of the information that she had just received. How did this all fit together? What did

Smallmarshes have to do with C19?

'And just how, pray tell, did you know I'd spoken to this Jana Kristan, eh?' She turned and looked at John-Paul, now running around in his cage. 'Tell me that?'

John-Paul, obviously, had no answer.

It was six minutes to three. The wall-clock outside the office, which overlooked the Square, chimed three times. It was deliberately set early. That way any errant MPs, civil servants and administrators who worked in the Houses of Parliament could, in the current Speaker of the House's vernacular, 'get their arses in gear'.

'Sir John, you are due at Lord Blake's reception in fifteen minutes or so.'

Sir John Sudbury sighed. He knew that. He knew where he was meant to be, when he was meant to be there, why he was meant to be there and even how he was meant to be getting there.

'What I do not know is what I have done in the eyes of the Lord to be presented with you, Clive Alexander Fortescue, former Secretary to the Chief of Defence, as my own private pain-in-the-posterior. Fortescue, if you continually take valuable time telling me I am going to be tardy, then tardy I will be, simply because you have distracted me. In other words—'

'Yes, sir. I know. "Shut up, Clive."' Fortescue shuffled some of Sir John's papers into a black briefcase.

'Exactly. "Shut up, Clive." Words spoken, no doubt, a great many times by the Chief of Defence over the years.'

Fortescue nodded. 'Yes, Sir John. Familiar sentiments. Nevertheless, you are due there in—'

'Clive. Belt up.' Sir John stared at him. 'There. A new phrase for you to learn.'

Clive Fortescue was in his early forties, physically slight in direct contrast to his master's portly frame. Thinning grey hair, over-sized horn-rimmed glasses and a slight moustache were the only ones of Fortescue's attributes which might be considered appropriate for a secretary. His clothes veered towards the flamboyant; his old school tie of yellow-and-black stripes was a permanent fixture at his neck, and his white silk shirt had the slight patterning that suggested something of a dandy. Fortescue closed the briefcase, and picked up Sir John's hat and scarf. 'Consider it heard, absorbed and learned, Sir John.'

Sir John stared at Fortescue. 'Good grief, man. Why on Earth do I need a hat and scarf? It's the middle of the summer, and I'm only going to my car!'

Fortescue seemed to have prepared an answer to that, much to Sir John's disappointment: 'Appearances, Sir John. There may be members of the press or television crews out there.'

Sir John crossed to the window and waved Fortescue over to join him. He pointed outside at throngs of people with cameras and notebooks at the ready, then indicated his own attire, formal black jacket and grey tie, pinstriped charcoal trousers and gold cufflinks. 'Bearing in mind that the Prime Minister is honouring us with his exalted presence, you know damned well that the press are there. I still fail to see why I should go out looking like a refugee from the Sad Old Men's Rest Home for the Bewildered.'

Fortescue shrugged. 'My apologies, Sir John. I just assumed that you'd want to look as though you were suitable for a position in the House of Lords.'

Sir John finally let his face crack into a smile. 'Oh, all right, you win this round. But –' he waved a finger at Fortescue – 'I vow to make you smile first this evening.

You are not going to win four rounds in a week.' Throwing his arm around Fortescue's shoulder, the older man led his friend and colleague downstairs.

They passed a few other Parliamentary figures and their secretaries scuttling about, and nodded at a few peers. As they went Sir John received a running commentary, *sotto voce*, from Fortescue about each peer and how long they were expected to remain alive.

'Do you know how many non-hereditary members of the House of Lords got there without being Members of the Commons?' Sir John asked. 'Very few indeed,' he answered himself. 'The opportunities simply aren't there. And—'

'"And frankly,"' quoted Fortescue, '"being Head of Department C19 is not a meal ticket to those comfy seats and long lunches." I know, but we both need to dream about something.'

Sir John smiled again. 'Ready to face the public, Mr Fortescue?'

'Whenever you are, Lord Sudbury of... of...?'

Sir John shrugged. 'I don't know, Fortescue. Where shall I be Lord Sudbury of?'

Fortescue pushed past a couple of people and caught a glimpse of Sir John's car, the driver standing by the near-side passenger door. 'Lord Sudbury of Late Appointments, I think. Why don't these reporter people bugger off back to Fleet Street and invent some copy like they normally do?'

Sir John raised a hand to acknowledge his driver. 'Good. It's that young Glasgow boy driving. What's his name?'

'Morton, Sir John. Try to get it right if you speak to him. Last time you called him Hughes, your previous dogsbody. Poor Morton didn't know whether to correct you or not.'

Sir John was astounded. 'Of course he should have. Poor chap must think I'm a beast or some such, ready to eat him alive. Never fear, young Morton will be correctly appellated, acknowledged and complimented on his driving.'

Fortescue passed the briefcase over as they reached the doors of the House. 'And if he's a bad driver?'

'All the better. It'd knock a few of the others off the road, eh?'

Fortescue nodded. 'You won't get anywhere if you don't tie your shoelace up, Sir John. Going head over heels in front of the BBC will not do any of our careers any good.'

'Thank you, Fortescue. What would I do without you?' With some difficulty, Sir John bent down to tie his lace.

'You're putting on weight, Sir John,' Fortescue laughed as he regarded Sir John's doubled-up form from the rear. He was still smiling when, less than a second later, a bullet entered his head at the bridge of his nose and punched its way through the back of his skull, showering blood over the Parliamentary stonework.

In an instant, the orderly crowd became a frenzied mob. Screams and shouts went up. The Prime Minister was pushed out of view by his personal secretaries, their side-arms drawn and ready. Sir John was pushed towards the ground as a middle-aged reporter dived into him.

Before either Sir John or his alert saviour had landed, two more shots rang out, both hitting Morton in the chest. He was hurled back against the car with enough force to crack two of the windows, and slumped to the ground.

As people rushed about, Sir John lay on the cold gravel, staring at Morton's dead body directly in front of him, the young man's shirt now more red than white. Shifting slightly, he turned to see if Fortescue was all right. It took a few seconds for him to realise that the headless corpse beside him was wearing Fortescue's distinctive black-and-yellow striped tie.

He heard the crack of another shot, and felt a sudden pain in his right shoulder. His brain registered the facts in an instant. He had been the target, not the Prime Minister. As the pain began numbing his arm, Sir John tapped the journalist lying across his back. 'Thank you, I think you saved my life.'

There was no answering movement. Sir John rolled slightly and the journalist flopped off, the last shot having gone straight through his body, killing him instantly, before burying itself in its intended victim.

As sirens began to wail and people ran towards the House, Sir John looked up. He was staring into the sun, but he could swear he saw someone moving at one of the high windows of an office building. It was a tiny figure, and at that distance he could not tell whether it was male or, heaven forbid, female. But the spring sun glinted off the long rifle it carried as it moved out of sight. Other hands pointed at the figure, and policemen dashed across the busy road to try and hunt down the assassin.

All Sir John could do, as an ambulance crew hurried towards him, was stare at the three dead men surrounding him. Guilty of nothing more than being in the way as he dropped out of the assassin's cross-hairs. He looked down at his still untied left shoelace, wondering whether to consider himself the most fortunate man alive, or whether his conscience could carry those three innocent lives and let him sleep at night. He doubted it.

Liz stared, transfixed as the BBC News logo gave way to

the familiar face of news-reader Corbett Woodall.

'Three men have died, and another was seriously wounded, in an attempt on the Prime Minister's life at the Houses of Parliament this afternoon. Shaken but unhurt, the Prime Minister told journalists later that the perpetrators of this outrageous act would be caught and punished. He would not rule out the possibility of a Northern Irish connection.

'Shortly before three o'clock, four shots were fired at the Prime Minister as he left the House of Commons. Sir John Sudbury, a junior Defence Minister and MP for Woodhaven, was wounded in the shoulder. The three dead men have been named as Sir John's private secretary, Clive Fortescue; Alan Morton, a Parliamentary driver; and Michael Wagstaffe, defence correspondent for the *Daily Chronicle*. Sir John is currently undergoing surgery in St Thomas's Hospital, but it is understood that his wound is not life-threatening.

'The Prime Minister has tonight reaffirmed his Government's anti-terrorist commitment, suggesting that he believes this attack to be the work of the IRA. The shots seem to have been fired—'

Liz switched the set off. The phone rang and she snatched it off its cradle.

'Yes?' she snapped.

'I'm sorry, Elizabeth, but I did tell you that something would happen.'

'Were you responsible for this? Is this some kind of attempt to get at me through people I know? People I work with?'

There was a pause, and then the old voice continued, sounding horrified: 'No. No, I assure you not. I just knew this was going to happen. It's following a pattern. I know who is responsible, and it's got nothing to do with Northern Ireland. It's all to do with UNIT, the Glasshouse, C19 and everything else you're involved in.'

'So, it is my fault. It's because of me—' Liz was almost hysterical.

The old voice was shouting: 'No! It's because of you, and your unique status in UNIT, that I need to rely on you. I've provided you with an associate, a real investigator, who can use her talents to help piece things together. She knows nothing about you, or where you work. Her independent view could help you sift through things.'

Liz swallowed. 'And why can't you do anything?'

The voice laughed. 'I'm an old man, Elizabeth. I've sat on the sidelines all my career. It's what I do best, manipulating people and situations. I thought I could contain them, you see, but I was wrong.'

'So,' said Liz, slowly. 'So, you know who "they" are?'

'Of course.'

'So why can't you tell me?'

There was a sigh on the other end of the telephone. 'Elizabeth, consider this to be a game of snakes and ladders. Yes, I could put a ladder leading from Square Two to Square Ninety-Nine. But you need to play the game, get through every square, find everything I found. Otherwise what I know, what you two find out, won't stand up to scrutiny, and won't stand up in court. If you confront them without having amassed every shred of evidence, they'll cover their tracks. They're very good, you know.' He stopped. 'Oh,' he said suddenly. 'You'll be pleased to know that Sir John Sudbury is going home tomorrow morning. He's fine, just a flesh wound.'

The telephone was dead again. The mystery man had gone. Liz found herself pulling her knees up onto the sofa, and hugging them. Suddenly the world seemed much larger and nastier than it had the day before.

The old man was waking up. The monsters had dressed him in one of those stupid-looking string vests although at least it was warm. They had piled the old man's clothes up next to him, but only after they had rummaged through his pockets and made a pile of the peculiar things they had found.

The monsters were sitting on the other side of the strange vehicle they were in. When Marc had first seen it, parked on the beach, he'd thought it was one of those funny electric vans, like milkmen used, except with solid sides and twice as big. The monster that had held him prisoner had used the calling-box and the vehicle had rolled towards them, a door opening in the side.

Then the old man had appeared, shouting, by the cave. The second monster had come out of the sea and the old man had fallen down. The new monster had picked the old man up and carried him into the vehicle. The first monster had then pointed at the vehicle and, realising that he was meant to go in, Marc had done so.

He found himself inside a padded room. The redressed old man was lying in a corner, against some hard seats. There were no windows but a television was embedded in the wall opposite, and the two monsters sat in seats in front of it, waving their hands over tiny black things. A few seconds later, the vehicle moved. On the television, he could see the water getting closer.

They submerged, and time passed.

'Hello,' whispered a voice. It was the old man. 'Who are you?'

'Marc,' he whispered back. 'Marc Marshall. Are you all

right?'

The old man nodded. 'Yes. The Silurian just stunned me.'

'Si… Si-what?'

'Silurian. Them over there.'

Marc stared at their backs. 'What are they? Are they monsters? Will they eat us?'

'No, Marc. No, they're vegetarians.'

'Actually, we're not.' The newer monster, or Silurian, turned back to look at them. 'But unlike Apes, we synthesise all our food so as not to use up our planet's resources.'

The old man stood up. 'I see. I'm sorry, I was mistaken. Why have you captured us?'

The other monster turned. 'We are Earth Reptiles. This is our planet. You are an infestation and, by rights, should be wiped out. However –' it pointed at Marc – 'we have need of the hatchling.'

Marc frowned. 'Me? Why?'

The first monster turned away and watched the television. 'You will find out.'

The old man cleared his throat, and motioned for Marc to keep quiet. 'I have met your people before. Perhaps you know of Okdel. And K'to?'

'Were you responsible for their deaths?'

The first Silurian hushed the one which had spoken. 'Sula, do not say anything else.'

'No, Tahni, we need to know how they died. Chukk and the others must have their revenge on the Apes.'

The old man moved towards them. The one called Sula turned in its seat. Its third eye flashed red, and he stopped abruptly, his face showing pain.

'Please,' he gasped, 'please let me speak.'

The other Silurian nodded and the blue glow stopped.

'Thank you.' The old man rubbed his nose. 'I am called the Doctor. Okdel was my friend. He was the victim of an uprising within your own people and, I believe, was murdered by one of them. The Apes had nothing to do with his death.'

The two Silurians faced each other. 'Morka?'

Sula nodded. 'Probably. He always was a fool.'

The Doctor continued: 'This Morka, he released a plague to kill the Apes. Okdel helped me find a cure, but the Apes retaliated in the only way they knew how. Desperate and afraid, much as Morka had been, they fought back.'

'They murdered our people, you mean.'

The Doctor shook his head. 'No. Many of them died, I know. But some were put back into hibernation. K'to certainly was. The Apes sealed the caves up, entombing them. But I'm sure many of them still live. Indeed, a great many were never revived and are still fast asleep, unaware of anything that transpired.'

Sula stared at him. 'Why did you befriend Okdel? To betray him?'

'No.' The Doctor sat on a seat opposite Marc. 'No. I sought to find a way for the Sil- for the Earth Reptiles to live in harmony with the Apes. Okdel also wanted this, but paranoia on both sides ultimately doomed such plans. It was a terrible waste of lives, both Reptile and Ape.'

'Ape lives are unimportant,' said the other Earth Reptile. Marc watched as it, too, returned to observe the screen.

'I think all life is important, Sula. Okdel believed that, too.'

The other Silurian swung round again. 'Then Okdel was a fool. We shall be back in our Shelter soon. You will answer to Chukk and the Triad.'

There was only the faint sound of the strange vehicle's engine. After a few moments, the Doctor looked at Marc. 'I'm sorry. I tried.'

Marc tried to smile. 'Will these Reptiles kill us, then?'

'I really don't know, Marc. Why not tell me how you came to be here?'

Marc nodded and told his story, from his stay with his aunt and his visit to Dungeness, right up to seeing the Doctor appear on the beach. The Doctor listened intently and made him clarify a few points but after ten minutes or so, he seemed satisfied.

'Well, the policewoman is alive and in hospital, so that's something good I can tell you.' The Doctor paused, then indicated the Reptiles with his head. 'Now all we have to do is sit tight and find out where we're going.'

Fiona was beautiful, no doubt about it.

As she sat opposite, her hair highlighted by the flickering candles on the table between them, Alistair felt he loved her more now than ever before. Her blue eyes sparkled like sapphires, and when she smiled at him he felt an unquestionable glow spread in his chest.

Mr and Mrs Lethbridge-Stewart were having their first dinner together for far too long. They had experienced little trouble in convincing Virginia Ince to baby-sit Kate for the evening and, dressed up to the nines, they had headed into Old Beaconsfield, to their favourite restaurant, the Saracen's Head.

They were not entirely sure if the maître d' really did recognise 'such old and valued customers', but nevertheless they got an excellent table, secluded but not so invisible that the waiters could ignore them.

Alistair had ordered a salmon steak, Fiona had gone for

the veal escalope, and a simple Burgundy washed it down well – Alistair forgoing his usual house red.

They had talked about the house, Kate, and her forthcoming first year at school. Alistair wanted to make plans to send her to a boarding school when she was old enough, but Fiona argued that the girl would be just as well educated closer to home. Not wishing to get into a 'you just want the girl away at boarding school to make things easier for you' row – which would have been untrue anyway – he consented.

In fact, so far, not a single cross word had been spoken. It felt like something of a miracle. Yet at the back of his mind Alistair knew that Fiona was keeping something back; she often seemed on the edge of saying something and then changed onto a totally different track.

'So,' she said, finishing off her last mouthful of veal, 'work must be very busy. The office seems to call a lot, or keep you there for days on end. London's not so far away that you can't come home, no matter how late, once in a while.'

And it had been going so well. If only Fiona knew that 'the office' was less than ten minutes from their front door and not in the City as she assumed. The only time he'd ever been completely truthful with her was during the period he was based in Guildford, while the central complex was being built. If Fiona had known he was spending his days inside a massive aircraft, inside a military hangar... Even now, he occasionally had to visit it as they used it as a green-field HQ. Young Captain Walters excelled in looking after the hardware...

His mind was wandering. 'Sorry, Fiona, but at this time of year, things do get very hectic. Foreign clients arriving at odd hours, and wanting to be entertained, and such things.'

Fiona nodded and took a sip of her wine. 'And just who is this Miss Hawke who keeps phoning you up?'

Alistair tried to laugh. 'Maisie? Oh, she's been with the firm since day one. I suppose you'd call her my Girl Friday—'

'Really? And what does being a Girl Friday entail?'

'Oh, honestly, darling. She's married,' (well, she was engaged, he thought), 'to one of the young... accountants,' (he was a captain, actually), 'Sam. And he's an ex-boxer,' (true), 'who'd flatten me easily.' (Also true, but at least he wouldn't have dared.) 'Please don't start inventing fantasy women to keep me at the office.'

Fiona shrugged. 'Just a thought, darling. Apparently Eric Pike is cheating on Monica, and they've three teenage sons.'

'No,' he laughed. 'I expect poor Pike just has a gorgeous wife, whom he rudely takes for granted much like I do, and who has a vivid imagination working overtime.'

'You're a spy, aren't you? Something to do with the Government. And your Maisie Hawke is some kind of Miss Moneypenny.'

Alistair stared at her, unsure whether to laugh at the absurdity or admit the proximity of her guess. Then he saw her eyes. They were glittering sapphires no more. Now they were hard chunks of ice, daring him to argue.

'I think that's... well—'

'Spot on, darling?'

'"Preposterous" was the word I was looking for. Darling.' This was going wrong. Alistair knew with a sinking feeling that it was going to get worse. 'I mean that's just so ridiculous.'

The maître d' appeared beside them, like a genie from

a lamp. Alistair actually jumped. 'There is a phone call for you, Mr Lethbridge-Stewart. A Miss Hawke from your office of work?'

Fiona smiled tightly and gestured across the restaurant towards the phone by the coat-rack and the gents.

With a mumbled 'Excuse me', Alistair got up and followed the maître d' to the telephone. He picked up the receiver, there was a click, and Corporal Hawke was there.

'Sorry to disturb you, sir. We are now scrambled.'

'Hawke, how in blazes did you find me? D'you know how inconvenient this is?' The Brigadier found himself whispering despite the scrambled line. Across the restaurant, his wife was finishing her wine, looking anywhere but at him.

'Terribly sorry, sir. You weren't at home, and your baby-sitter said you had gone out with Mrs Lethbridge-Stewart for dinner. Having been your Administrative Assistant since we were based at Guildford, I have booked more than one table for two at the Saracen's Head.'

'Don't get funny, Hawke. What is it?'

'A Navy sub in the Smallmarshes area has reported detecting strange underwater movement, sir, possibly a submersible.'

'In what area? Why is this worth interrupting a very expensive dinner, Corporal?'

There was a silence. The Brigadier imagined that Hawke was pausing, unwilling to continue, fearful of her master's wrath. 'Well?'

'Something came up yesterday, sir, while you were lunching with Sir John Sudbury. The Doctor said he was going to show you the report and discuss it with you before he left. It involved Smallmarshes, a seaside town in Kent, near Hastings. In Sussex.'

'I know where Hastings is, Corporal. I can also tell you that I didn't see the Doctor at any time after Sir John left. Now tell me what the Doctor has gone to see, find or do.'

'I'm sorry, sir, I know I should have told you earlier but—'

The Brigadier sighed. 'Corporal Hawke, you have already ruined my evening out. I suspect my wallet is going to have to stand another two or three evenings out if I am to pacify my wife. You, it would appear, have kept something from me, but not from the Doctor. As briefly as you can, Hawke, what is going on?'

The one-word reply chilled the Brigadier. After a second's pause, he began to chew his lip. 'Are you sure, Hawke?'

'Yes, sir. I've got the original report here. Miss Shaw has seen it as well, although she asked me not to tell you that. I have tried reaching her on the London number you gave me recently, but it has been engaged for a while. I think perhaps you should see this report before we go any further.'

The Brigadier felt himself going red, and fought to control his voice. 'I think I should have been shown it a day and a half ago, Corporal, so that UNIT could have reacted properly. This has all the hallmarks of what Sergeant Benton would term a "cock-up", and believe me, right now the Doctor is in very deep water. I shall be with you as soon as I've dropped Mrs Lethbridge-Stewart at home. Now, as if this evening wasn't ruined already, is there anything else?'

There was a slight but audible pause. Then: 'Have you seen the news this evening, sir?'

'No, Corporal. I have better things to do than watch television. What Earth-shattering event have I missed?

Michael Parkinson interviewing one of the Silurians?'

'Someone tried to assassinate Sir John Sudbury. The bullets used were C19-issue. The grapevine is linking it, tenuously, to Sir Marmaduke Harrington-Smythe and the Glasshouse team.'

'Wonderful news, Corporal. All I need now is Scobie to accidentally launch an all-out nuclear strike against the Chinese, and my day will be perfect. I want everybody in the Operations Room in forty-five minutes.'

Without waiting for a reply, he replaced the receiver. Silurians. The Doctor must have gone off chasing them, probably assuming that UNIT would follow and try to blow them up. Typical of the man. Never thought of the bigger picture. And then someone tries to kill Sir John Sudbury who, despite his inflated opinion of his role in Parliament, was hardly a prime target. If the Glasshouse set-up was compromised, all hell would probably break loose.

Which, frankly, was nothing compared to Fiona's reaction to his having to return to 'the office'.

As Alistair walked back towards his alcove, he realised he was approaching an empty table. The candle had been put out, and was currently playing host to their bill, impaled halfway down its length, torn and soaked in red wax.

The maître d' had the decency to try and look anguished as he walked towards him, carrying his long fawn overcoat.

'The lady has, er, departed, sir. She hailed a cab. She said you would pay the, ah…'

Alistair de-speared the bill, flattening the torn centre to try and read it. He took out his wallet and gave the maître d' a twenty-pound note. 'I imagine this covers everything,' he said curtly.

The maître d' coughed in surprise. 'More than adequate, sir. Are you really sure you want to—'

But Alistair Gordon Lethbridge-Stewart was gone.

And it was the Brigadier who got behind the wheel of his Daimler, and headed onto the A40 towards Denham, and UNIT HQ.

The pale young man was waiting for the blond man when the latter returned to his bed-sit that night.

'Well, you botched that, didn't you?' was his first comment. 'And I was led to believe that you were one of the best.'

'I am the best,' the blond man replied emotionlessly.

'Oh, tosh and nonsense, old chap, tosh and nonsense. You're a second-rate East End hood whose reputation is probably bought rather than earned.' The pale young man poured himself a drink. 'Scotch?'

'Please.'

A moment later and they were both drinking. The blond man helped himself to a second. His employer declined the offer.

'Now, what are we to do with you?' he wondered. 'Sir John is still alive, and although the evidence neatly points to the Glasshouse thanks to the tit-bits we left for the Parliamentary internal investigators to find, we have three innocent corpses in a morgue and one blighter with a bit of a scratch on his shoulder. Harrington-Smythe is going to find it quite easy to squirm out of this one.'

'The sights on the rifle you gave me were mis-aligned.'

The pale young man turned his face to him, his expression unreadable, his eyes invisible behind the thick lenses of the sunglasses he always wore. After a second he nodded his head a fraction of an inch. 'I'll have the armourer reprimanded for that.' He dug into his suit pocket and passed the blond man an envelope. 'I think it's time to get daring. Do the job outlined in here and then lie low for a few days. After that, I think we'll go get our policewoman back from Sir Marmaduke's grubby little mitts.'

With a sudden and jarringly fast movement he grabbed the bottle of Scotch, smashed it against the doorframe and jammed the jagged end into the door itself. 'And if you screw up once more, next time the bottle goes into you.'

After he had left, the blond man tried prising the bottle out of the wood, but it was stuck fast. As he grasped the broken neck, he felt unusual ridges in the glass. He looked closely. Gouged into the glass were five clear fingerprints. But to have the strength to do that… the pressure needed would require someone with the strength of about ten men. And there was no way that the pale young man was that strong, surely?

In a cage, kept away from too many smells, sights or sounds was a Dobermann pinscher. At least, once it had been a Dobermann pinscher. Now it was something more, something extra special.

One day a man it had trusted had come into its cage with a large syringe of a thick green ooze, which bubbled slightly. The man had injected the substance into the dog's neck, right into the jugular. It had hurt, and the dog had tried to snap at his former friend, but collapsed as it tried.

The transformation had taken about eight minutes. Waves of pain swept over it as it felt its body and mind twist and alter. Its senses were heightened it could see things previously hidden from its limited spectrum of vision; it could hear the breathing of people a hundred yards further down the cavern; it could smell the particular scent of sweat on a man standing next to a woman he was attracted to.

And this sudden in-rush of new perception snapped its mind, sending it insane and insensible.

The man watched the transformation from a safe distance, and reported back to his masters that the Stahlman Hound was ready to be trained. To become the Stalker. And over three months, he trained it, using a mixture of drugs, conditioning and basic cruelty.

The Stalker was the first living thing to be deliberately infected with a modified sample of Stahlman's gas from the aborted drilling project nicknamed the Inferno. The man was justifiably proud of the aberration of nature he had designed and engineered. He considered himself almost god-like; he had created a new form of life in the name of science, research and the future.

Then one day he woke from a dream of being chased through dark tunnels, and realised that he had helped to create not a new species, but a new weapon – one with untested and terrifying implications. What if it escaped? What if it could infect other dogs through breeding, or biting? What if it could infect humans? Rabies would be the equivalent of a slight cold in comparison to the Stahlman Hound's fearsome mutations. He decided it was time to stop those experiments, and vowed to do what he could to make the workers in the Vault see the error of their ways. And if they would not, he would find another way of stopping their work.

Now, all that was left of the man and his good intentions was a pile of well-gnawed bones and a shattered skull, scraped clean of all meat and marrow, their surfaces scarred with deep gouges from canine incisors. Around them lay pieces of torn and tattered clothing. One, a sock, lay discarded in the corner of the cage. Inside was a neatly stitched label that read 'Grant Traynor'.

The creation had eaten the creator. And it was still hungry.

Marc Marshall stood beside the nice old man, the Doctor. Both of them were dressed again in their own clothes, which had been washed and dried. The reptile who had returned them explained that they had needed to wear the mesh vests to protect their bodies from the pressure caused by the depth. The explanation had taken a while and Marc had not understood any of it, but the Doctor had remarked on its cleverness.

'And very thoughtful, too.'

Now they stood in a cavern deep under the sea, facing a whole group of reptile people. Earth Reptiles, they seemed to call themselves. The Doctor had explained to him how they had ruled Earth at the time of the dinosaurs. How their cities had sprawled across the world. How they had cars and planes, ships and submarines, and had been working on spacecraft. The Doctor also said that they had art and literature, sports and games. A complete civilisation.

They were the same as humans, but much, much older. The Doctor told him that the entire race had gone into hibernation when their astronomers saw the moon approaching the planet. Thinking it would suck away the Earth's atmosphere as it rushed by, they built vast shelters underground and went to sleep, waiting for it to pass and return to deep space. Instead the moon went into orbit and the Earth Reptiles never awoke.

The Doctor also explained how thousands of their shelters had been destroyed over the millions of years that had passed, but hundreds more must still exist somewhere. He explained how he had met the Earth Reptiles before, and how they had fought and ultimately lost a battle because they were too similar to humans. At least, that was how the Doctor put it.

Now the two humans were being examined by these seemingly hostile Earth Reptiles in their shelter. And from a large screen mounted on one wall, three others stared down. They appeared slightly different, slightly older, than the ones in the room.

'I have to say, Sula, there are marked differences between your group here, and Okdel's group.' The Doctor was staring at Sula and Tahni, the two Reptiles who had been in the submersible. 'You are very different from the older Earth Reptiles. You have what seem to be fins rather than ears.'

'You are correct, Ape. And before you prod and poke us any further,' said Tahni, slapping his hand away, 'we are different. We are hybrids. We are—'

'Enough, Tahni. The Apes do not need to know anything.'

'Of course, Baal.'

Marc looked at the newcomer. If what he had gathered from the Doctor's comments was correct, this must be another hybrid Reptile, because he too had fins for ears.

The new hybrid, Baal, pointed at him. 'Sisters, you have done well. The Ape hatchling is exactly what I need for my experiments. Take it away.'

Marc was petrified, but the Doctor stood between him and Baal. 'What are you going to do with the boy?'

134

Baal shoved the Doctor aside with astonishing strength. 'It is no concern of yours, Ape.' He looked back at the screen. 'If the Triad has no objections, I will start breaking this one down. Interrogate the old Ape as much as you like; just ensure that it is killed afterwards.' He looked across at an older Reptile, who resembled the three on the screen. 'Is that all right with you, Chukk?'

The one called Chukk nodded slowly.

Baal grabbed Marc's arm tightly, hurting him. He was determined not to cry out. He would be brave. 'And Chukk, be sure to disinfect this area. I can feel the Ape's fleas crawling all over my skin already.'

As Marc was dragged away, he heard the Doctor calling out, 'Noble Triad, please guarantee the safety of the Ape hatchling. I implore you not to—' but his voice was muffled by the rocks.

'What are you going to do to me?' Marc asked Baal.

Sula, who had followed, laughed. 'Make use of you, Ape. You never know, you may be our only way of surviving.'

'I'd like to help. Really I would. Just tell me what to do,' Marc said.

Baal stopped in front of a rock wall. His third eye glowed green for a moment and the rocks seemed to melt away, revealing a cavernous laboratory inside. He pulled Marc in, and Sula followed. She used her third eye to replace or rebuild the solid wall, Marc couldn't work out which.

'How did you do that?' he asked.

Baal ignored the question. 'Stand there.' He pointed to a far wall, where something that looked like a large movie camera was mounted near the ceiling, pointing straight down. 'Under the encoder.'

Marc stood. Opposite him, Sula waved her hands over a console.

'Begin,' she said out loud.

Marc's body began to tingle as he was enveloped by a pale light, emanating from the camera-like object above him.

'It is working,' said Baal, from the right side of the room. 'Observe.'

Marc looked. In Baal's hand a tiny figure seemed to shimmer into existence, about six inches high, mounted on a black disc.

Baal sneered at Marc. 'See, Ape. You do not possess such technology. This is a hologram, and it has reproduced every facet of your body. Your inferior mind cannot begin to grasp the concepts involved.'

Marc was positive he was not going to give in. He would not cry, or let Baal or Sula or anyone know how frightened he really was. He'd been frightened when Tahni had dragged him into the cottage, but that had been surprise more than anything else. He would try to resist whatever they were going to do. Somehow in his mind the memory of the cottage seemed like years ago, but it was only yesterday, surely?

'Tell me about the technology anyway,' he said.

Sula shrugged. 'It has spirit. For an Ape.'

Baal pointed at the hologram, and Marc saw a tiny copy of himself stare back. It glowed slightly, and flickered. 'Here it looks like you. But now –' and Baal tapped a stud on the base of the holo-thing and the copy of Marc vanished, to be replaced by a Marc-shaped image, composed of a series of lines and circles – 'we have a wire-frame image of you.' The stud was pressed again and this time, the Marc-image was filled with glowing primary colours. 'Here, you are in infrared. We can see your inner body, and trace your genetic codes. Here we can see it all.'

Marc was aware that Baal was not really talking to him, or to Sula. He was talking to himself.

'Here we can find the chromosomes that make you different from us. We will separate them, bind them with our own and create new ones.' Baal looked up from his console. 'We needed a young hatchling, on the brink of puberty, while its body chemistry is in such a marvellous state of flux. With you, we may be able to single out the exact piece of genetic material that can save us all.'

'When will you do this?' asked Marc, looking at Sula, as Baal turned back to his console, engrossed in data.

Sula looked at Baal and then back at Marc. 'Very soon, Ape. Very soon.'

'And will it hurt much?'

Baal looked up suddenly and laughed. 'Oh, probably. But you shouldn't worry about the pain. Whether it hurts you or not, it will most definitely kill you.' He turned back to Sula. 'We can proceed immediately. Let us start.'

FOUR

The Brigadier strode into the UNIT Operations Room, watching the chaotic scene before his eyes. Eight people were engaged in frenzied activity, each studiously avoiding eye-contact with their commanding officer, if they had even noticed his arrival.

Only the staff officer for the night, Sergeant Benton, managed a quick salute before grabbing and scanning a series of messages that had come through on the telex. Corporal Bell was on the red phone, linked directly to UNIT'S headquarters in Geneva. Private Parkinson was doing a round of teas and Corporal Hawke was sticking small red flags into a map of the Hastings area. Others gathered files, brought chairs and made themselves busy. It was chaos, but a structured chaos.

'Well?'

Everything went quiet and still as the Brigadier spoke. He moved to sit in a chair behind his desk as Bell stepped into the next room to continue her conversation with Geneva. Hawke broke the silence, pointing at her map.

'This, sir, is the cottage outside Smallmarshes where the Silurian activity is reported to have taken place, and where WPC Redworth was found.' She pointed to the next flag along, very close to the first. 'This is the Smallmarshes police station, the Doctor's last reported location.' She indicated a third flag. 'And this is Hastings General Hospital, sir. The policewoman apparently injured by the

Silurian or Silurians was taken there, and later abducted during an armed assault. The kidnappers caused enough other distractions to cover the abduction for a few hours.'

'Any casualties?'

'A few concussions, a few cuts from broken glass and one fatality. A strange one, sir.'

'Don't stall, Corporal.'

Hawke shrugged. 'A woman in a nurse's uniform was shot dead in the hospital's reception. She was not on the hospital's staff, and her uniform wasn't recognised by any Hastings staff. Which is hardly surprising.'

The Brigadier raised an eyebrow. 'Why?'

Benton chipped in, holding up a photograph of the dead woman, allowing the Brigadier to see the neat hole in her forehead. 'She was wearing a Glasshouse uniform, sir.'

'And the gun,' the Brigadier continued, mostly for his own benefit, 'was a Compacta 25 calibre, judging by the entry-wound. Any rear damage?'

Benton shook his head. 'Apparently not, sir. The bullet entered her brain and lodged there.'

'As I said, Compacta 25 calibre; a toy unique to the Glasshouse. Was the weapon located?'

'On the reception desk, sir. It looks like she was shot with her own gun,' Hawke replied.

The Brigadier stood up and coughed. 'Let me get this straight. We have a possible sighting of a Silurian; a category A plus, UNIT-eyes-only threat. Instead of UNIT's commanding officer being informed, the report is intercepted by his scientific advisers and they act upon it. One goes to Smallmarshes and talks to the police, one of whom has seen the creature and has been hospitalised as a result. The other adviser disappears. Neither of them are contactable. Meanwhile, the policewoman in hospital is kidnapped and only one clue is left behind: a potential Glasshouse staff member murdered with her own gun.' The Brigadier glared at the group around him, as if daring someone to speak. 'And I wasn't briefed on any of this until an hour ago. Anything else?'

'Just two things, sir.' Benton picked up a sheaf of papers from beside the telex. 'The Smallmarshes police have reported that they were due to meet the Doctor at seven thirty this morning at the cottage where the Silurian was seen. He didn't turn up, and they want to know if he was really attached to UNIT. Secondly, a teenage boy has been reported missing from the same town. His name is Marcus Marshall.'

'So?'

'A duffle-bag, belonging to a Marc Marshall, was found near the same cottage. And Marc Marshall is Alan Marshall's son.'

'So apart from the Doctor passing out the telex number of a supposedly top-secret defence agency, and the son of a prominent MP vanishing, I trust everything is going well?' The Brigadier paused as Corporal Bell re-entered the room. 'And what joy from our Swiss paymasters?'

Bell glanced around the room, but a look from the Brigadier told her to carry on. 'Well, sir, it's bad news. Because C19 won't release any information on our operations over the past twenty-four months to the UN, and both the Dutch and French Governments are being equally tight-lipped, the UN Secretary has cut UNIT's budget by almost half. If we're to get any more money, it must come directly from C19 and the British Government, not the UN.'

The Brigadier wandered over to Hawke's map, deep in thought. He studied the position of the flags for a moment, then turned to face his staff. His face was hardened with the resolve of a man determined to face any slings and arrows that fortune threw at him. 'Our funding is a C19 matter, and until Sir John Sudbury returns from hospital we will just have to carry on as best we can. I will take a small group down to Smallmarshes to look into things and find the Doctor. Benton, call up Yates and ask him to get a squad together. You're staying here to co-ordinate everything. In my absence, you have command.'

'Sir.'

'Hawke, you liaise with Smallmarshes and Hastings police. I want total assistance from them. Put out a complete D notice on everything relating to this. If the media boys give you any trouble, pretend we're bigger and far more powerful than we currently seem to be, and shout a lot. Scare them. Blackmail them. Threaten to shoot their families if necessary, but I want absolutely no press involvement.'

'Sir.'

'Bell, you're with me. Use the Austin, not the Daimler. I want this to be a discreet operation. Benton, ensure Yates does the same. No Rovers, no uniforms. Handguns for the troops. This is going to be a subtle operation, ladies and gentlemen. And there will be no further cock-ups. Is that understood?' He looked around and smiled mirthlessly. 'Dismissed.'

As the troops began to disperse, the Brigadier waved Maisie Hawke over. 'Corporal,' he whispered, 'find Miss Shaw. Contact Private Johnson and ask if he knows where she is.'

'Sir?'

'Hawke, it is my job to know about my staff, and their personal as well as professional lives, much as I don't like it. I believe you have his number. Don't make me turn a suggestion into an order.'

'Sir.' Hawke saluted and left the Ops Room.

The Brigadier followed, heading for his own office. He had to make a phone call himself. A more personal one, a more difficult one than he would ever have imagined. He had to telephone his wife and say he wouldn't be home that night.

He entered his office and looked at the clock. Ten o'clock, an hour and a half since Hawke had rung him in the restaurant.

More importantly, an hour since Fiona had taken herself home, and an hour since Alistair had collected a few odds and ends from the spare room, and then pushed open the door of his own bedroom. She had been in bed and asleep, or pretending to be. Either way, the message was clear.

Then Alistair had popped his head into Kate's room. Lying on the floor, presumably having fallen out of her bed, was Aloysius the bear. He had crossed the room, picked up the soft toy and slid it back under the covers. Kate's arms had instinctively grabbed for it and hugged it closer.

As he had turned to leave the room, a sleepy voice had murmured, 'G'night Daddy. I love you.'

'G'night Tiger,' he had whispered back, and shut the door.

A knock on his office door broke his reverie.

'Brigadier?' It was Bell.

'Yes, Corporal?'

'The cars are ready. Mike Yates will be here with his troops in about ten minutes.' The Brigadier realised he had never seen Corporal Bell out of uniform. She was dressed in a thick grey fisherman's sweater and black jeans.

Perhaps aware that he was staring at her, she coughed. 'I thought it might be cold down there this early in the morning. If it's not appropriate, sir, I can—'

'No. No, it's fine, Corporal.' He stared at his own clothes, realising he was still dressed in the suit and tie he had worn to the restaurant. 'Glad you reminded me. Could hardly go traipsing around Sussex in this get-up, could I?'

Bell smiled and shook her head. 'Are you needing anything else, sir?'

The Brigadier shook his head. 'No. I'll get changed now, I've spares here somewhere.'

'Left-hand cupboard, behind the black filing case, sir. Three shirts, four pairs of casual trousers and two pairs of light shoes. Plus assorted sweaters.'

The Brigadier smiled at Bell. 'What would I do without you, Corporal?'

Bell went red, and was smiling as she left.

The Brigadier looked at the cupboard she had indicated. 'No,' he muttered. 'Displeasure before business.' He picked up the phone and dialled his home number. It rang twice before Fiona answered, her voice crisp and clear, without a trace of tiredness. The phone had clearly not woken her.

'What do you want, Alistair?'

'Hello, darling. How did you know it was me?'

'Fifteen years of late-night calls saying I won't see you for the next week, that's how. What do you want?'

Alistair sighed. 'To apologise?'

'Oh, fine, darling. I'm supposed to forgive you for abandoning me for the millionth time, leaving me embarrassed and unable to explain to our daughter exactly what is going on.'

'I really am sorry.'

There was a pause and then Fiona sighed. When she spoke, all trace of sarcasm had gone. The only thing Alistair could detect was a sudden tiredness. She must have been holding back. 'I can't go on, Alistair. It's all too much.'

'What do you mean, darling?'

'Don't bloody "darling" me all the time!' she shouted. 'Stop saying that as if it excuses everything, explains anything or justifies something. Just stop "darling this" and "sweetheart that".' She paused again and then continued, more quietly, 'What I mean, Alistair, is that you come home now. You drop everything and get back here. Your job can survive without you for one evening. You tell Miss Hawke to keep the office running for the next three days or so without you. Is that so impossible?'

Alistair coughed. 'Well, yes, darling, it is impossible. I'm an important person here. I have staff to manage. I can't just—'

'Can't or won't?'

'Can't. Absolutely. I'll try and get a weekend off in the next couple of weeks. Mike or John can hold the fort. But not right now.'

Fiona took a deep breath and exhaled noisily down the telephone. 'Alistair, you know as well as I do that you won't leave Mike, John, Miss Hawke, Uncle Tom Cobbley and all in charge. I still don't understand what is going on there, but I do know it's more important to you than your family.'

Alistair interrupted her: 'Now hold on, darling. That's not true at—'

'It is true, Alistair. Absolutely. One hundred per cent true. If I was some faint-hearted little wifey who did not have a life of her own, I'd probably sit back and accept it.

But I'm not, and I won't.'

'Shouldn't we discuss this face to face—' tried Alistair, but Fiona cut him off quickly.

'No! You had your chance for "face to face" this evening. You blew it. This is it, Alistair. Kate and I are off. Don't try to contact us – if there's one thing you do know, it's that my father will ensure you get nowhere near us.'

Alistair felt a sudden pit in his stomach deepen. 'What are you saying, Fi? Your parents are in Chichester. Why are you going that far away? Why are you going at all, damn it?'

Fiona sighed. 'If you don't know that now, Alistair, you never will. Goodbye.'

Click. A disconnected hum.

'Fiona?' said a small voice into the phone. 'Fiona, Kate? Please?'

Alistair Lethbridge-Stewart realised that the voice was his, abruptly lost and cut-off.

She was going. Away. Leaving him? But, no, she couldn't. Surely not. It wasn't fair. Not to him. Certainly not to Kate. What chance had he had to explain himself? Fiona couldn't just drop eight years of marriage over something as pointless as this. People didn't just give up on married life, abandon their families because of a few long weekends away and a disrupted dinner.

Except, said the demon in the depths of his stomach as it churned up bile, it wasn't just about long weekends or a ruined dinner, was it? It was about the last eight years of lies and evasions. It was about how his life had altered following that meeting with Air Vice-Marshal Gilmore after the 'London Event'. How secrecy had become his watchword, at home as well as work.

Kate. Had Kate just been the result of some attempt by

both of them to solidify a partnership that had never had any concrete base of its own?

Was he destined to be on his own for the rest of his life? He remembered what Doris had said in Brighton that day all those years ago: 'Never take a woman for granted, Ali. You never know when familiarity has become boredom; when what one accepts as normality means depression and tedium for the other. That's what destorys marriages. Not one sudden argument, but a slow eroding of love because two people don't realise they have drifted apart, Their mental image of their partner becomes far removed from reality. Beware that, Ali.'

She'd given him a present then; a watch. It lived in a box, tucked away at the back of the cupboard Bell had pointed out. Doris had been a friend from Sandhurst, where she'd been a WRAC-in-trianing and he'd been a young lance-corporal, He'd thought they loved each other but he'd let her go, to drift away from him into the arms of George Wilson.

They'd met up a few years later on the pier in Brighton, the day after his marriage to Fiona. She gave him the watch, ostensibly as a wedding gift, in addition to the Wedgwood dinner set from both of them. But he knew it was more than that. It was a reminder of what might have been. Perhaps what ought to have been.

Wilson had been killed in Northern Ireland a couple of years ago. Alistair had sent a brief letter of commiseration to Doris. Just a few lines crammed into a few moments between a battle with Cybermen and Autons or some such threat. Thinking back, he realised how impersonal the letter had been. No more meaningful than the frighteningly regular letters he had written to the parents or wives of young privates who died under his command at UNIT.

No wonder Doris had not written back.

What kind of unfeeling monster had this job turned him into? Was he any better than those Cybermen or Autons? Did they have more feeling or conscience than him?

The phone's hum had become a high-pitched whine, indignant at not being used, and he gently placed the receiver,

He undid his collar and slipped off his tie. Then off came the jacket, trousers and shoes. He crossed to the cupboard and took out a blue cardigan and grey trousers. After that, on went a pair of comfortable black leather Hush Puppies. On the back of one cupboard door was a half-length mirror, and he stared at himself in it. Behind him on the floor lay the suit and tie, the wreckage of an identity, something that had been but wasn't any more. He turned back, scooped them up and shoved them roughly into the cupboard, screwing them up to make them fit. He put his black leather shoes on top. Then, after a moment's though, he reached into the back of the cupboard and pulled out the box and stared at it for a long moment, debating whether to put it on. Then he closed the lid and returned the box to its resting place.

He looked at himself in the mirror again. Alistair Lethbridge-Stewar had been put away.

The Brigadier was ready for action.

It was lunchtime.

People milled through the streets, butling their way around the shops, pushing and charging, and generally acting like headless chickens.

Liz Shaw did not feel like one of them, or like a part of

the human race. She was just an observer, brought down from an alien planet and forced to watch the silly things mankind did.

She was not sure exactly how long she had been feeling this disjointed, but it had certainly started since joining UNIT. There were so many other life forms out there, amongst the stars, millions of miles away. Each of them, too, lived day to day, enrapt in their own little worlds, unaware that she or her race, even existed.

When she was small, Liz's parents had walked her around the shops of Nottingham. It had occurred to her even then that each of the hundreds of people she saw in the old market square had homes, families and friends that she would never know. Everyone had lives that she could not know, and her own existence would touch only an infinitesimal proportion of the world's population. Although that knowledge had scared her a little, it had also fascinated her. Since then she had devoted herself to other people. It was that which had driven her towards science at school, college and eventually university. Receiving her doctorate from Cambridge was, she had thought, the pinnacle of her career.

Yet now, as she still stared at the unknown throng around her, she realised not for the first time that there was more to the universe than a few billion people on Earth. There were Nestenes, and Delphons and something called the Great Intelligence. There were Cybermen and Daleks and Zarbi and Drahvins according to the Doctor. There were even Time Lords.

So many different races, so many different cultures, attitudes and moralities. And Earth people could barely maintain a fragile peace with each other. Liz once asked the Doctor why UNIT had to be secret, why it couldn't use its resources to find benign races and bring them to Earth, to show mankind the folly of arguments, disputes and wars.

'And if they came, Liz? If they arrived on Earth just to say hello, what would you do?'

'I'd shake their hands. Or fins. Or tentacles or whatever. I'd say hello.'

The Doctor had looked dubious. 'Would you, Liz? Wouldn't you wonder what they were doing here? Query their motives? Distrust them? Why, if they had the technology to travel to Earth, would you assume they wanted to share it?'

'Because… because…'

'Because,' the Doctor had said, 'you are a trusting soul. But a vast majority of people aren't. And the least trusting of all are those in power, those who would be responsible for meeting the aliens. They'd be driven by paranoia to blow them up, I think. Earth has been visited countless times by harmless, inquisitive visitors, or by those unlucky enough to be stranded here. Many have left unnoticed, but those who have been discovered are usually persecuted, hounded and often killed. And some, who wanted nothing but peace, were forced to kill to defend themselves. No, Liz. Mankind is not ready to know the truth. Just look at the Silurians and how they were treated by the Brigadier.'

'But they were killers. Well, some at least.'

The Doctor had nodded. 'But so were a lot of humans. Should the entire human race be wiped out because of a few Hitlers, Genghis Khans or Magnus Greels?'

Now, as she sat outside a small café, sipping at her mug of hot tea, Liz found herself agreeing with the Doctor's sentiments. Mankind was not ready. But one day it would be, one day it had to be or they were all –

'Doctor Elizabeth Shaw?'

Liz stared up at the woman who had spoken. She was a good six feet tall, her blonde hair cropped in an unusual manly cut. An ample bosom was encased in a red sweater, and her extraordinarily long legs were barely concealed by a very short black miniskirt. Slung over her shoulder was a large black holdall.

'Yes, I'm Liz. You must be Jana?'

The newcomer smiled and sat beside her. 'Yeah, hi. Good choice of location. Easy to find for a newcomer to London like me. Amsterdam is full of street cafés like this. I almost feel at home.' Jana placed her bag on the ground. 'Can I get you anything?'

Liz declined, and watched as Jana walked – no, strode – into the cafe to get something to drink.

While she waited, she resumed her observation of the lives passing her by. There was an old woman carrying too much heavy shopping. A young couple, who looked as if they'd been arguing about something. They were together physically but obviously not mentally; both looked at different shops for prolonged periods, determined not to catch the other's eye. A young woman caught Liz's attention, her clothes and make-up a little too over-the-top to be fashionable. Still, this was Soho, and people had to earn a living. Just across the way was the Palace Theatre, and beyond that a congregation of German or Swiss tourists were disembarking from a coach parked illegally outside the famous 84 Charing Cross Road bookshop.

'Books. Everywhere you go round here, there are books. But do people read them? No, the young today listen to rock 'n' roll. This peace, love and free sex stuff. Drugs, that'll destroy them all. In ten years, they'll all be dead and this will be a wasteland. And then where will we be, eh?'

Liz, startled, stared at the shabby tramp who faced her, his hands in mittens despite the warm summer day. He shook a tin cup at her. By the sound of it, so far he'd scrounged a couple of old shillings and a ring-pull from a coke can. In his other hand was a tatty plastic shopping bag.

'Still,' he continued as if she'd shown some interest, 'at least the birds will survive. One day, we may see a fox in Piccadilly again. Or hear a nightingale in Berkeley Square. Do you know the old song?'

Terrified that she was about to be subjected to a rendering of it, Liz dropped a fifty pence piece into his cup.

He put the bag down beside her table and touched a matted lump of his grey hair. 'Bless you, miss. May God smile on you today, and guide you on your journey.'

'Oh yes, and which journey is that?' asked a strong, slightly accented female voice beside Liz. The scientist looked up, pleased to see Jana return.

The old tramp held his cup out optimistically, but he obviously saw something in Jana's returned stare that made him wilt. His arm dropped and for a second Liz thought he would spill his money.

'Careful,' she said.

The old man looked back at her. 'God bless you again.' His voice was suddenly very quiet and hoarse. 'I'd best be going.' He turned away and disappeared with surprising speed along Old Compton Street.

'Well, I suppose this is hello.' Jana was drinking something that looked and smelled like rich hot chocolate, with a dollop of cream on top.

'That looks nice.'

Jana nodded. 'My absolute favourite. Chocolate is a true gift from the gods. Energising, exotic, erotic and very tasty. Do you want a sip?'

Liz shook her head. 'So why are we here? Literally rather than philosophically, if you don't mind.'

Jana laughed, loud and strong, yet feminine and hearty. Liz realised that she had instantly taken a liking to this Amazonian journalist. 'It's a good question. I suppose we're here to discuss our mysterious nameless friend and his strange notes. You're with UNIT, aren't you.' It was a statement, not a question. 'So I thought it must be something to do with them, or at least with the United Nations. Maybe someone is defecting to Russia.'

'We're not MI5, you know. It's sometimes a little deeper than that.'

Jana nodded. 'Yeah, all right. So we're talking about little green men with three heads.'

Liz chuckled quietly.

Jana frowned. 'What did I say?'

'The same as me when I first started working for UNIT. I said I wasn't interested in spies, invisible inks or anything like that. Nor little green men with—'

'Three heads,' finished Jana. 'OK, I'll tell you what I know about UNIT. Bugger all. Zero. Zilch. Nought. I once had lunch with a UNIT officer called Jan-Dick Heijs but all he said was that it was top secret, and fobbed me off with the usual cover story.'

'Nice man,' Liz murmured. 'I met him at a reception at… Westminster. He said that one day he thought UNIT personnel would all be integrated and working all over the world.' Liz paused to sip her tea. 'I said I hoped he would come and work in Britain.'

Jana nodded intently. 'Did he?'

'He was killed in an... accident a few weeks ago.'

'Oh. God. How awful. I didn't know...'

Liz shrugged. 'How could you? It was a UNIT thing. Hush-hush.' Something at the back of her mind was jabbing at her; she was not allowed to speak about UNIT affairs so openly. Least of all with a journalist, no matter how pleasant her company might be. But she pushed it down. She was fed up with UNIT red-tape. With being denied the freedom to talk.

'I need to talk.'

Jana looked over. 'Did you say something?'

'No. Just day-dreaming.' Liz finished her tea. 'OK. To business. I can't say I like getting strange mail or phone calls, but I admit I'm intrigued. I thought our anonymous source was a hoaxer until you called.'

'Hoaxer?'

'Sorry. Prankster? A man making stupid calls for the hell of it. Putting me on.'

Jana smiled. 'Ah, right. Hoaxer. I'll remember that. My English isn't bad, but there's always room to learn.'

Liz laughed. 'Actually, I think your English is excellent. I forgot it wasn't your first language.' She looked along Old Compton Street. 'Do you fancy a bite to eat? I didn't have breakfast this morning and I know a place that does a good brunch. That's a—'

'A cross between breakfast and lunch. Believe me, Liz, where food's concerned, I know the language.' Jana also got up and looked off towards Charing Cross Road. A police siren could be heard wailing above the general hubbub of the crowd. 'I can't think here. I need to be inside something like a restaurant and what's that?'

Liz looked down at her feet. The old tramp's bag was lying there. 'The old fool must have left it here. It's probably got all he owns in it. We must find him and give it back.' She looked around, as if expecting to see him pushing his way through the crowds to retrieve it. 'Oh, the poor man.'

Jana reached over and took it. 'Maybe we can see if there's anything in here that will help us find him.' She put her hand in and pulled out a long manila envelope.

DR SHAW. MS KRISTAN.

It took a few moments for it to sink in and then Liz opened her mouth to speak, but no words came out. Jana just shrugged. 'He's cleverer than we thought.'

Liz looked at the bag. 'And being a tramp almost guaranteed that we wouldn't look too hard at him. He knows human nature.'

'Yeah, that's as may be, but let's see what he left us. I doubt he was just saying hello for the hell of it.' Jana dug into the envelope and yanked out a small letter.

Hello to both of you.

If you've got this, then everything is going well. The Glasshouse has been framed for the assassination attempt on Sir John Sudbury. They're moving in for the kill now. The Minister has begun an investigation into the Glasshouse and Sir Marmaduke. Beware, both of you. Few people are what they seem. Except me, of course. I'm exactly what I seem: a faceless mystery that no one notices.

Enclosed is a map. It shows an island in the Channel Isles. That is where the trail is leading. Something is there, connected with what is going on in Smallmarshes. I don't know what exactly possibly because of my connection with Grant Traynor, my supply of information has been 'diverted' to other people and I'm left in the dark. Something dangerous is going on up North, and this island is linked to it.

One final thing. Beware of Sir Marmaduke Harrington-Smythe. He's a tricky bugger and will not let anyone get in his way. Like all vicious animals, he's at his most dangerous when he's cornered.

I believe someone is aware that I'm feeding you two, and I may have been betrayed. Perhaps that's why my information has dried up. Either way, you're on your own now. I've given you all I can.

Good luck, my angels.

A friend

'He's given us nothing!' shouted Jana, causing a few heads to turn. She ignored them, but spoke more quietly. 'A map of an island and vague references to the "North". Of England? Europe? The Arctic circle?'

'And why worry about the Glasshouse?' chipped in Liz. 'They're hardly dodgy.'

Jana scratched her chin, aware that her voice was still raised to make her words audible above the sound of the police siren which had stopped nearby, and was now joined by the ululation of an approaching ambulance.

'Except they've been implicated in the attack on your jolly politician. Perhaps we should go there first. Can your UNIT connections get us in there?'

Liz nodded. 'I'll arrange some transport.'

Jana smiled. 'Won't you get into trouble for taking a journalist there?'

'Right now,' Liz said, 'I'm more concerned with finding out the truth behind all this.' She pointed at the letter. 'I'm afraid brunch will have to wait. We'll get something on the motorway.'

'Where do we go from here?'

'I need to make some calls from my flat, to arrange things. So Piccadilly Circus tube station.'

They set off down Old Compton Street, heading to the junction with Wardour Street. A thought struck Liz. 'Do you have a car?' she asked.

Jana failed to respond. Liz turned to look at her, and saw her companion staring down the road, towards the junction of Wardour Street and Brewer Street. A police car and ambulance were parked there, with uniformed police pushing the crowds back. Intrigued, both women moved forward to get a better view, and Liz inexplicably felt a shudder run down her spine. 'This is going to be bad,' she muttered. If Jana heard, she failed to respond. Instead she shot Liz a glance and indicated with her head towards the crowd.

Liz stared through the mass of onlookers and caught a glimpse of what seemed to be a body lying in the road. She immediately thought someone had been knocked down.

Something inside egged her on. 'Let me through please,' she heard herself say. 'I'm a doctor.' Jana was following close enough behind her to get through the gaps in the crowd, and if anyone closed in, her muscular frame soon eased them out of her way.

The body was dead, there was no question, but it was clearly not the victim of a car accident. Three cavities disfigured the upper chest and left shoulder, and Liz recognised them as bullet-wounds. A fourth bullet had gone through the temple and another into the throat, making the face unidentifiable. The body was a mess, soaked with blood. This hadn't been an accident, or even a killing. It had been an execution.

'Poor old guy,' muttered a woman laden with bags of shopping. 'What a way to end his life.'

'Probably the best thing for him,' replied someone else; a man. 'I mean, who'd want a tramp's life anyway?'

Liz stared at the crowd in surprise and disappointment. A man a human being had been shot. Deliberately. A life gone in seconds. And they reckoned it was for the best?

She was about to give someone a piece of her mind when Jana grabbed her arm and pointed. Under the front of a nearby parked van, where it had rolled away, was a bloodstained tin cup. A few small coins were scattered nearby.

Liz looked again at the dead body, and then at Jana who had clearly reached the same conclusion.

'Well.' Jana tapped the envelope against her hand. 'I guess that was our last message. We really are on our own now.'

The Reptiles' base was a fantastic piece of architecture. Deep below the island, it had been built to circulate air from the surface, equalising pressure naturally. Its passageways and ducting were designed to optimise the heat and humidity without the interior becoming stuffy. Condensation formed on the walls and drained into grated gutters, providing a constant supply of pure water in which the inhabitants could bathe and replenish their natural oils. It was also salt-free, and therefore drinkable.

Some of the walls were rough, jagged and unfinished. However, closer to the living areas, their surface was so perfect and flat that the walls became almost reflective. Stunningly vivid paintings adorned the walls at intervals, and tiny holographic images had been placed in recesses almost invisible until one encountered them. These artworks all represented reptile-people; some, the Doctor noted as he passed them, of hybrids or sub-species that he had not yet encountered.

Most of the reptiles the Doctor had seen so far bore little resemblance to those he and UNIT had met in Derbyshire. Just as humans varied in hair and skin tones, height and weight, so the reptiles differed in physical characteristics. Some seemed adapted for underwater life, others for extreme cold or life on high plateaux. Although it was untrue to say that no two reptiles looked identical, it was easy to group them together into families or clan groups.

However, the Doctor realised, if that was true then the group which currently held him prisoner, was the most mixed possible. They were also not represented in the art.

As Chukk led him towards a food area, the Doctor allowed himself to be the subject of stares and inspections and, sometimes, hisses from the various reptiles he encountered.

'My people,' Chukk had explained earlier, 'have no respect for Ape life. I apologise.'

'No need, old chap,' the Doctor replied. 'I don't blame them at all.'

The journey so far had been following a downward path, leading further into the depths of the Silurian complex. Although he was capable of resisting extreme temperatures far better than any human being, even the Doctor was beginning to find the heat a bit stifling.

'Much further, is it?'

Chukk shook his head, his thin ears flapping slightly. 'Not far. There is much you need to understand. You will appreciate why Baal is doing what he does to the Ape hatchling.'

They emerged from the narrow hot corridor into a room very different from it and indeed the rest of the Shelter. It was a massive cavern, reminding the Doctor of the Panopticon on Gallifrey. Or, in more human terms, of St Paul's Cathedral. The room's enormous domed ceiling was decorated with beautiful paintings showing Silurians battling and taming dinosaurs.

'And I thought the Sistine Chapel was the pinnacle of Earth's architecture,' murmured the Doctor.

Chukk pointed upwards. 'There you can see Masz K'll, legendary warrior chieftain from our Third Dynasty fighting the legendary Two-Face Lizard, his evil alter-ego. And to the left is Panun E'Ni, leader of the Southern Clan, who conquered much of the world and ruled it cruelly, although briefly. To his right is Tun W'lzz, who ultimately brought about Panun E'Ni's downfall. The lower end of that wall shows the celebrations that followed their destruction as the previously imprisoned and cast out tribes reconverged into a new, unified civilisation, eating their foes' mindless warrior beasts, the Myrka.'

The Doctor nodded. 'Folk stories, or historical fact?'

Chukk laughed; the sound was alien and abrupt. 'Does it truly matter, Doctor? They inspired our race for a millennium, that is all that counts. We copied these paintings bit by bit from the Hall of Heroes at the centre of our world.' The reptile-man shrugged. 'I doubt it still exists. Very little of our civilisation has been found by our few scouts or your fellow humans.'

The Doctor had wandered into the centre of the cavern, standing right below Masz K'll. 'Firstly, I'm not human. I'm not from this planet. Secondly, I fear you are correct. Nothing of your civilisation exists at all. Millions of years of erosion and plate movement have seen to that.' He paused and examined the paintings as best he could from the ground. 'I find that rather sad.'

'As do my people. Those entombed here, especially.'

The Doctor looked at Chukk. 'Entombed? So you weren't placed here voluntarily, then?'

Chukk surveyed the ground, the walls and his own feet before apparently deciding to confide in the Doctor. He moved towards a handful of benches roughly hewn out of the walls, and waited for the Doctor to join him before he continued speaking.

'Look at me, Doctor. What do you see?'

'A person,' replied the Doctor. 'Alien to mankind, but not this planet. A member of a race I have thought of as Silurian, or *Homo reptilia*. Both inaccurate, I imagine, as your records here would indicate you are much older than we previously imagined.'

Chukk shrugged. 'Your human terms are unknown and irrelevant. No, Doctor, what I am is an outcast. Despised by my peers and loathed by the other inhabitants of this Shelter. I am a go-between if you like, leader by order rather than design. In truth, one of our pure Marine cousins should be leader of the Shelter, but he died during hibernation and I assumed control.

'You met one of my closest hatchlings in what you call Derbyshire. Like me, he foresaw that co-operation between the Apes mankind, or whatever they call themselves and us has to be the only viable option for survival. Others here would rather see us dominate and destroy to reclaim our territory.' Chukk sighed. 'I fear my attempts at conciliation are destined to fail. Most of those here are young and idealistic. Auggi, the former leader's mate, is a charismatic opponent of any kind of deal with Apedom.'

The Doctor scratched his neck. 'I see your problem.'

'There is more,' Chukk added. 'The worst part. I am unfamiliar with Ape culture – indeed I am one of the few who can imagine using those two words together – but I doubt it is much like ours.' He indicated the passage through which they had entered. 'You have seen the different forms of our people. By far the biggest genetic and physiological differences lie between my clan and our Marine cousins, the Sea Devil Warriors. You may have noticed that you did not see any paintings or holograms of people who look like Baal and his sisters. Or any of the hundreds of their generation still hibernating here.'

'Indeed, it had crossed my mind. Do I assume that inter-breeding is frowned upon?'

'You might say that. "Punishable by death" is far more accurate. The pure eugenics of our people are considered our race's most important principle, and our most sacrosanct belief. Those cast into this Shelter were guilty of abandoning those teachings.'

'So Baal and the others were conceived by a union of your clan and these Sea Devil Warriors?'

'Correct. Normally their eggs would have been crushed, and the parents executed. But our scientists knew that many millions of our people would die in the cataclysm that caused us to hibernate. They allowed the hybrids to live here for the twelve years before the great hibernation. We went to sleep like so many others, and awoke a few years ago.' Chukk stood up, indicating for the Doctor to follow him. 'Let us return to my laboratory. Now you have seen something of our culture and history, let me hope you understand our quest.'

Her reddened eyes were reflected in the glass of the school photograph. It showed a group of twenty-three boys aged between 13 and 15, on a rugby pitch, all wearing House colours, all smiling, with a small trophy in front of them.

All bar one were at home, safe and secure with their parents.

'It's our own fault, constable,' she said, still looking at the picture, feeling tears building up in her eyes once more, stinging the sore rims. She sniffed. 'We sent him down to Eve's because it was Alan's most important season. Lots of constituents all swarming around. the place. Marc would have hated it, so we thought a few weeks down at the seaside would be great. Kids love the seaside. I always did.'

'He's 14. He's not 6.' The Right Honourable Alan Marshall, member of Parliament for Irlam o' th' Heights, was sitting on the sofa, staring at a blank television screen. He wouldn't let her catch his eye, nor those of the two police officers who had come to collect Marc's photograph for the papers. 'The Opposition will have a field day with this.'

She lost focus on the photo of her son instantly. She just saw a blur of red, felt her cheeks glow and her hands clench into fists. She didn't remember turning or moving across the room, but suddenly she was pummelling her husband as he sat on the sofa, tears of fear and rage spraying off her face as her head twisted ferociously.

The two police officers moved swiftly and efficiently to pull her back, letting her sob, uncontrollably, against one of them. It was the woman officer, the one with the soft Irish accent who had spoken at the door, offering condolences and apologies and suggesting that a photograph of their son would greatly increase the chances of finding him.

As she raised her damp face from the equally damp white blouse, Sarah Marshall threw a look at her husband. She saw astonishment – presumably at her fury – etched across his face.

And at that moment she knew she hated him. She hated his job, his politics, his friends and his need to socialise. She hated the tea parties, the endless public meetings, the local constituency arguments at the town hall. She hated wearing a fake smile as complete imbeciles turned up on her doorstep with petitions signed by twenty people from the local fish and chip shop. She hated wearing blue jackets, blue trousers and a silly blue rosette in public. She hated having to be present as he opened fêtes and donkey derbies.

'I just want my little boy home,' she screamed suddenly, falling to the floor in what she knew was an undignified heap and hoping that it would embarrass him further.

Again the strong arms of the two police officers helped her up. The woman spoke again. She was the only one of the two who ever had. 'I think, Mr Marshall, it might be best if we talked to your wife alone for a few moments. Allow her to calm down a little. Could you make us all a cup of tea, perhaps?'

'Tea? Oh, right. Yes.' Alan Marshall left the room.

'He… he doesn't even know how to turn the kettle on,' sobbed his wife as they led her to the sofa.

'He'll find out, Mrs Marshall. Men are remarkably adaptable.' The Irish policewoman indicated to her companion that he should go into the kitchen. As he went, the policewoman began massaging Mrs Marshall's shoulder. 'Tell me about your son. Why would someone kidnap him? Has he any enemies? Or your husband, perhaps?'

Of course that was it! Alan's bloody job again. It had to be. She had no enemies, and Marc was only 14. But Alan, his politics. The IRA? The German lot? Someone from the Labour Party even?

'I don't know, but it's possible.'

The policewoman nodded. She understood, of course. In their line of work they must come up against this all the time. They'd find him.

'Has there been a ransom note?'

Good God! There had been nothing at all. But the abductors must know how to contact them, or why would they bother kidnapping Marc? Unless it was being done through the House. 'Maybe Alan should go to London. See if there's anything there?'

The policewoman frowned. 'Unlikely. And we don't want to draw attention to this yet. We need to let the kidnappers think we're relaxed about this. Any signs of panic and, well, we just don't want to risk anything in these situations.'

She was so reassuring. 'Have you done this a lot?'

The policewoman stopped smiling. 'Once. A long time ago, in Eire. My older sister was kidnapped by one of the anti-IRA groups. I had to help negotiate her release.' She smiled again. 'But that was different. We're unlikely to be dealing with terrorists here. It's probably someone who's after your money.'

'But we haven't got any. Well, not cash to speak of. I know Alan's an MP, but he doesn't make much. Most of it goes to charities and other worthwhile causes.'

She looked up as the door opened and the policeman walked in with a tray. He smiled at her as he put it down. Sarah was convinced she'd seen that smile before, and then it hit her. The Irish policewoman – these two must be related. Their smile, their eyes and features were perfectly matched. The way they moved in unison with each other. But he hadn't spoken, hadn't said a word, so she didn't know if he too was Irish.

'Where's Alan?' she asked.

The policeman shot a look across at the policewoman. She just shrugged.

Sarah was confused. 'Is he in the kitchen still?' She raised her voice. 'Alan?'

There was no reply and she got up, narrowly avoiding the outstretched hand of the silent policeman. She found herself in a hurry to get to the kitchen, to Alan, to –

'Oh God,' she whispered.

On the floor... blood... he... he...

Something hit her between her shoulders and she found herself on her knees.

It hurt. She wanted to turn around but couldn't, wanted to... to... reach out to Alan. Why was he on the floor with her? Why was he wearing red?

Where was Marc?

Where

A small, dark-haired woman looked up as two police officers walked towards her car. As they reached it, they both took off their caps and the male got into the driving seat, the female joining the owner in the back.

'They were useless. Totally useless,' the policewoman said. 'They don't know where the boy is. They think he's been kidnapped.'

'What did you do, Ciara?' The dark-haired woman. tapped Ceffian's shoulder and indicated that he should drive.

As the car started to go forward, Ciara smiled, her blue eyes sparkling with joy. 'The usual, of course. She actually lasted about eight seconds.' She placed a silenced revolver on her lap. 'The gas ought to go up in about fifteen minutes. There's enough to take out a couple of other houses. It'll be ages before they piece the bodies back together.'

'Nevertheless, Ciara, we have to move quickly. The Government wants to investigate your employer over that Sudbury incident. He's been framed for something he didn't do, and my people don't want him to be cleared.' The dark-haired woman smiled at Ciara. 'In the meantime, let's see if Peter has had any luck with our artist from Sussex.'

Doctor Morley was aware that he was not having any success with WPC Barbara Redworth. Despite his best efforts, she had remained almost completely comatose since her arrival. He had decided not to ask too many questions about exactly how she was removed from a public hospital. He doubted he could stomach the answer.

Dick Atkinson had pulled himself away from whatever had preoccupied him for the last few days to examine her chart.

'Her temperature is up quite badly, Peter. Whatever happened to her, she's picked up some kind of infection.' He shrugged. 'Oh well, it's your project.'

'Hey,' Morley started, but Atkinson was gone, back

through the long strips of plastic sheeting that separated Morley's patient from anyone else in the basement area. OK, he consoled himself it wasn't exactly Barts, but she was clean and sterile down here. Sir Marmaduke's obsession with hygiene had ensured that. Only Morley was officially entitled to go near her, but he had invited all of his team to make periodic visits if they wished. Atkinson, he guessed, did it to relieve boredom. Not of his job, but of having to work with people he considered no better than lab rats, with lower IQs. Griffin occasionally popped in, and his chirpy Newcastle accent was, at least, not as monotonous as Atkinson's Midlands drawl.

Of Cathy Wildeman, Morley had seen nothing for a couple of days. Jim Griftin said that she'd been down to work for a few hours but had done nothing but complain of a headache, and so had gone back to bed.

'Peter,' Jim had suddenly asked that morning. 'Peter, what are we doing here?'

Morley had continued examining the policewoman's charts – it was the question he had been dreading for the last few months. He was surprised it had taken three intelligent people so long to ask, but nevertheless, he knew from experience that geniuses were often so absorbed in their work that they never stopped to ask 'why?' Just look at Oppenheimer. Or Mengele.

'How do you mean, Jim?'

'What is Sir Marmaduke paying us for? All we do is research a few odds and ends he brings us, but we never see an end product. Why?'

Morley hated that word.

'Because,' he began, and then stopped. How much could he actually say? Was this a test? Was Sir Marmaduke stirring up the others to test his loyalty? 'Because he's paying us not to ask questions of him. Only science. Only those new and unique things he provides us with. Those are the only questions we're paid to think about.'

To Morley's total surprise, Jim Griffin seemed content with that answer and had wandered away. But should he be surprised? If this was a test, he might have given him the right answer and everything would be all right. Wouldn't it?

He returned to ministering to his latest charge.

'So who exactly are these Glasshouse people, then, Liz?' Jana was staring at Liz's guinea-pig, although Liz was not sure whether it was out of affection for small, furry animals, or incredulity that Liz could own such a worthless pet.

Liz was actually quite proud that she did. Having seen a life wiped out not an hour earlier, she was rather happy to arrive back at the flat to find Mrs Longhurst out shopping and the guinea-pig excited to see her. It had raced around its cage for a good fifteen minutes while she made coffee and Jana began flicking through their dead contact's papers and photos.

'Presumably they're not on this Channel Island?'

'No,' called Liz from the kitchen. 'No, they're somewhere in Gloucestershire, I think. I only went once. I'll give UNIT a call sometime and sort out that car.'

'OK,' was Jana's response. Then: 'Are you sure you want to go on? I mean, if he's dead, well, what are we doing this for?'

Liz walked into the lounge with a tray and placed it on the occasional table near the sofa. She sat down. 'I don't know, really. I have some idea of a reason in my head, but I'm not convinced it's a good reason.'

'Air it,' said Jana.

Liz poured two coffees. After passing one to Jana, she took her own and slumped back in the soft. 'OK, stream of consciousness, so beware.

'I work for UNIT, a supposedly top-secret organisation, yet apparently everyone, including Dutch journalists, knows who they are.'

'Permission to interrupt,' interrupted Jana. 'I don't know what they are at all. I just know they exist. Part of my brief to myself when all this started was to find out what they are. Before our late informant contacted me, I had no idea they even existed.'

Liz nodded. 'OK. Granted, but nevertheless, having signed the Official Secrets Act, I'm not blowing my future by talking about them. Sorry.' Jana smiled, and Liz carried on. 'So, anyway, I'm feeling a bit under-used. I'm a quite well-qualified research scientist. But, as more than one person has pointed out recently, the string of letters after my name are barely recognised at UNIT.'

'So? Leave.'

'To do what, Jana? I suppose all this –' she waved towards the photographs and letter 'was my attempt to get involved a bit more. To do something of my own.'

'To impress your superiors at UNIT?'

'Not really. No, to impress myself, I think. To prove I still had it in me to research and follow things up, even if they're not strictly scientific.'

Jana swigged down her hot coffee in one gulp and replaced the mug on the tray. She leant over and grabbed the telephone, passing it to Liz.

'Seems a good reason to me. Let's get investigating. But we have a decision to make.'

'What's that?'

'Revert to Plan A: the Glasshouse. Or go with Plan B: the Channel Islands. Which I'd prefer.'

'Why?'

'I could do with a holiday. A bit of sea air. The Glasshouse, whatever it is, probably isn't going away. But things do leave small islands slightly more regularly. Let's go south.' Jana picked up the tray and took it to the kitchen. 'Book us a flight to Jersey. Use my company charge-card. It's in my handbag.'

Liz shrugged and began to probe Jana's bag.

Then she saw the pistol. Its unmistakable outline was pressed against the thin cloth of an inside pocket.

'Jana?'

'What?' came the reply from the kitchen.

'Jana, why do you carry a gun?'

Jana hurried out of the kitchen, drying her hands on a tea towel. 'Oh God, that. I'm sorry, I forgot I even carry it now.' She smiled reassuringly. 'When I first said I was coming to England, one of my photographers gave it to me. It's a replica he bought in Rotterdam, I think.'

Liz stared at the outline of the gun. It was… familiar somehow. A strange design she was sure she'd seen before. 'So it's not real?'

'Good God, no. I wouldn't know what to do with a real gun. Horrible things, terrify me. No I keep it there to warn off muggers.'

Liz passed the bag to its owner. 'You'd better find your charge-card thingy. I don't like guns either. And after this morning…'

'Hey, yeah, you're right. I'm sorry, I should have warned you.' She rummaged in the bag and then passed Liz a small plastic card. 'My charge card. Just give them the number, my company will pay. She wandered back into the kitchen. 'Oh, and Liz?'

'Yes?'

'First class, if possible. If it's someone else's money, I want to go in comfort.'

The typically restrained English tourist guides merely described them as 'pleasant, rolling hills' that were 'ideal for all rambling enthusiasts'. That, and the 'charming, unspoilt beauty' and 'opportunities to view rare and diverse wildlife in its natural habitat' were usually enough to have the area swarming, during the summer months, with tourists from both Britain and abroad.

But what the tourist guides frequently forgot to mention was that the Cheviot Hills in Northumberland were also famous in English mythology for their connection with Arthurian history as well as the more fanciful folklore of the type Shakespeare had brought into his play *A Midsummer Night's Dream*. The hills were famous for their sightings of faeries, goblins and unicorns. Many students of English legend flocked to the area to see if they could be the ones to finally photograph or paint members of the Otherworld community.

In the mid-sixties, however, a massive blot was built upon the landscape. The Darkmoor Experimental Nuclear Research Station was opened amidst a blaze of bad publicity and open hostility from nearby businesses. Partly funded by money from the private sector, the project took far longer to complete than the British Government had anticipated and, after a serious assault by a terrorist gang known as the Reavers, the plant was closed down. The resulting publicity, organised jointly by the Northumberland Health Authority, CND and Greenpeace, was massive. Having been shamed, the

Government agreed to leave their nuclear capabilities in the proven hands of Dungeness, Sizewell and Windscale. The plant was dismantled four years later.

The ground upon which it was built, however, was still owned by the Government. Nestling conveniently in the vale between two hills, with an entrance disguised by a tunnel between them, a new, far darker project was born.

In the late fifties Department C19 had been established. It was primarily a little brother to M15, an off-shoot of the Civil Defence programme instigated in the defence boom of the Cold War. As the decade progressed, C19 acquired a reputation for involvement in some of the less well-documented paramilitary excursions. After what was referred to in ministerial papers, all marked Top Secret and Eyes Only, as 'The Shoreditch Incident', the responsibility for the Intrusion Counter Measures Group was handed over to C19 with a recommendation that it be used as the foundation for an entirely new organisation. An organisation set up to deal with those out-of-the-ordinary events which fell outside the remit of the regular army.

A decision was made to mix military and scientific measures and an experienced Air Force Group Captain, Ian Gilmore, was promoted and asked to lead the new unit. He in turn requested the scientific help of an adviser called Rachel Jensen whom he knew to have been pivotal in Turing's work with computers during the war, expanding upon the aborted Judson Ultima Machine.

Although she had retired to write her memoirs in Cambridge, Jensen agreed to help Gilmore, also suggesting the recruitment of a number of her Cambridge protégés, including Allison Williams, Ruth Ingram and Anne Travers. A few years later, London was evacuated, reportedly due to a nerve-gas explosion that froze the capital, focused on the area within the Circle Line of the Underground system. That incident was handled by an army officer, Colonel Lethbridge-Stewart who, on Gilmore's recommendation, was instrumental in setting up the organisation known as UNIT – the United Nations Intelligence Taskforce. As its moniker suggested, this set-up had a wider remit than the Intrusion Counter Measures Group, and was answerable not just to C19, but also to a central governing body in Geneva.

Throughout, the population of Britain, indeed the whole UN, remained blissfully unaware of the existence of these organisations. The few ministers aware of, or responsible for, C19 were sufficiently well briefed to remain silent. For most of them, all it took was a reminder of wartime slogans about careless talk costing lives to ensure their loyalty and discretion. That, and their signature on the Official Secrets Act, any breach of which was tantamount to treason.

What no one in the British Government, the United Nations or even Lethbridge-Stewart's UK branch of UNIT knew was that there was more to C19. Far more.

Like any organism, natural or social, it possessed a dark side: a cancerous, repressed side that made the light seem all the brighter. Only those who directly worked for C19's darker half knew of it. They were ensconced deep within those Cheviot Hills, reporting directly to someone who, on the rare occasions the matter was discussed, did not appear to possess a name. He was a pale young man with a vicious scar disfiguring his face. His eyes were forever hidden behind a pair of expensive silver-rimmed dark glasses and he always wore the same pale grey suit. Or perhaps he had a wardrobe full of identical ones.

On the whole, the people there turned a blind eye to the implications of their work. Most had been selected, signed up body and soul, and brought to the base because, apart from lacking family ties and loyalties, they also lacked two other things considered essential by the more public side of Cl9: morals and integrity.

Grant Traynor had once been such a person, and as the pale young man viewed Traynor's record of employment on the screen of a so stateof-the-art computer that no one outside the Vault even knew it existed, he smiled broadly.

'Employment terminated. Benefits rescinded. Private pension payments reinserted into our funds, I think.'

'Don't get too complacent,' said a voice that seemed to come from just behind him.

'Complacency is the beginning of the end.'

The pale young man switched off his computer. 'Of course, sir.'

'And is the Doctor dead?'

'No.' The pale young man coughed slightly. 'Our agent claims that he succeeded but no body was found. I believe he's lying. The Doctor seems to have disappeared.'

'He's probably sharing lunch with the Reptile People. Knowing the Doctor, he'll try negotiating a peace settlement like last time. Ensure that his efforts fail. And ensure we get at least one of the Reptiles here. I haven't seen a good dissection in months.'

'Yes, sir.'

'Oh, and one last thing. I'm going away for a while. You might call it a round the world cruise, if you had a sense of humour.'

'I don't have, sir. Sorry.'

The voice laughed. 'No, that response was a joke within itself.'

'Was it, sir? I'm glad. May I return to work?'

'Yes. I will return in a few weeks. I expect to find lots of records about Reptile physiognomy when I return. One last thing.'

'Sir?'

'The Glasshouse. Questions have been asked within the House about its validity. Ensure those questions are answered to our, to my, satisfaction. I want it closed down until I'm ready to take it over.' The voice laughed. 'I can't stand private enterprise, unless it's mine. Goodbye.'

'Goodbye, sir. Enjoy your trip.' There was no reply.

The pale young man switched off his computer and pressed a button under his desk. A portion of the desk slid back silently and the unique computer slowly lowered into the gap. Once it was out of sight, the hatch slid back seamlessly and only someone with exceptionally good eyesight, who knew exactly what they were looking for, would have spotted a slight mark on the mahogany. He shuffled a few papers around, then got up. He walked to the cabinet that had a tray of glasses and a whisky decanter on top and poured himself one. Bailey was due in exactly eighteen point six minutes, and they always shared a Black and White.

He swallowed his drink in one, letting the Scotch roll over his tongue and down his throat in one fluid movement. He pictured himself, as he had been five years previously. Sitting with his mates in the Bullfrog after work on Friday night. He had been drinking, as normal, watching those same mates playing billiards. Occasionally one or two of them had turned and looked at him in sympathy, their eyes automatically drawn to the stump which was all that remained of his right arm, or the livid scar down his cheek. And he'd hated them all for it.

OK, so he could no longer join in. He could no longer play cards, read on the train comfortably or even toss a coin. But he could still work. And drink. His firm had been very good after the accident, all sorts of benefits and continued employment, although at a desk rather than on the shop floor. He couldn't handle all that complex electronics or even screw the back on a transistor radio with great precision, but he could take and place orders, work out schedules and timetables. Really, he had been very lucky.

He could also still taste Scotch. And steak. And roast potatoes, ice cream and cigarettes.

But all that had changed that Friday evening, five years ago. When the boss had unexpectedly wandered into the pub, with a couple of his middle management types.

The boss had sat beside him and asked him how he was getting along. Was the work fulfilling? Questions like that. And as his mates continued their game, he sat and listened while his boss outlined a new scheme, explaining that some foreign investors had placed a vast amount of money and research opportunities with the company. The boss suspected that this would go down as the silver age of prosperity for the firm, and there would be chances for all, especially those who were willing to take a few risks.

And he would get a new, fully operational arm out of it. Capable of doing everything his original arm could do and, as he discovered later, able to break a billiard table into fragments with just one finger.

Intrigued, he had agreed to join the Special Projects Team. In fact, he was to lead it.

There had been an operation, he remembered. He remembered feeling the strange detachment as the anaesthetic took effect. He remembered gowned and masked doctors and nurses and then… then…

Then he had awoken. Complete with a new right arm. And a left one. And two new legs and, he was told, an infallible new set of internal organs. His skin felt cold yet he was perfectly warm and comfortable. He had been given food and drink, but couldn't taste any of it. Initially, he assumed that was the result of the anaesthetic, but no, he was later told that it was a by-product of the complete body replacement he had undergone. The only reason he had to eat and drink was to keep his head and facial skin healthy looking. All the nutrients, vitamins and everything else he needed would be diverted to keeping everything from the neck up in prefect health. His new internal organs would sort out the residue.

From that day, he had never grown a minute older. Sometimes, such as when he and Bailey shared their Scotch, he felt a twinge of remorse at having lost the pleasure of taste, but his heightened strength, resilience and stamina more than compensated.

He had continued working for a few more years until the company was finally declared bankrupt after his boss, the man to whom he owed his new life, was apparently killed at an out-of-town warehouse.

But his boss hadn't really died and, before long, the pale young man found himself with a position in a Government paramilitary department, a move arranged by his boss. There, he was able to carry on his boss's wishes right under the Government's noses, without them suspecting a thing. He had redirected money and resources into setting up this whole sub-section of Department C19, deep beneath the Cheviot Hills, codenamed the Vault.

His task was a simple one. Collect as much information, hardware and software as possible from UNIT operations around the globe (his boss was very interested in UNIT's work), store it, experiment with it and learn from it. Or use it.

The Vault was staffed by a lot of good, hard-working people, all of whom the pale young man could rely upon. Among them was Bailey, a Nigerian munitions expert who had been seconded from one of the boss's companies in Ottawa. Now he doubled as the pale young man's chauffeur. As he entered the office and took the proffered tumbler of Black and White, he passed over a sheaf of reports.

'I think you'll find everything we need for the current project is there. The room is set up, the conditions seem perfect. In fact, it's bloody hot in there. But it ought to make our guest feel right at home. Any ideas when it'll arrive?'

'None yet.' The pale young man swallowed another tumbler of Scotch in one go. 'But I don't think it'll be long. I've sent people in to fetch it.'

Bailey nodded and sat down underneath a portrait that showed the head and shoulders of a man in his late fifties. The combination of swept-back silver hair and thick black eyebrows gave him a rather disturbing appearance. His right eye was half closed but the left gazed straight forward, wide-open with a cold blue iris and huge black pupil. He was wearing a collarless black jacket over a high-necked Nehru-style white shirt, buttoned at the neck with a gold clasp. His gaze seemed to follow people around the room, no matter where they stood. The pale young man assumed that Bailey had noticed this a long time ago, because he always sat directly below it.

'And how,' Bailey continued, 'are the plans regarding the Glasshouse progressing? We're beginning to find a few projects here increasingly difficult because the Glasshouse are taking most of our – how can I put it? – raw materials.'

The pale young man smiled. 'It won't be long now. The assassination trail we laid to Harrington-Smythe and his lot ought to at least result in the Government suspending their licence. All we need to do is go down there and, using our tact and diplomacy, remove anything we need. In fact, I already have a man in mind for the job.'

Bailey drained his tumbler. 'Well, I'd better get back to work. The Russians have put in a bid for the Nestene energy weaponry, by the way, and it tops the Saudi one. Which do you want to go for?'

'Neither, at the moment. There are more pressing things to worry about. Play them off against each other for a few more days.'

Bailey nodded. 'You're the boss,' he said and walked out.

'Oh, if only you knew…'

The Doctor and Chukk were eating a porridge of what appeared to be crushed nuts and various fruits. It was very sweet, but the Doctor had not been ill-mannered enough to complain.

'This is very nice, Chukk, but I really do need to get back to the mainland. Could Sula or Tahni possibly give me a lift?' The Doctor put down his spoon. 'And then there's that young man I came here with.'

Chukk swallowed hard. 'If it were up to me, we would return you, Doctor, but that decision is not mine to make.'

'No. It is mine. And everyone else's, Chukk.'

The Doctor turned as a newcomer strode into Chukk's office. 'How do you do? I am the Doctor and—'

'I know who you are, Ape. I am Auggi, mother of the tortured ones. This,' she indicated a massive Reptile Person standing behind her, 'is my friend Krugga.'

Chukk seemed to frown. 'Krugga? Why aren't you at your station?'

Krugga walked forward and the Doctor almost did a double-take – Krugga was so heavily muscled that he was almost as broad as he was tall. The Reptile pointed at the Doctor. 'I believe that it is my duty as a citizen of the Shelter to guard this Ape. That responsibility is more important than the task to which I am normally appointed.'

Chukk stared at him. 'I see.' He then looked straight at Auggi. 'And how long did it take for you to write that little sermon?'

'I don't know what you mean.' Auggi walked towards the Doctor. 'But I'm sure the Triad would not approve of your showing the lowly Ape our Shelter. Our tools and equipment. Our defences.'

The Doctor mutely observed as Chukk crossed to a monitor screen and waved a clawed hand over it. Immediately, a flow of unreadable script darted across it, of a style the Doctor had glimpsed in Derbyshire. He was impressed by the level of technology the Reptiles had. One-touch, possibly even voice-activated, equipment littered Chukk's office. He would have enjoyed the chance to study it, but Auggi and Krugga seemed fairly determined not to let him do anything except be a 'lowly Ape'.

A few seconds later, three faces appeared on the screen, high-resolution, the Doctor noted. Almost holographic.

'Where is this Triad of yours based?' he asked.

'Silence.' Auggi pointed at him. 'You are to remain quiet, or Krugga will quieten you.'

'Oh, well. In that case, I'll keep quiet.' The Doctor smiled at Krugga, unsure whether Krugga was smiling back or not. 'Wouldn't want to upset you of all people, old chap.'

Chukk had greeted the Triad and was telling them about the Doctor. He heard one of them demand to speak to him, and Krugga pushed him into clear view of the screen.

'Greetings, noble Triad. I am the Doctor.'

One of the Reptiles on the screen, clearly the leader, was standing (or sitting, the Doctor could not be sure) slightly proud of the other two.

'I am Icthar, Leader of the Triad. This,' he pointed over his right shoulder, 'is my Second, Scibus and with him is Tarpok, my Science Adviser.'

'Then I am greatly honoured, noble Triad.' The Doctor bowed slightly. 'To speak with three such learned people is a great privilege.'

Tarpok leant forward slightly on the screen. 'So, you are the Doctor. You knew Okdel L'da. Were you responsible for his death?'

'No. I am truly sorry that Okdel died. I would not be arrogant enough to say we were friends, but we were associates. We worked together.'

Tarpok nodded. 'He supplied you with the antidote to cure the virus. We know this. We are not without sympathy for his actions.'

The Doctor took a step forward, and felt Krugga's hand grip his arm. Icthar also noticed this and waved Krugga back.

'Thank you.' He cleared his throat. 'What Okdel did certainly caused those in his Shelter who did not share his views to lead an attack on the research centre in an effort to stop me finding the cure. That led indirectly to some deaths and the eventual entombment of the others. However, had the virus run unchecked, mankind would have struck back in a far more violent way. That Shelter would never have been able to defend itself against their weapons of mass destruction.'

'You say they were entombed, not destroyed?'

'Indeed. The humans resealed the caves rather than commit mass murder.' It occurred to the Doctor that it might not be wise to go any further into that. The Brigadier had wanted to raise a full military expedition to slaughter the Reptiles but the Doctor had talked him out of it. Then, apparently on direct orders from C19, the Brigadier had resealed the caves, stopping the Doctor from going back down, and attempting to make peace.

'Why?' asked Tarpok.

'Because there were still a great many of your people in hibernation, including the scientist who developed the virus. A large number of the colony never awoke in the first place and, should they be revived, will not even be aware that Okdel, Morka and the others had ever fought mankind.' The Doctor let himself look proud. 'I was, indeed still am one day, hoping to revisit the Shelter, revive your people and talk to them. There are great areas of this planet mankind does not use. The deserts, the ice tundras. All places you can live and build and co-exist with each other.'

'Mankind, these Apes, they are a vermin. This is our planet,' spat Auggi. 'I will never co-exist with them. I should rather die.'

The Doctor turned to her. 'That, madam, if I may say so, is a totally irrational and inflammatory thing to say. Even if you fought mankind, even if you unleashed virus after virus, there are billions more "Apes" than there are of you. It would be a long and bloody war and one that you could not win. Once mankind at large begins to know of you, if they see you as hostile, your Shelters will be sought out. If you antagonise them, they will locate every sleeping Reptile Person on this planet and kill them.' The Doctor paused and stared at her unflinching eyes. Then he continued in less aggressive tones: 'Madam, if you want a war with mankind, you will certainly get one. And you will receive your wish. You will surely die.'

Auggi took a step towards him, Krugga also moving nearer. 'Are you threatening me, Ape?'

The Doctor stood his ground. 'No. No, I am simply stating a fact.' He turned back to the screen. 'Great Icthar, you have survived so many millions of years. Why throw all that away in a war? Seek peace, I beg you.'

Icthar spoke again. 'You speak well for an Ape. The Triad will consider your words carefully. Chukk, we shall communicate soon. Until our next conversation, take care, all of you.'

The screen went blank.

Auggi circled the Doctor a couple of times and then stopped in front of him. 'You can take off that smug look, Ape. The Triad might be swayed by rhetoric, but they are three old cowards. My prime concern is for my young, and their continued existence, no matter what the cost.' She turned away and, with Krugga, walked out of the office, throwing a parting remark over her shoulder. 'I, too, shall consider your words, Ape. Very carefully indeed.'

After she had left, the Doctor let out a deep breath. 'She is a very powerful woman, Chukk.'

Chukk nodded. 'She would be Shelter Leader, if I let her. I see it as my main job to be a counter balance to her extremist views. Nevertheless, Doctor, she has many followers here. Especially amongst the young ones. They see her as some kind of potential saviour. Her and Baal, her son. He is a science student. A very good one, but very determined.'

'How careful, though? I have known many scientists, all "very good ones", but they all lack one important thing necessary to be a really good scientist.'

'What is that, Doctor?'

'Morals, Chukk. The ability to judge right and wrong, and not to live by the old credo that the end justifies the means. Is Baal like that?'

Chukk looked down at his feet for a moment, and then straightened up. 'I think we should go to his laboratory, Doctor. Quickly.'

The Doctor followed Chukk as they raced down some corridors, and through areas the Doctor had not seen before. Past more walls of art and holograms. Through a more open area, with benches and chairs and a fountain which sprayed a fine mist over them. They rounded blind corners, almost crashing into Reptiles going about their business, and nearly knocked one off a ladder as he repaired a burnt-out lighting circuit.

As they went round another bend, Chukk nearly sent Sula flying.

'What is the hurry, Chukk?'

Chukk was breathless by now. 'Baal. Has he experimented upon the Ape hatchling?'

Sula nodded. 'Yes. But sadly he won't know the results of—'

She stopped as the Doctor thundered past her, shouting Baal's name. As he entered Baal's laboratory, he was able to see everything. The holograms, the charts on the screens (the ones he could understand at least), the particle disseminator in the corner.

'Baal!' he shouted. 'Baal, what have you done?'

Baal swung around, angrily. 'Who let this Ape in here? Sula? Sula, where are you?'

Sula and Chukk scurried in. Baal was livid. 'How dare you let this… this thing into my workplace, Chukk! What were you thinking of? Think of the contamination!'

'Balderdash and rot,' snapped the Doctor. 'Where is Marc Marshall?'

'Who? Oh, the Ape hatchling.' Baal suddenly stopped and sat in a chair in front of a hologram. 'Do you know what this is, Ape? Has your puny science achieved this yet?'

'Yes, of course it has. If you'd stop being so blind about mankind, you'd understand their science is on a par with yours in many respects.'

Sula hissed. 'Nonsense. If the Apes are so advanced, why do they have diseases? Why could they not build a Shelter like this? Why do they not live on the moon yet? We have all that technology; they have nothing.'

The Doctor looked at her. 'My dear young lady, you are so very wrong. Mankind has that ability, it just has not made use of it yet. Or doesn't realise it has it. But the ability is there.'

Baal coughed. 'But to my question, Ape.'

'He is called the Doctor, Baal,' murmured Chukk. 'He is a scientist also.'

'My apologies, Doctor. As one scientist to another, do you recognise this?'

'It is the double helix. The basic structure of genetics and all life.'

'Very good.' Baal wiped a hand over a nearby screen, and the helix was replaced by a wire-frame model of a Silurian, like Chukk. 'This is one of my people. As is this.' A variation appeared, looking like the Reptiles the Doctor had seen on the screen when talking to the Triad. A further eight or nine variations appeared in the room, each one twisting slightly on its holographic axis, making the room appear to be full of dancing Reptile People.

'We, on the other hand, are different.' All the images vanished, to be replaced by a wire-frame model of a Reptile which looked more like Baal or Sula. 'We are hybrids. The byproduct of genetic interbreeding. Two genetic strains which are too different to breed true when crossed. Maybe Chukk has explained that our aquatic caste and all land castes are forbidden to mate. The genetic structure is too impure. Well, the mating happened, shortly before the Great Hibernation. And we are the result.'

The Doctor frowned. 'You're alive. I presume you're healthy. What is the problem?'

'Correct, we are alive,' said Sula. 'But we are sterile. We are the end of our line. And you are most certainly wrong about our health. Most of our people live to be two hundred, maybe two hundred and fifty years old. Our research into our sterility has proven we only have another eight or nine years before our cellular structure collapses and we die.'

'I'm truly sorry. But how does that involve Marc?'

Baal got up. 'Ah, that's my great discovery, Doctor. The Ape chromosomes, vile as they are, contain the genes we need to survive, to correct the imbalance and give us longer to develop a cure for our sterility.'

'I imagine your mother does not approve.'

Chukk agreed: 'Auggi would be horrified if she knew you were actually implanting Ape material into your own bodies.'

'Then she must not know,' said Tahni, emerging from a side room, closing the door behind her. 'And if she finds out, Chukk, our revenge will be very swift indeed.'

'Look, this is all very well, but your inter-Shelter politics are of no interest to me. Where is Marc?' The Doctor began to cross the laboratory, towards the other door through which Tahni had entered, but she stepped into his path.

'Our politics ought to interest you, Ape.' She placed a hand firmly onto his chest. 'Auggi, our mother, would prefer you dead. Chukk would prefer to let you go and tell the other Apes all about us. But the three of us well, we'll see. And as you are here now, I rather think it will be our decision.' Tahni moved to one side. 'And if you want to see your Ape hatchling, it's in there. I remember how attached to each other you lot were. It's disgusting, all that groping and mauling each other. How primitive.' She went and stood to one side of Baal. Sula stood on the other.

Looking at them, the Doctor was suddenly reminded of the way Scibus and Tarpok had stood slightly behind and to each side of Icthar. He hoped that these three never got those particular reins of power.

He gave a last glance at Chukk who, once again, was examining his own shuffling feet upon the floor, presumably unwilling to catch the Doctor's eye. He, therefore, knew what the Doctor was going to see.

The Doctor looked across at the particle disseminator, and thought of the hologrammatic double helix. What had Baal done to the child in the name of science? If, indeed, Baal's experiments could be placed under that heading.

He pushed open the door, surprised at its weight, and decided Reptile females must be stronger than they looked. A point to remember, a point to file away for future –

He saw Marc Marshall, lying on the rough ground, curled up in a foetal ball. Even in that position, his bloated skin was obvious, hanging from his body in swollen folds. Most of his hair had fallen out.

The Doctor was at his side in a second, his long legs crossing the room in three strides. He bent over him, checking for a pulse through the distended skin of his neck. He found one, but it was very slow.

Marc's mouth, nose and ears were caked in dried blood and his eyes were closed; he was unconscious. The Doctor tried moving some of the skin, feeling for the bones underneath. They seemed to be strong and unbroken. The Doctor concluded that the particle disseminator had somehow disrupted both Marc's hormonal and glandular state, causing the skin mutation.

He tried to lift Marc up, but couldn't get a firm enough grip on the horribly loosened skin. Instead, he stroked the boy's head. His caress dislodged the last few strands of hair.

'Oh, Marc,' he murmured.

The boy's eyes fluttered open and the Doctor could see he was holding back some immense pain. 'Doctor? Is that… you?'

'Yes, Marc. Just sleep. You've had an accident but you're going to be fine. I'll look after you.'

Marc swallowed gingerly as if he had a very bad sore throat, his eyes watering. 'The man Reptile said it would hurt. He… he was right. I want to go home.'

The Doctor rubbed the back of his neck and tried to look apologetic. 'I don't think we can yet. But as soon as we can, I'll let you know. Now, just sleep. Sleep. Sleep.'

The Doctor stared hard directly into Marc's eyes,

silently mouthing the word, until they rolled up and his eyelids closed.

The Doctor spent another couple of moments collecting his thoughts. Then he stood up, prepared to confront Baal.

Facing him in the doorway was Tahni.

The Doctor almost snarled at her as he pointed towards Marc. 'Was that necessary?'

'Yes. Remember, we are not savages or primitives. We do not experiment on vermin just for the fun of it. We do not kill, maim or fight for fun. We needed this sacrifice to try and find a cure.'

'And have you?'

'Baal will not know that for a while. That is why the hatchling is still alive.' Tahni stared down at Marc. 'We may need to study his DNA more closely.' She looked back at the Doctor. 'And you will stay here as well, for now.'

'Now just a minute—' the Doctor started, but was interrupted by Tahni's third eye glowing green. He suddenly felt pins and needles shooting up through his feet and legs. With a gasp of surprise, he dropped to the floor, unable to move the lower half of his body at all.

He rolled onto his back, trying to lever himself up, but his legs simply would not obey. It was as if the commands from his brain were encountering a brick wall as they reached his thighs.

As he stared at the damp ceiling, Tahni's face loomed upside down above him. 'It will pass,' she said. 'In time.'

'How… how long?' The Doctor found it hard to speak. The paralysis had already spread through his stomach and was reaching his chest.

'A few hours. Maybe a day. By then, we may have retaken our world. That depends on Auggi. All I will say is that with you here, this time, no one can stop us.'

The last thing the Doctor was aware of was that he could not answer her. The paralysis was swamping his brain and everything was going dark. Like sinking into a pool of thick black ink, he was floating down, down, down...

FIVE

The tall, blonde woman, dressed in jeans and a red T-shirt watched as the police frogmen went under the water for a fourth time.

The lake was not particularly large and was almost completely surrounded by shrubbery and trees. Only the gravelled area on which she and the ageing and rather tubby inspector stood provided a clear run up to the water. The car simply had to have been driven in at that particular spot.

Maya der Voort glanced around the countryside in an effort to stop watching the surface of the water, waiting for the tell-tale black-encased arm to point up and indicate that the discovery she had so long expected had finally been made.

'Mrs der Voort, it has been eight months now.' Inspector Hoevern was doing his best to be sympathetic, as he had been ever since the investigation began, but Maya could tell he was beginning to lose his patience.

'I know, I know,' she said. 'And it is costing a small fortune in your time and resources.' She lit a cigarette, offering him one as well, which he declined. 'It's just that everything my husband and I have discovered leads us here.'

'With respect,' said Inspector Hoevern, lighting her cigarette, 'you and Mr der Voort are hardly experienced investigators.'

'Unlike my sister,' Maya said. 'Yes, I know. Hans has been at me to give this up already. But it's my sister – his friend – who we think is down there. I have to be sure we're right.'

'Do you know how many people deliberately vanish every year, Mrs der Voort?'

'Hundreds.'

'Thousands. Most of them turn up again, even if only to say they're all right, but sometimes not until months, even years, later. If your sister chose to vanish, she could do it with consummate ease. Especially with her background. How do we know this isn't some assignment she's on?'

'Because her editor would have told us. Oh, he might not say what she was doing exactly, but he would have put our minds at rest. According to him, she was taking a break after exposing that military cover-up.'

'I remember.' The inspector scratched his head. 'And the awards she won were impressive. For the third year running, I think.'

Maya nodded. 'Each one meant something to her. She never quite believed she could really win one, let alone three. That's why I can't believe she'd run away. She loved life, her job, her family.' Maya sat on the bonnet of the inspector's car. 'She hadn't argued with anyone, had no enemies—'

'Ah, well, that's where you might be wrong, Mrs der Voort. In her line of work, she was bound to make enemies. And after her last case blew open that corruption ring in the army, well, she must have upset a lot of influential people.' He looked at his watch and then back at the crystal-clear water. 'I'll give you until six, and then I'm calling it off. I'm sorry.'

Maya gave a resigned shrug. 'Thank you. You've already

done more than I expected.'

Inspector Hoevern joined her on the car bonnet. 'To be frank, I admired your sister. That's what keeps me going on this case. I'm as intrigued as you, but out of respect for her rather than family loyalty. I want her to be living it up in Spain or South America. The last thing I want is for you to be right. But if she is under this,' he pointed at the water, 'then rest assured, I'm going to find out why.'

A car suddenly slewed to a halt beside them, skidding on the gravel. After a second, the driver got out, cursing.

'Blasted roads. No sign to say it turned into gravel. Hit that at forty-five kph and you'd be under water in a moment. Brakes would just throw you in.' The newcomer stared at Maya. 'You must be Mrs der Voort. I met your husband a few months back at a charity do. The Art Gallery.'

Maya frowned, shooting a look at Inspector Hoevern.

'I do apologise,' he said. 'Mrs der Voort, allow me to introduce you to Doctor Moere.'

Maya raised an eyebrow. 'I remember my husband talking about you. You made a nice donation to his project. He was very grateful.'

'A police doctor's wages aren't high, Mrs der Voort, but I'd rather see young people's art on my walls than their drug-filled corpses at the mortuary.'

Maya was about to ask why he was there, when an arm suddenly shot up from under the water, sending spray everywhere. All three of them were at the water's edge in an instant. The diver was walking towards them, pulling off his mask.

'Well?' asked Doctor Moere.

The diver nodded. 'There's a car there. One occupant, a driver.' He shot a glance at Maya and then to Inspector

Hoevern. 'It's been there... well, quite a while.'

The doctor tutted. 'ID will be difficult. It'll take a couple of days to sort everything out.'

'Is it a woman's body?' Maya was surprised to hear herself ask the question. Her legs were turning to jelly and all she wanted to do was get back inside the Inspector's car and sit still.

The diver looked again at the inspector, who nodded. He turned back to Maya. 'I'm sorry, Mrs der Voort. I believe it is. It's a dark car, probably a Mini, imported from the United Kingdom.'

'As I said.' Maya sat on the bank. 'It's hers. I knew it.'

'We don't know if she's the one inside it, yet, though.' Inspector Hoevern looked back at the diver. 'Anything else?'

Again the diver looked towards Maya. She stared up at him. 'Please,' she said, 'don't spare me anything. Inspector Hoevern will tell you, I'm no shrinking violet. And I'll find out eventually.'

'But we don't want to make you assume the worst until Doctor Moere can do an autopsy.'

Maya smiled stiffly. 'Yeah. But you know it's her just as I do. That's why you called a police doctor here.'

'Just a formality. Just in case,' the inspector said.

Maya again looked to the diver. 'Well?'

He took a deep breath. Behind him, the surface was broken by the other two divers. One of them was carrying something. He swallowed. 'It is definitely a woman. I can't say more than that, except...'

'Go on,' urged Inspector Hoevern.

The diver held his hands out, apologetically. 'It's up to Doctor Moere really, but—'

Moere nodded sharply. 'No, go on. In your opinion, if

you like. I can make my formal report later.'

The diver nodded. 'All right. From what I could see, the victim had been shot. At close range, in the back of the head. This was no accident; this looks like murder.'

'Back of the head, eh? Well, that's suicide out.' Moere looked across to the other divers. 'What's that?'

Inspector Hoevern took a wet bag from the nearest, who reported: 'On the seat beside the corpse, sir.' He shot a sad look at Maya. She recognised him as someone who had been on the inspector's team from the beginning.

The inspector opened the handbag with a piece of clear plastic he took from his pocket.

Maya stared at the bag. She'd seen it so many times before. On her sister's shoulder. In her car. On her sofa. 'It's hers,' she breathed. 'My God, it's hers.'

The inspector produced a purse and an ID card from within. On the ID card was a photograph of a blonde woman with a strong bone structure, and piercing blue eyes.

Maya couldn't stop the tears coming. She felt Doctor Moere's hand on her shoulder. 'I'm sorry,' he said.

Inspector Hoevern waved the divers back under the water and dropped the bag onto the back seat of his car. Then he crossed to Maya, holding out the ID card.

'Your sister, I presume?'

Maya glanced at the photo, and the signature beside it. 'Yes,' she said, a little hoarsely. 'Yes, that's Jana.' Maya looked back out to the disturbed water. 'And this is where she died, isn't it? Murdered.'

Finally, she gave way to tears.

The career of Sir Marmaduke Harrington-Smythe was finished, he realised, and there was nothing he could do about it. It had all been a set-up, a deliberate attempt to wreck his life. And all for revenge. Oh, yes, of course, it all fitted now. It was Lethbridge-Stewart's fault. He had Sir John Sudbury, in fact the whole of C19, eating out of his hand.

He'd always been manipulative, that soldier, right back to their days at Sandhurst, when a very young Sapper Lethbridge-Stewart had been caught making an error on manoeuvres. A careless rifle shot that had nearly killed one of the training marshals. The marshal had tried to bring a charge, to teach the young man a lesson, but of course, Lethbridge-Stewart had everyone eating out of his hand even then. Charmed the disciplinary board with assurances that it was an accident, that the rifle was at fault, not the operator. And that the training marshal had overstepped the bounds of safety by being ahead of the manoeuvres instead of watching them from behind.

As a result Colonel Harrington-Smythe had been forced to resign. What else could he do? Lethbridge-Stewart had betrayed him, stabbed him in the back. His life as a training marshal was over and he had to leave the Armed Services and return to civilian life.

From there, he had got together the funds (from his accrued inheritance) and set up the Glasshouse. A marvellous concept, a private paramilitary nursing home, caring for the sick and injured from the likes of M15, UNIT and other 'discreet' organisations across the United Kingdom. With the help of the Ministry of Defence, C19 in particular, he had made quite a go of it. Only last year, they had agreed to extend his contract.

And so here he was, sitting in one of those marvellous oak-panelled briefing rooms that littered Britain's corridors of power, listening as six or seven sad old men dictated his future. Of course, Sudbury had made it all sound jolly pleasant when he'd called him to London. Talk of an early retirement: 'Old Marmaduke's abdication' he had called it, oh so very wittily. And all because of that failed assassination attempt. And a tape sent to Sudbury's office that morning that the old fool had not bothered to listen to until after the attempt.

Sir Marmaduke now sat, both rapt and appalled, listening to that very tape. On it, he heard the unmistakable sound of his own voice, discussing with someone a plan to kill 'those C19 asses who are wrecking my Glasshouse'.

'That is a fake. A forgery. It's all a plot by someone who wants to discredit us, break up the alliance between your Ministry and the private sector.' Sir Marmaduke straightened his back, trying to look relaxed at the same time, as if none of this could possibly be upsetting him. 'It's a complete fabrication, and it will never stand up in court.'

'We are well aware of that, Sir Marmaduke,' one of the faceless bureaucrats said. 'But it does not alter the fact that three men died that day, and Sir John Sudbury is only sitting here due to the bravery of one of those men.'

Sir John Sudbury pushed himself up from his chair with obvious discomfort. Sir Marmaduke momentarily felt sorry for him and then noticed that the expression of pain on Sudbury's face was not quite realistic. He was faking it. Faking it in an attempt to get sympathy.

'I regret that these events, whatever Sir Marmaduke's involvement in them, have forced our hand in this matter. After all, I was responsible for persuading all of you here, as well as the Minister, that Sir Marmaduke's Glasshouse project was worthwhile. I still believe it is.'

Sir Marmaduke was puzzled. Surely Sudbury was after

his blood, irrespective of that tape? They all were. They always had been.

'However,' Sir John continued, 'I do believe that it would be appropriate for there to be a change in management. The Minister has allowed me to arrange to buy Sir Marmaduke out of the Glasshouse at, I might add,' and he looked pointedly at Sir Marmaduke, 'a very fair price. Enough to keep you comfortable for the rest of your life.'

Sir Marmaduke decided enough was enough. 'I accept that offer, Sir John, in the spirit in which it has been offered. Unfairly, unnecessarily and spitefully. Yes, take the blasted Glasshouse project. I would not wish to work for, indeed ever see, any of you again after today. But for the record –' he looked directly at the young man sitting at the back of the room, transcribing the proceedings – 'I believe you are all in error. I have been framed. Someone is out to get me, or obtain my facility for their own ends. That tape is forged and somehow I shall prove it. And when I do, I will drag this quorum through the slander courts so fast, you'll end up paying me six times the offer currently on the table.' He looked at Sir John. 'You, sir, I believed to be my friend. You have destroyed my faith in this Ministry and our relationship in particular. Take the Glasshouse and everything involved in it. I don't want your blood money, because I have my pride. Goodbye to you all.' He took his case from the floor, rose and walked towards the door. 'I hope, young man, you got all of that on record.'

The young recorder looked up, and smiled. It struck Sir Marmaduke that he would have been quite a handsome young man if it hadn't been for the scar down his face, made more livid by its contrast with the paleness of his skin. Perhaps he was some poor wretch Sudbury had found in the dregs of the working classes, scarred and injured. Maybe he was partially sighted, hence the dark glasses. 'Trust no one,' Sir Marmaduke warned him.

'Whatever you say, Sir Marmaduke,' the pale young man replied.

Sir Marmaduke walked into the corridor and slammed the door behind him. On a bench further down the corridor were the Irish Twins, dressed in their Glasshouse medical uniforms. They stood up together, Ciara reaching for his briefcase, Cellian passing him a plastic cup of water. Sir Marmaduke shook his head at them both. 'Thank you, but no. If you can bring the car round, I'm going to walk outside for a few moments. Meet me outside County Hall in fifteen minutes.'

The Irish Twins nodded and looked up as the door which Sir Marmaduke had slammed shut was reopened and a gaggle of old men traipsed through it. Sir Marmaduke shot them a stare of open hostility but it was only seen by the young recorder, who followed them out.

Sir Marmaduke hugged his briefcase closer and headed for the stairs that would take him towards Parliament Square. A few minutes later, he stood on Westminster Bridge, looking back at the House. He allowed the slight breeze blowing down the Thames to ruffle his tie and hair. He liked the feel of the wind – it was something he had not appreciated for too long.

The air was warm, the sun blazing down onto the river, sending beautiful streaks of reflected yellow across the water, like tiny bolts of lightning. A River Police boat was chugging downstream from under Lambeth Bridge, tearing through the calm waters and leaving a churning wake behind it.

A disturbance, he decided. A breaking of the river's

natural form. Rather like his life, he supposed. What to do now? Twenty minutes ago, he had been the head of a powerful organisation.

Now, he was abandoned, with nothing to look forward to but returning to the Glasshouse, and facing his staff. Telling them that he had been dismissed from his own company and that they would soon be working for a new, as yet unknown, leader.

He looked left, towards the South Bank and County Hall. He could see his distinctive Mercedes parked there, but there did not appear to be anyone in it. Perhaps the Irish Twins were also getting a breath of fresh air. Probably worried about their jobs. No, nothing fazed them, really. Peter Morley, though, he was potential trouble. He was weak enough as it was, but news like this might send him off… oh, what did it matter? Why should he care? If Morley didn't finish his work, it was no business of his any more. It was behind him. One day he'd been in charge, the next, he was out without so much as a thank-you for everything he'd done. The last few years' work meant nothing to the men in power. They would take everything he'd done and use it quite happily, and within three months, he would be nothing more than a hazy memory.

He saw Ciara walking across the bridge to meet him. Strange, that was unlike her. Oh well, he'd find out what she wanted soon enough.

'There's someone who wants to talk to you, Sir Marmaduke,' she said, pointing back towards the car. Sir Marmaduke could have sworn it was empty a moment ago, but there were two people in it now. Cellian was presumably in the driving seat, but who was in the back?

He and Ciara crossed the bridge and got to the car, Ciara side-stepping and getting into the front passenger seat before Sir Marmaduke could. He shrugged, but before he could climb in behind her the door was opened for him from the inside.

Sitting comfortably on the back seat was the pale young recorder.

'What do you want?' Sir Marmaduke asked him, annoyed. 'Why aren't you typing up your copious notes? Is this Sir John's attempt at an apology? Because it won't—'

'Shut up, Harrington-Smythe!'

Sir Marmaduke stared at the back of Ciara's head. How dare she speak to him like that! 'Ciara—'

The scarred young man reached out and grabbed his wrist with amazing strength. Before he knew what had happened, he had been pulled off his feet and into the car.

Sir Marmaduke looked across at his assailant in astonishment. 'Who are you?' he growled, rubbing his bruised wrist.

'Me?' said the pale young man. 'I'm the new owner of your Glasshouse, Sir Marmaduke.'

'But you're just... just a...'

'Oh Sir Marmaduke, I'm a great many things.'

Sir Marmaduke gasped in horror as the pale young man removed his dark glasses, revealing a face without human eyes. In their place were two black discs criss-crossed with microscopic filaments. Sir Marmaduke found the artificial eyes fascinating. 'What happened to your... I mean...'

The pale young man replaced his dark glasses, and tapped Cellian on the shoulder. 'You are a fool, Harrington-Smythe. We've been using you for months now, preparing to take over your little nursing home, preparing ourselves.'

'But... but you're with C 19?'

'Am I? I suppose in a way I am. But I'm also involved in

far more interesting things.' The pale young man smiled, his perfect white teeth almost glinting in the sunlight as Cellian drove down Millbank, towards Victoria.

Sergeant Mike Yates stood and stared across the greyish-blue water of the English Channel. A slight breeze was blowing his hair, but he was not particularly cold. Cool, but not chilly. To his right was the road that ran through Smallmarshes towards Hastings. Dotted along it were various shops and guest houses. Out of sight but, he knew, further along was the police station where Bell and Osgood would be making their investigations. The Brigadier was at the railway station. The five other men they had brought with them were searching the village. Only Hawke was not out and about. She was sitting in his car, using a short-wave radio to keep in touch with Benton at HQ. On the side of the car had been stencilled the name and address of a fictitious taxi firm, just in case anyone saw her with the radio.

This was Yates's first civvies-job since joining UNIT and he was rather enjoying himself. Being in the army was all very well, but wearing a khaki collar and tie or rough fatigues every day could get a bit tedious. The chance to wear his own clothes while at work was rare enough to be savoured.

He was dressed in a brown roll-neck, under a brown check sports coat. His tan flannel trousers flapped in the breeze as he started back towards the car, stuffing his hand in his pocket.

Cunningly deepened and reshaped, the pocket was actually a holster containing a small Browning automatic, loaded and ready. Mike Yates was not taking chances.

As he approached, Maisie Hawke stuck her head out of

the window, smiling. 'Hey, Michael. I don't think any of the locals are going to attack us. No need for the pistol, eh?'

He got into the passenger seat. 'Can't be too careful, Maisie. You never know. The Brig always says to be prepared.'

'You sound like a boy scout.' She was still smiling. 'When you've been with UNIT a while longer, you'll relax a bit more.'

Mike shrugged. 'Yeah, but how long is that? The life-expectancy of a UNIT soldier isn't exactly known to be high.'

'We all know the risks when we sign on the dotted line. No one forces us here, you know.'

Mike opened the glove compartment, taking out a bar of Dairy Milk. He broke off a piece, offering it to Hawke. She took it and began munching.

He did the same. 'I know, but it sounds quite glamorous when you're in the regular army, pounding some parade square. Or going on endless manoeuvres in Germany.'

Hawke shrugged. 'So. Why did you join up?'

Mike stared out of the windscreen. 'A long story involving family pressure, peer-group pressure, university pressure and personal inability to say no to anyone who thought they could run my life better than I could.'

'Wow. Anything you do actually like in your life?'

Mike looked at her in concern. 'No, don't get me wrong. I actually like it. I mean, UNIT is great because it has an element of risk. Of the unknown. I've done things here that I could never have dreamed of. I've travelled through time rips, I've arranged for top-secret objects to be locked away. I've seen more weirdness here in two months than I could have hoped for in ten years in the regular army.

I'm not leaving this place unless it's on a blanket-covered stretcher.'

'How grim.' Hawke held her hand out for more chocolate. 'Best I've done is book restaurant tables for the Brigadier and the Doctor, order sandwiches for Sir John Sudbury and have a Nestene Energy Unit delivered to the National Space Museum.'

'Huh. Didn't know such a thing existed.'

'Nor me.' Hawke demanded more chocolate. 'You're a weird one yourself, Michael.'

'Why?'

'Most of us are doing a job. OK, I'm a glorified telephonist and radio ham, but I probably know more about UNIT and what it does than any foot soldier here. But it doesn't greatly interest me. You, well, you're sort of odd. You like all this crap. Aliens, killer robots, space missions bringing back alien plagues and all that. It actually interests you, doesn't it?'

Mike Yates nodded. 'I think so, yes.'

'Do you know why we're here?'

'Silurians. That's what Benton said when he rang. I had a quick flick through the files and gather that they're—'

'Reptile people, who had a civilisation upon this planet millions of years before mankind could even talk clearly. Recently located in some caves in Derbyshire. Research, however, has caused some speculation that a similar colony was found in the Antarctic during the twenties, although the UNIT station subsequently set up there has yet to provide any concrete evidence. Unlike most Reptiles, they appear to be able to adapt both to extremely hot and extremely cold temperatures. They are dangerous when roused and are a Code 1101 menace.'

Mike was impressed. 'How did you learn all that?'

'I typed the file you read.' She paused, staring forwards. 'I also lost my fiancé to them, at Wenley Moor.' She turned to face him. 'Possibly out of consideration for my feelings, or maybe because Sir John won't extend his budget, the Brigadier has not had a captain since Sam was killed.'

'I… I'm sorry, Maisie. I didn't know.'

'No reason why you should. Even his family don't know. They think he died in a military car accident in Switzerland. Do you know how many lies I have to type, Mike? How often I have to write and tell someone that their son or daughter has been killed while on attachment to UNIT? I can't say they died when an Auton shot them in Essex, or a supposedly friendly alien shoved more radiation through their body with one touch than they'd get if they sat in a reactor at Windscale for six months. No, they die in car accidents, or swimming accidents. Or missing after manoeuvres in the Gobi desert have gone awry.' She looked at her hands and Mike could see they were gripping the steering wheel too tightly; her knuckles were white. 'I had to write to George Hawkins, a man I spent Christmas with last year, and tell him Sam died in an accident when he actually died protecting us all from a bunch of reptilian killers.'

'I thought the Brigadier wrote to people,' Mike said suddenly, and immediately wished he hadn't.

But Maisie Hawke laughed and let go of the steering wheel. 'Oh, Michael, you're so sweet.'

'Oh. Thanks. I think.'

'Yeah, he signs them. But I research who they go to and actually type them up.' She shook her head, letting her hair whip around her face for a second. 'Right, that's enough about that. What next?'

Mike just stared at her. 'That's the first time you've talked about Sam's death, isn't it?'

'Not allowed to talk about it, am I? Official Secrets Act and all that.' She touched his hand. 'Thanks for listening.'

'Thanks for talking. If you want to do it again, I'm always around.' Mike gave her the last piece of chocolate.

She ate it and then pointed out of the window. 'Here comes Tom.'

Mike sighed. Why did he have to bring Corporal Osgood? The chap meant well but he was, frankly, a bit of an egg-head. Ah well.

Osgood opened the door and slid into the back.

'Sergeant. Corporal Hawke.'

'Well, Tom? Anything from our helpful local constabulary?'

Osgood consulted the spiral-bound notebook he always carried. 'I left Corporal Bell talking to a Sergeant Robert Lines. It appears he knew the Doctor.'

Hawke sighed. 'We knew that. That's why you went to find him.'

'Oh. Yes, right. Well, he knows nothing more, it seems, but he wants to help. The Doctor obviously took him into some confidence.'

The radio crackled and Benton's voice came out of the dashboard receiver. 'Trap One to Greyhound Two. Over?'

'Greyhound Two to Trap One, receiving.'

'Hello, sir. News for you from Sir John Sudbury. The Glasshouse has been closed down pending an inquiry. Sir John wants us to oversee the removal of sensitive materials. Over.'

'Oh great,' Mike muttered. 'Roger, Trap One. Will inform Greyhound One of the situation. Do nothing until contacted. Over and out.' He looked at the other two.

'We'd better find the Brigadier.'

The Glasshouse receptionist looked up as the doors opened, briefly letting the bright sunlight in. She blinked slightly and her eyes readjusted.

A man in a cream jacket and black roll-neck sweater stood in the doorway. He had a neatly centre-parted cluster of blond hair above a richly tanned face. He was wearing dark glasses. She felt herself relax until she saw the hefty pistol in his hand, a large stubby silencer on the end. She reached for the alarm button but didn't make it – the man smacked her in the chest.

No he didn't, he was standing by the door…

Then wha –

The blond man walked past the reception desk, glancing at the dead nurse as scarlet red spread across her breasts, stark against the bleached white of her uniform.

A male nurse came out of a room, carrying a sheaf of papers. Seconds later, he was on the floor, the papers soaking up the blood from a massive hole through his neck. His arm twitched violently, but he was already dead.

Moments later, the blond man entered Doctor Peter Morley's laboratory. It was empty apart from a man in a white coat and a young woman, both sitting in a corner. The woman was drawing something on the wall with a pen while the man watched. Neither was aware that he had entered.

He fired twice, almost severing the man's head from his body. The woman swung round and looked up, uncomprehending.

'Hey, who the hell—' Another man in a scientist's jacket had entered from an office at the rear.

The blond man turned almost imperceptibly, firing casually as he did so, not bothering to take careful aim. The shot took the newcomer through the groin, slamming him back against the far wall. White with shock, the injured man tried to get up until a second shot hit him between the eyes.

Before he had hit the floor, the blond man strode across to the woman, grabbed her roughly and threw her over his shoulder.

Ten minutes later they were on their way to Northumberland.

Brigadier Lethbridge-Stewart stared at the timetable pasted up at Smallmarshes station. One train every hour passed that way, heading either for Dover or Hastings. The railway was a one-track job, like the famous Marlow Donkey near his home.

Home, Fiona and Kate, and all those problems, seemed frighteningly far away at that moment. It constantly amazed the Brigadier how easily he could set aside his worries about his domestic life. It was a kind of schizophrenia, he decided, a deliberate leading of a double-life to try and keep Queen, Country and Fiona happy. He didn't need to remind himself that he had failed. Fiona was going to divorce him. Even her Catholic grandparents wouldn't be able to stop that one. Maybe she was right. Maybe he should just give in and let her go, let her get on with her life. Find a real city businessman, with a real city business who could give her real excuses for working late and have real affairs with real secretaries.

No. He would not get bitter. Separation was, frankly, inevitable. It had been ever since that business in the Underground a few years back, when everyone else was talking about being evacuated from London. Fiona had wanted to know why he had 'stayed at the office apartments in London' instead of leaving for the safety of the countryside with her. Kate had not even been a gleam in their eye then, but nevertheless, Fiona had been pregnant within eighteen months. It had been a reminder that his place was at home.

But Lethbridge-Stewarts had been in the military since the battle of Waterloo when Major General Fergus Lethbridge-Stewart had been right-hand man to the Duke of Wellington. And family tradition was something the Brigadier had never kicked against. Like all Sandhurst lads, he'd learnt another trade in case he ended up in Civvie Street, but there had been little doubt that the army was to be his life.

And so here he was, standing on an empty railway platform on the Kent/Sussex coast, wondering what had happened to two of his staff. The Doctor was not known for his adherence to rules and regulations, but for him to have vanished so totally seemed more than a little suspicious. And if those reptile monsters were involved, well, there could be an element of revenge thrown in. After all, the Doctor had been around in Derbyshire. Mind you, it had been the Brigadier and not the Doctor who tried to blow them all up, all on orders from C19 of course, but he would hardly blame them for bearing a grudge.

Then there was Miss Shaw: acerbic, spiky and just a little frightening. Nevertheless, the Brigadier valued her, not just for her mind but for her ability to keep the Doctor in check. She had just vanished without trace. Maisie Hawke had not been able to track her down at all, not even through Jeff Johnson.

'Can I help you, sir?'

The Brigadier found himself facing a ticket collector.

'Not another train for a while, sir. Sorry. I'm just about to lock up while I nip out and get a bite of lunch. Do you want to stay, or come back later? It's due in about twenty minutes, if you're wanting Hastings. Over an hour before Dungeness and Dover.'

'Oh. No, I'll go.'

'Right you are, sir. See you later.'

The Brigadier followed the ticket collector off the platform and back onto the short path leading up to the coastal road.

'Mr Lethbridge-Stewart?'

He looked up. There was Yates in his car with the two corporals. He walked over to them and Yates relayed Benton's message.

The Brigadier snatched at the radio transmitter and paged Benton back at UNIT HQ.

'Afternoon, sir. You got my message? Over.'

'Certainly did, Benton. What the hell is Sudbury up to? We need the Glasshouse. Over.'

'No idea, sir,' came the reply. 'But I think he wanted us there quickly. To be frank, sir, I think he was worried that Sir Marmaduke HamngtonSmythe would go back there and, well, scuttle the ship as it were. Over.'

The Brigadier thought about that. Harrington-Smythe was a spectre from his past who somehow always reared his ugly head at inopportune moments. He'd been there at Sandhurst, always trying to get him and the other sappers into disciplinary cases; he had been there after that business with International Electromatics, offering to buy the company up, and when that failed (the Government bought it out itself), he set up the Glasshouse. It was generally believed in the better circles that both his knighthood and CBE were pacifiers to keep him quiet and sweet. He had a knack for finding out the truth about less-than-public-interest events – that was how he'd known that an institution like the Glasshouse would be useful.

If Sir John Sudbury had upset him too much, he was malicious enough to make trouble. 'Do as Sudbury asks, Benton. Take a small squad of men you trust implicitly. I don't want a word of this getting out. Remember not even everyone at UNIT knows of the Glasshouse's existence. Over.'

'Understood, sir. Over and out.'

The Brigadier passed the transmitter back to Yates. 'Where's Corporal Bell?'

'Still at the police station, sir,' replied Osgood.

The Brigadier looked back towards the town. 'Not much to learn, is there?'

'No, sir,' said Yates. 'I suggest that a couple of us stay here for the night. See if anything unusual turns up.'

'Good idea, Sergeant. You keep a couple of your men here. I'll go back to HQ with the corporals. Osgood, can you drive the other car?'

'Yes, sir.'

The Brigadier swapped places with Yates to leave the sergeant standing outside the car, next to Osgood. 'We'll pick Bell up at the station. Got your radio, Yates?'

The sergeant produced a small walkie-talkie from under his jacket. 'And I'm armed, sir.'

The Brigadier told Yates that he was to observe, not take any risks. When the sergeant agreed, the Brigadier started the motor and began the long drive back to London.

He watched Yates and Osgood's figures fade into the distance as he and Corporal Hawke sped out of Smallmarshes on the road to Dover.

'Do you mind the long way round, Corporal?'

'No, sir. I like the Kent countryside.'

'Good girl.' He watched the road for a few moments before clearing his throat. 'Good man, Mike Yates, don't you think?'

Hawke smiled. 'He's a good officer, sir.'

'Oh come on, Maisie. I'm not asking about just his military skills. He's intuitive. He's got exceptional leadership qualities, don't you think?'

'I think, with respect sir, that those are military skills.' She opened the glove compartment, producing another bar of chocolate. 'A bite, sir?'

'No thanks. My wife is on at me not to put on weight.' He paused. 'On the other hand, some chocolate would be very nice right now. Thank you.'

He could see Hawke relax a little more. Good, that was what he wanted. He tried a different tack.

'We've served together quite a while now, Corporal, haven't we?'

'Three years, sir. I've enjoyed it. For the most part.' Hawke nibbled on some chocolate and broke a piece off for the Brigadier, passing it as she spoke. They were about twelve miles from Dungeness, and another ten from the road that led towards London. 'Corporal. Maisie. I'm thinking it is time for some promotions within UNIT. Possibly a captain.'

Hawke let her head fall back against the head rest. 'I appreciate what you're saying, sir. Really I do. But I think you're right, you do need a captain. The troops could do with some stability as well. A handful of sergeants and corporals are all very well, but the command structure needs to be strengthened.'

'Yates? Benton? Someone from outside?'

'Mike Yates would make a fine captain, sir. As I said, I appreciate your waiting this long, but Sam is dead and life has to go on, for everyone.'

The Brigadier felt himself flush slightly. She had caught on. In fact, she'd probably caught on ages ago that he was putting off making any promotions to avoid upsetting her. 'That means there'll be a sergeant's job up for grabs. It's yours if you want it.'

She turned sharply and smiled. 'A nice idea, sir, but I'm not one of the troops. If someone like myself or Carol Bell went for a sergeant's job, we'd have to move away from UNIT. I know I speak for her by saying that neither of us want that.'

The Brigadier nodded. 'I could try for a special dispensation. You'd be one of the few female sergeants in the British Army.'

They were passing through Dungeness now, and they could just make out the distant bulk of the nuclear power station, dwarfing a nearby cluster of terraced houses.

'No thanks, sir. I like what I do. Tom Osgood would make a good sergeant. He's a technical wizard and although he can be a bit eccentric at times, the lads like him a lot. He'd be popular.'

The Brigadier steered the car into the turning for London. 'Thank you, Corporal, for your appraisal. As usual, I expect I will act upon it.'

After five minutes he switched on the radio, and Radio Four filled the silence that had blanketed the car's interior.

'I feel sea-sick. Just thought you ought to know.' Liz Shaw tried smiling at her companion as their motor boat was tossed like a salad by the twenty-foot-high waves. At least, that was what it felt like. In fact, the sea wasn't that choppy, but the constant motion and the drone of the engine had made Liz feel very unwell indeed.

'Nearly there, Doctor Shaw. And I thought you looked sturdier than this.' At the back of the boat, steering it, Jana Kristan looked for all the world like a misplaced figurehead, her jaw set firmly against the buffeting wind and spray, her brown overcoat billowing behind her. All Liz wanted to do was hide under the tarpaulin she had found tucked under seat, and emerge when they reached the island.

Sturdier? She had never felt worse. She just hoped she would not have to use her favourite hat as a sick bag.

They had flown from Southampton to St Helier on Jersey, taken the ferry to Guernsey, and then hired the outboard to take them across to their mysterious island which, the man at the boat-hire company told them, was called L'Ithe. It was not until they were on the boat that Jana confessed she had accidentally left all the notes given to them by their mysterious correspondent back at Liz's flat. However, she had remembered enough for them to work out which island was their destination.

'It's a very small lump of rock,' Jana yelled over the noise. 'Only a couple of miles across. It shouldn't take long to find whatever it is that he sent us after.'

Liz just nodded, trying to keep the aeroplane snack down, and praying that they would get there soon.

'Where exactly are you taking me?' asked Sir Marmaduke Harrington-Smythe. 'Not back to the Glasshouse, I imagine.'

'Oh, certainly not,' said the pale young man. 'By now, UNIT will be crawling all over it, and searching for various things they won't find.' He pointed at the trees at the side of the road. 'This is a very nice part of the country. I used to enjoy walking though the trees and fields when I was younger. Especially when it was dark.'

Sir Marmaduke wondered if they were going slowly enough for him to jump out. He looked forwards, and saw Cellian's eyes reflected in the rear-view mirror. Piercing blue, they stared straight back. As if he was reading Sir Marmaduke's mind, the car sped up a bit.

Damn.

'How long have my trusted aides here been working for you?' Sir Marmaduke asked.

The young man opened up a small wooden box built into the floor of the Mercedes. He took out a small bottle of Gordon's gin and another tonic.

'Ice?'

Sir Marmaduke bristled. 'I don't want a drink. I would like an answer to my question.'

The pale young man shrugged and flicked his finger at the top of the bottle. The vacuum-sealed metal cap flipped off and up, embedding itself in the roof. Sir Marmaduke stared as the pale young man extracted a glass from the same box and mixed himself a drink. He then looked Sir Marmaduke straight in the eye, swallowed the drink in one gulp and replaced the grass. He picked up the empty gin bottle and held it upright between the palms of his hands.

'This, Sir Marmaduke, is your career.'

Sir Marmaduke watched open-mouthed as he slammed his palms together. Instead of shattering and cutting both of them to ribbons, the bottle seemed to vanish. The pale young man opened his palms, revealing thousands of fragments of powdered glass.

'How—?'

His kidnapper shrugged. 'Just a knack. No, that's a lie, I'm stronger than the average human. My reflexes are faster than the average human's. My life expectancy, barring accidents, is longer than the average human's. Oh, and–' he removed his glasses again, revealing his mechanical eyes – 'my eyesight is better than the average human's. It extends beyoned the normal spectrum into the infrared. I can see colours that the average human doesn't even dream exist.'

'Are you human?'

'Oh yes. But I'm also much better than human now. Augmented by a technology the rest of you can't begin to imagine. And before you ask, yes, alien technology.'

Sir Marmaduke again asked how long Ciara and Cellian had been working against him.

'Since before you employed them. I… well, created them I suppose, about seven or eight months ago. Using technology that you had a hand in.'

'Me?'

The pale young man smiled. 'You'll find out very soon. Now, tell me everything you know about the United Nations Intelligence Taskforce that I don't already know from working at C19.'

The car drove on as the sky began to darken with the fall of night.

Sergeant Benton stood in the doorway. Three UNIT soldiers were hovering by the reception desk, including Corporal Tracy and Private Boyle. Benton looked at the body of the receptionist, but Boyle shook his head.

'Is there anyone left alive?' Benton asked.

'Not on this floor,' said Tracy. 'All the patients and nursing staff were in the wards, on the top four floors.

They weren't even aware of any of this until an hour ago.' The corporal pointed to the receptionist's telephone. 'One of the staff nurses heard it buzzing and came down to see why it hadn't been answered. There –' he pointed at the body – 'was the reason.'

Benton stared at the carnage, holstering his gun. 'Yes. But why, Tracy? What was there here that she had to die for?'

Corporal Champion approached from the corridor opposite. 'I think you'd best see this, sir.'

Benton and Tracy followed Champion down the corridor, briefly staring at a dead male nurse, his blood drying on a sheaf of scattered papers. They passed two more bodies at the junction of the corridor before Champion pointed at an unremarkable door.

'A cupboard, corporal?'

'Not exactly, sir.' He pushed at the door and, with a hum, it slid upwards.

Both Sergeant Benton and Corporal Tracy allowed their surprise to show. 'Well, I've been here a few times with the Brig,' said Benton, 'but I've never seen this part before. Either of you?'

'Absolutely not, sir.' Corporal Champion led them further on. They were now in another corridor, which seemed to be sloping downwards. At the bottom was a series of connecting routes.

'It's like a maze, sir,' said Tracy. 'Shipman and Farley went exploring a few moments ago. They should be back soon.'

No sooner had Champion spoken than Farley's voice called out from the left-hand corridor. Sergeant Benton led the way towards him, noting the various doors and sub-corridors leading off the corridor. 'This must extend for nearly a mile. Impressive.'

They met Farley outside an oak-panelled door. Sprawled in front of it were another two bodies.

'In there, sir. It's not pretty.'

Farley opened the door and Benton found himself looking into a large laboratory, lights in the ceiling illuminating various areas, like spotlights in a circus.

He saw the man on the far side of the room first, but the bullets which had blown away most of his head had rendered him unrecognisable.

'Shame that,' said Benton. 'He's not nursing staff, so we can't ID him.'

Corporal Champion stared at him. 'We can't identify any of these poor blighters, then. None of the people in here were nurses.'

'No, Corporal, we can't. The Glasshouse is top secret. Frankly, only the Brigadier and his main staff, and Doctor Sweetman of course, officially know about it.'

Farley coughed. 'Actually, sir, just about everyone at UNIT does. It's always been…'

'A bit of a joke to be sent here. Yes, Private, I know. I was a private too, once.' Benton pointed to the opposite wall. 'And there's another.'

Champion stood upright with a start. 'Sergeant Benton, what was that man doing over there?'

Benton strode over to examine the unrecognisable corpse by the far wall. 'Nothing… Wait a mo! Oh, this seems a bit stupid, but there's a pen and someone's—'

'Drawn pictures on the wall, Sergeant? Mammoths, tigers, that sort of thing?' Champion hurried over.

Benton nodded. 'That's about the size of it, Corporal. Why?'

'Just remembering something, sir. From those caves

in Derbyshire, when me and some of the lads went up there with Captain Hawkins. Steve Robins was drawing pictures like that when those Reptile things trapped us there. Silurians, I think the Brigadier called them. And Sergeant Yates mentioned them when he rounded C Patrol up this morning to go down south. Come to think of it, Steve ended up in here for about six weeks before going back to the regular army.'

'All right.' Benton thought for a moment. 'And apart from the Doc, they're looking for some missing policewoman who drew similar pictures.'

Tracy vocalised what they were all thinking. 'So that policewoman must have ended up here, then.'

Suddenly, Boyle bustled in with Private Shipman. 'We found a large office, sir,' Boyle said. 'Look at these.'

Shipman handed over a sheaf of photographs that seemed to have been pinned up, judging by the tiny holes in the top of them.

'Let me see those.' Benton swiped them from the private's outstretched hands. 'Yes, look at this. Whoever came here probably didn't murder all these people out of hand, then – they had a far greater purpose.' He passed the two corporals one of the photographs. 'Either of you recognise her?'

'That's the policewoman the Brig's been hunting for.'

'Yes, Champion. And that's why he couldn't find her down in Kent. She was here and, as we haven't found her body, she's probably been taken away, possibly by someone who wants her alive and ready to talk about your Derbyshire Reptiles.' Benton looked around the huge room, trying not to focus on the two bodies and the drawings. 'I reckon this is a medical or biological lab of some sort.'

'Looks like it, sir.' Tracy was hurriedly examining the papers and equipment scattered across the benches. 'I'm no Sherlock, Sarge, but I don't think these were the only two working here.'

'Why?'

'Well, I'm trying to picture the Doctor's laboratory at UNIT. I mean, he has loads of things on the go at once, right?'

'Usually,' Benton agreed.

'So he's a bit cleverer than your ordinary bloke. But there are four or five different bits of equipment set up here, like the Doctor has, but spread about more. Like individual work stations.'

They were interrupted by a shout from Shipman, who had returned to the small office. Leaving Tracy to examine the worktops, Benton and the others went to investigate.

'Hey Sarge, what's that policewoman's name?' Shipman was leafing through a box file.

Benton paused. 'Red-something, I think.'

'Not Wildeman, then?'

'No. Why?'

Shipman held up a piece of paper. It looked like a personnel file, with a photo clipped to the top. 'Cathryn Wildeman, sir. Worked here, presumably. She seemed to be some sort of animal boffin. Zoology, and genetics. Seems she came from Cambridge. And she's not dead out there, is she?' He waved the paper in the direction of the main laboratory.

Benton looked over Shipman's shoulder. 'That's one of the men out there, though. James Griffin. Perhaps the other one is this bloke, Atkinson.'

Shipman dug to the bottom of the file. 'Or, sir, he could be this bloke. I saw this report first. Peter Morley. He seems to have been in charge, and it's him that the other three had to report to, according to their files.'

Benton paused for thought and then stuffed all the papers back into the box. 'We'll take this lot back to HQ for the Brigadier.' He turned to the others. 'Right, I want all the other staff questioned and everything on this level sectioned and, if it can be carried, taken back to HQ as well.' As the other soldiers began following his orders, Benton followed them out of the office, and stared ahead. Boyle was covering the unrecognisable body with black plastic sheeting. Above it, he could make out the pictures on the wall. 'Blimey, where's the Doctor when you really need him?'

The Doctor was surrounded by Reptile People, all staring at him. They had stripped him of his cloak and smoking jacket in case they concealed any weapons. A shaft of light and power that beamed down from the ceiling held him helplessly in place.

He was in a massive chamber, even larger than the one Chukk had shown him earlier. This one was filled with stone benches, arranged in a semi-circle. Some kind of debating chamber, he guessed. Behind the benches, directly facing him, a huge screen had been carved into the rock. To either side of it were two entrance tunnels. The Doctor guessed that when decisions were made the Ayes went one way and the Nays went the other.

His nose itched, but he could not move. He wanted to speak, to say something, but that was impossible. All he could do was stare straight ahead. Straight into the jubilant eyes of Auggi.

Twenty minutes earlier, she had come to the lab and demanded of her son that he release the Doctor into her care. This he had agreed to do on the understanding that the Doctor wasn't harmed and would be returned later. Auggi had said that would not be a problem and Krugga had carried him away.

Now he was standing in what he took to be some sort of council chamber. Chukk was there, and one of Baal's sisters, Tahni probably. She seemed to be more politically inclined than Sula, who appeared content in her role as her brother's assistant.

'The Ape is an abomination generally, but this one is particularly vile,' Auggi was saying. 'It was involved in the destruction of Okdel L'Da's Shelter.'

'Entombment,' Chukk said.

'I'm sorry?' said another Reptile Person. 'Explain?'

'The Doctor is adamant that a majority of Shelter 873's population are still hibernating, alive but entombed. The Apes sealed them inside their Shelter rather than kill them. This Ape that Auggi is so keen to blame for everything is actually responsible for keeping our people alive rather than letting the other Apes destroy them.'

Thank you, Chukk, thought the Doctor, but I doubt that will help.

'So, even if this Ape is in some way benign,' another said, 'the majority are still murderers. Typical Ape behaviour.'

Auggi nodded. 'Indeed. And anyway, this Ape is what passes for a scientist among the Apes. He probably wanted our people to experiment on.'

Chukk sighed. 'Auggi, you know that is not true.'

Auggi turned to him. 'I do not know whether it is true or not. Neither do you. This Ape has fooled you and you are blinded by its apparent sincerity.' She walked to him and took his hands in hers. 'Dear Chukk, understand this. You are a good person, with a deep belief in right and wrong. You became our leader after Daurrix died and have seen us through the last few years with great wisdom and sense. But I believe these Apes present a terrible threat to us all. To our hatchlings. We need an Ape-free world for them to grow up in.'

'Why?' The Doctor forced his jaw to open, his vocal chords to vibrate. The word emerged as a hoarse whisper, but it was enough to make everyone stop and stare at him.

'Turn the beam up!' yelled Auggi.

As Krugga moved to obey, Chukk shouted: 'No! No, I believe we should hear this Ape. If we consider ourselves the leaders, the decision-makers of this Shelter, then we need all available information, no matter how unpalatable.' He walked to stand beside the Doctor, and held his arms outstretched. 'We need to know everything we can.'

Slowly, one by one, the Reptiles sat on their benches. The Doctor hoped this was an indication of agreement, and realised it must be as only Auggi and Krugga were left standing. Then Krugga sat, despite a sharp look from Auggi. She remained standing even after Chukk switched off the beam.

'Thank thank you.' The Doctor massaged his throat. 'Thank you for giving me the honour to address you all today. Everything you have heard about me in this chamber today is true. I was present at Shelter 8…?'

'873,' prompted Chukk.

'Yes, Okdel's Shelter. Many of his people died because they attacked mankind. The Apes, as you call them. Mankind was stronger because they were afraid. And fear is a huge asset in a war, because it makes people fight harder. Dirtier. Believe me, mankind has weapons far dirtier than you. Mankind has split the atom, created nuclear weaponry capable of destroying millions of you in a second.'

One of the elder Reptiles stood. 'We discovered the power of nuclear fission and saw its potential for destruction, but we chose not to develop it further. Why have the Apes done something so foolish?'

Other Reptiles nodded at this question, daring the Doctor to answer.

'Yes, well, you're right. Mankind is foolish. It could wipe itself out in half a day if it so chose.'

'Good,' Auggi said. 'We could live with high radiation levels. Perhaps we should rediscover nuclear power.'

A shocked exclamation rippled through the chamber.

'I am, of course, joking,' she said quickly. The Doctor eyed her carefully. She was clearly a consummate politician, capable of judging opinion and changing tack instantly. Very shrewd. Very dangerous, too.

'But know this as well, noble Reptiles,' said the Doctor. 'Mankind has a thousand other skills as well as making war. For every weapon of destruction, it has ten cures for diseases, sicknesses and accidents. For every war that breaks out, another two or three groups demanding peace spring up. Mankind is resilient.'

Another Reptile stood. 'Could the Apes cure the genetic disorder in our hatchlings?' A murmur went through the crowd. The Doctor guessed that many of them had wondered this, but in the face of Auggi's determined verbal assault on mankind, were unwilling to risk her wrath. Now that he had been freed to speak, Auggi's control had slipped a little.

'Possibly. Mankind faces similar problems and finds ways to overcome them.' He wondered if he should disclose Baal's secret experiments. Angry as he was about

Baal's torture of Marc Marshall, he knew it was a weapon to be used against Auggi only at the right time. This was probably not it. Instead, he glanced in Tahni's direction.

'Possibly. It is an avenue that ought to be explored and—'

A Reptile came crashing into the chamber, almost knocking a couple of the older members to the floor.

'Chukk! Auggi! There are two Apes upon the surface of the island.'

No! This was precisely what he did not need.

Unsurprisingly, Auggi leapt at the opportunity to discredit him. 'See! See how the Ape lies. He knew we were to be attacked.'

The Doctor decided that he would achieve little by pointing out that two people, probably local fishermen, hardly amounted to an invasion force.

Krugga used his third eye to activate the huge screen at one end of the cavern. On it, two figures could be seen tying a boat to a rock. Or rather, one was tying it up, the other was sitting on another rock, face in hands.

There was something familiar about that posture, the Doctor thought.

'Zoom in on them,' Auggi said to the screen.

Agitated voices travelled around the chamber like fire through dry bush. 'Are they hostile?' 'Should we destroy them?' As the picture closed in on the two humans, the Doctor saw Auggi staring at him. He was becoming very good at reading Reptile facial expressions but even a rank amateur could have seen what she was thinking. She had won her people over. The Apes were invading.

Chukk tried to reason with the crowd but no one was listening.

'Fellow Reptile People.' Auggi spoke quietly but

forcibly enough to silence everyone. 'We are under attack. Bring those two in for questioning.' She addressed the last remark to Krugga and he walked off down the right-hand tunnel. Auggi then pointed at the Doctor. 'This Ape has tried to fool you. He has lied and betrayed you all. Chukk, tell me you don't still believe him. He has distracted us all in the hope that we would remain unaware of these others.'

'I'm not sure, Auggi.'

The Doctor stared at Chukk. If he was faltering, then the Doctor had lost his only ally here.

Then a human face filled the screen. It was the face of the person whose posture the Doctor had thought familiar a moment earlier.

'Oh no,' he said quietly. 'Liz!'

Auggi switched off the screen.

'Damn cold, isn't it, Liz?'

Jana had finished tying up the boat and was rubbing her hands together.

Liz nodded. 'Yes, but we're here to find out what was important enough for our mysterious friend to die for. Let's take a look around.' She stuffed her hands into her green duffle-coat pocket. 'Experience tells me that the longer you stay near the unknown, the more dangerous it gets.'

Jana laughed. 'I'll tell you one thing. I'm dying for the toilet. I bet there isn't a handy ladies here anywhere.'

Liz laughed. 'I think it'll have to be those bushes.'

'I'll be quick,' said Jana and scurried off.

Liz pulled her hat further down onto her head to try and keep the wind from whipping her long hair into her eyes. Thankfully she'd exchanged her usual miniskirt for a pair of slacks, and had worn them over tall boots. As a result, her legs were probably the warmest part of her.

What was taking Jana so long? Where exactly had she run off to anyway and –

Liz stopped worrying about Jana in an instant. Emerging from a hole by some rocks was a Silurian, a massive one. For a second she thought she had not been seen, but then the Silurian turned to her. And stared.

Must get to the top of the tree. Have to hurry. The Devilbacks cannot reach us up here, they do not have the head for heights. The only way they can reach us is to use a Long Neck, but they rarely use them. Too stupid to be trainable, even when the Devilbacks use their third eye to hurt them. They don't even know they're being hurt!

The Devilback is coming, but it has not seen us. Wait. No! No, it saw someone's foot and is pointing us out to another Devilback. The eyes! Not the eyes. No!

Liz shook her bead. No, she was stronger than that. She had faced them before and would not let the race-memories overwhelm her. What would the Doctor do in this situation?

She knew the answer. Pushing down her feelings of fear, of nausea, she stood up and held her hands outstretched, palms up.

'I know you can understand me. I am not armed and I come in peace.' The Silurian turned its head slightly, as if considering her words.

'There were two Apes,' he said slowly.

Liz shivered at his voice. She had forgotten how cold, how completely alien they sounded.

'My friend will be back any second now,' said Liz. 'She too comes in peace.'

'Like hell I do!' shouted Jana from a rocky plateau

slightly above and behind the Silurian.

'No!' screamed Liz, but it was too late Jana was firing her pistol. One, two, three shots slammed into the Silurian's body. It staggered slightly and then swung round, its third eye glowing. Jana dived at it, catching it behind the knees.

The Silurian was on the floor in a second, bleeding from two injuries to its shoulder and a third in the back of the neck.

Liz glared up at Jana. 'What did you do that for?'

The answer she got was an action, not a word. Jana aimed the pistol straight at her.

'It's a Silurian, right?'

'Yes, but how—?'

'That hole, there. Did it come from that?'

Liz nodded. 'I still don't understand.'

'No, you don't. Just as well.' Jana jumped down beside the fallen Reptile, still keeping her gun trained on Liz. 'I only needed you for your knowledge of these things. Now, down the hole.'

Liz took a deep breath, and did as she was told.

Moments later, they were climbing down a ladder carved from the rocks, into a dark and damp tunnel.

'Where now?' Liz stopped, folding her arms. 'I mean, I presume you have a plan of some sort. You obviously knew what to expect.'

Jana, still training her pistol on Liz, stared around the phosphorus-lit tunnel. 'Nope, not really. I just followed my orders.'

'Our anonymous informant's?'

Jana smiled. 'Don't be pathetic, Doctor Shaw. I work for your people. C19.'

'You're with Sir John Sudbury?'

'Wrong again.' Jana pushed Liz along to the left. 'Our

mysterious benefactor thought he was safe from us, but we knew he wanted someone to expose what we do. We got rid of Traynor and I was sent down to pose as some stupid Dutch journalist he had written to. I followed his instructions, wound up in Smallmarshes and lo and behold, one Silurian gets the policewoman and the child. I make contact with you and go through the motions of being Jana bloody Kristan for a little longer.'

'You killed her, I suppose.'

'No, but someone did. Think yourself lucky I wasn't asked to impersonate you.'

'Probably because I'd be harder to kill at UNIT.'

Jana just laughed again, and pushed Liz into another corridor. 'I could walk into UNIT any time I wanted to with my credentials. No, impersonating you would have been difficult simply because we knew UNIT would become involved.'

'Stop, Apes!' A Reptile Person stood directly in front of them. 'I am Chukk, leader of the Shelter and I will—'

Jana shot him straight through the head, jumping over his body before it had stopped twitching.

In front of her, Liz saw a massive chamber, occupied by about thirty Reptile People. Standing in front of them was the Doctor. She shoved Jana out of the way and dashed through the startled Reptiles towards him.

'No you don't, bitch!' Jana aimed her pistol and pressed the trigger. As she did so, the third eye of every Reptile Person in the room glowed red.

Jana, or whoever she really was, was slammed back against the chamber wall, her mouth opening and closing in soundless agony. After a few seconds, she fell lifeless to the ground, her pistol skittering across the floor to stop at Auggi's feet.

The female picked up the gun. 'So Apes will help us, will they, Chukk?'

All the other Reptile People turned to look at the Doctor, waiting for Auggi to decide what to do with him and the other Ape.

And they saw the Doctor sitting on the floor, cradling the unmoving body of the other Ape in his arms, blood soaking into his shirt from the bullet that had gone straight through her back and out through her right shoulder.

A tear ran down his cheek. 'Oh Liz, no. I'm so sorry.' He stroked her hair. 'So very sorry.'

EPISODE
SIX

The Mercedes was waved to a stop at the tunnel's entrance by an armed guard standing in front of a red-and-white barrier. The guard wore a one-piece black boiler suit and a black belt decorated with various pouches and a pair of handcuffs. Hanging from it was a long black truncheon. He wore a matt-black helmet, attached to which was a clear plastic visor that covered his whole face.

The guard's machine pistol was held casually in his left hand, but it was undoubtedly primed and ready.

In the last few miles, they had passed so many 'Keep Out' signs that Sir Marmaduke had lost count. 'Since when have we had armed guards at tunnels in this country?' he asked. 'I thought I was in East Germany for a moment.'

Ciara did not turn to him as she explained that it was a safety precaution to protect the unwary as much as those working under the hills.

'You mean the place we're going is built inside these hills? But how?'

The pale young man showed a pass to the guard, who spoke into a walkie-talkie and then lifted the barrier. Cellian drove through. As the Mercedes entered the gloom, a series of red lights flicked on, dotting the roof in two parallel lines rather like, Sir Marmaduke thought, an airport runway upside down.

They carried on in silence for about half a mile before the two red lines became four as the tunnel forked. They took the right-hand turning and Sir Marmaduke swivelled round to watch all the lights behind click off, plunging their entry route into darkness. The glow from the lights through the windows cast unearthly shadows across his captors and for the first time Sir Marmaduke felt decidedly nervous.

'What exactly is this place?'

The pale young man smiled and settled back in the seat.

'OK, Sir Marmaduke, brief history lesson coming up. Why was UNIT set up?'

'I don't know. I wasn't aware of it until a few years back, after that business with the electronics firm with the dodgy components in their wirelesses.'

'Radios, Sir Marmaduke. Do try and keep up with the times. But that's by the by. What do you believe UNIT does?'

Sir Marmaduke focused on the red lights, trying to avoid seeing his captors' faces. 'I suppose it deals with things out of the regular military forces' purview. Alien invasions, extra-terrestrial infections, the paranormal, people with extra-sensory powers. That sort of thing. I only know that really because of the people we treat at the Glasshouse. It's just a job for me, a service I provide. I don't investigate that much.'

The pale young man chuckled. 'Oh rubbish, Sir Marmaduke. Why did you abduct the policewoman from Hastings? To continue your feud with Lethbridge-Stewart, perhaps? Or because you knew that she was connected with the Reptile People whose previous victims you had cared for?'

'What would I want with Reptile People?'

'A good question. We wondered that for a long time. Even Ciara and Cellian here couldn't find that out. None of my agents at the Glasshouse could work it out. Shall I tell you what I believe?'

Sir Marmaduke snorted. 'I'm sure you will anyway.'

'True. I think you believed that she would lead you to these Reptile People – UNIT's Silurians, or whatever they're known as colloquially. I think you believed that if you had one at the Glasshouse, you could begin to set up some kind of indispensable repository of… let's lump it together as alien paraphernalia. You'd go in after a UNIT operation and clean up. Gather the spare parts, dead aliens or whatever and sell them to the highest bidder. I believe you already have contacts, especially where UNIT, as a United Nations sub-division, has no jurisdiction. Behind the Iron Curtain, perhaps? Or the Middle East? Somewhere where the leaders would hope to upset the balance of power.'

Sir Marmaduke did not reply. Cellian had driven the car into a small side tunnel which flared with a bright light, revealing them to be in something no larger than a domestic garage. He turned as a mesh shutter dropped down soundlessly behind them. Then he realised that they were going up, on some massive hydraulic ramp. Eventually they stopped, the shutter lifted, and Cellian drove the car into a huge hangar-sized carport and stopped. About thirty other vehicles littered it, some recognisable as cars and vans, others looking decidedly unusual. Sir Marmaduke saw one craft which he recognised as Mars Probe Six.

'That?' said the pale young man, as if reading his prisoner's thought. 'We got that shortly after the British Space programme was abandoned. With James Quinlan's death and Professor Cornish's retirement, the Government put the whole thing into limbo. They're looking at moving part of it down to Devesham in Oxfordshire, out of the prying eyes of the public, but until then, we have their cast-offs.' He unwound his window and as he did so a black-clad armed guard rushed over.

'I understand that everything is prepared, sir. The woman is in the laboratory with the two science people.' The guard looked across at Sir Marmaduke, then back at the pale young man. 'We have also had a report from our agent on the HR Project.'

'Go on.'

'She reports that the targets are on a Channel Island known as L'Ithe. Mister Bailey decided that it would be inadvisable to send a force in because it would be difficult to avoid alerting people on the other islands. Traffic to and from L'Ithe is infrequent enough to draw attention.'

'Fair enough. What is his proposal?'

'He has sent some men down to Smallmarshes to wait in case the creatures return to the mainland, that way. He thought it safe to assume they would stick to familiar routes.'

'Probably right. OK, I'll review the situation later. Let me know if our agent contacts us again.'

'Yes, sir. Need anything else, sir?'

'No thank you, Mister Lawson.' Then he gently tapped his forehead, as if remembering something. 'Oh, Mister Lawson?'

'Sir?'

'Has anyone exercised the Stalker recently?'

'Not recently, sir, no.'

'Tell Bailey it will be going for a run sometime later today. I don't want it getting idle.'

'No, sir. Very good, sir.' Lawson nodded at the Irish Twins and walked towards one of the doors that dotted the huge car park.

'Now, Sir Marmaduke, where were we? Oh yes, I remember. You were veering close to queering my pitch.' The pale young man opened his door. In unison, Ciara and Cellian undid their seat belts, wound up their windows and got out of the car. Ciara then opened Sir Marmaduke's door for him, much as she always had.

'Ciara, why?' he asked quietly, but she ignored him.

Her real employer moved around to the front of the car. 'I think it might be best to incapacitate this vehicle. We wouldn't want Sir Marmaduke to attempt an escape.' He held his hand out and Cellian dropped the car keys into his palm.

With a smile, the pale young man closed his fist and dropped what was now a tight ball of metal onto the floor. 'And just to make quite sure…' Effortlessly, he thrust his arm through the bonnet, into the engine and started hitting things. After a few seconds, he extracted his arm, brushing off some minute fragments of metal. 'I don't think that's going anywhere.'

He looked at Sir Marmaduke again. 'Now, where was I? Oh yes, you asked what this place is.' He waved his arm around the area like an estate agent showing prospective clients around a house. 'This is the Vault. A – how can I put this – a side-line of C19. The sort of side-line that, should he be aware of it, would cause the likes of Sir John Sudbury to have a coronary. You see, I already do what you were hoping to.' He led them through one of the doorways and Sir Marmaduke found himself on a metal catwalk, high above another stadium-sized room built into the inside of the hill.

'The Vault takes up eight levels per hill. Two hills. Sixteen areas of research, storage and development, plus a few outlying areas where some of our more interesting experiments live. Look down there.' He pointed below, where white-coated men scurried about with clipboards. They were moving between various large computers with spinning tapes and other oddly shaped devices, while the double doors were guarded by more gun-wielding, black-clad men. 'Not everything here is extra-terrestrial in origin, Sir Marmaduke. Those men are building new computers, using man-made technology from a super-computer built during the sixties.'

'WOTAN? My God, I thought it was destroyed.'

'Oh, rest assured it was. But here at the Vault, we're very interested in any kind of artificial intelligence, especially an accidental one like that. Imagine the possibilities of an AI that could run businesses, administer hospitals and schools. And, of course, the Government. No need to feed it, water it, give it sleep. That's something we're working towards.'

The pale young man walked on, Sir Marmaduke trailing him, with the Irish Twins bringing up the rear. They went through a doorway which led to an airlock. Before the next door was opened, Ciara shut the four of them inside the cramped area and a fine mist sprayed all over them.

'Decontaminant. All perfectly harmless. But necessary between each section.' They entered the next area, which was a little smaller and was bathed in a blue light. Sir Marmaduke's captor continued his recital:

'Basically we go in after UNIT has done its job. We collect the dead, the detonated, the inanimate and the unusual. We strip away the ruined computers, the deactivated weaponry. Ostensibly it is all destroyed. Incinerated, under the Brigadier's strict orders. But what no one at UNIT, or the main part of C19, knows is that it all comes here. We sift through it, cannibalise anything interesting and store the rest. Nothing is disposed of.

'This area is devoted to flora. Every day millions of particles of dust enter our biosphere from outer space. Most of them are so microscopic that they are untraceable and irrelevant. But some attach themselves to plants on the planet's surface, causing interesting mutations. Did you know, Sir Marmaduke, that last winter eighteen people in Western Australia died after eating what appeared to be normal local fruits? They contained, however, appallingly high levels of mercurial duoxide, an element unknown to occur naturally on Earth. Over in that far corner is a new strain of the Venus flytrap. As you can see, it is large enough to catch a rabbit or small dog. It grew in someone's garden in Rhodesia a couple of months back. A unique specimen which, it has to be said, has created quite a stir in botanical circles. Among those who are aware of it, anyway.'

'This is obscene, you know.' Sir Marmaduke ran a finger round his collar. He was very hot.

'Obscene?' His captor pursed his lips in apparent confusion. 'In what way is it more obscene than that which you were planning? Or is it just that we've already done it, and on a scale, with resources, you could only dream about.'

'We were working towards something similar, I grant you, but we were nowhere near this audacious. Or secretive.'

'Pish and tosh, Sir Marmaduke. You had Peter Morley and his team working day and night on experiments that none of them guessed the end result of. Well, almost none.'

Sir Marmaduke stopped. 'How do you know about

Morley? Was he one of your spies?'

'Good gracious no, I wouldn't have employed anyone who was that big a security risk. The man is a positive liability. No stomach for what he was doing. But a genius, I have to say. Quite useful to me now.'

'So he is here, then?'

'Yes. Under protest. Come through to the next area and he'll tell you all about it. I think it might interest you.'

The pale young man pressed a button when they reached the far wall. The door slid up to reveal an elevator. 'Going down for ladies shoes and handbags,' he quipped, but the smile on his face couldn't extend to his artificial eyes. Sir Marmaduke shivered, wondering what awaited him at the bottom.

Liz Shaw was sitting on a swing in the back garden. Her parents' large back garden at their house in Burton Joyce.

The grass was a lovely rich green, the sky a cloudless blue, and a bright yellow sun bathed her in a warm glow. All the colours were very vivid, the heat too perfect. Something was not quite right.

And anyway, she was far too old to play on a swing.

She got off the swing and looked around. Definitely home, but everything looked too perfect, too neat and tidy.

But she did feel very safe. Very relaxed.

'That's because you remember it that way,' said a voice behind her. With a start, she turned, and saw a tall man in her place on the swing.

He had light brown hair shot through with strands of pure white. There was something she recognized about his pleasantly lined face and rather beaky nose, but his blue eyes were his most notable feature: the way they bored into her, as if seeing through her into, well, her soul.

He was wearing a silly black cloak, and a red velvet smoking jacket. That all seemed very familiar, Liz decided, but she could not quite work out why.

'Do I know you?'

'Oh yes,' replied the man. 'You know me as the Doctor. We work together. We are friends.'

'Oh. Right. So how come I don't recognise you properly, then?'

'Ah, that's a bit difficult to explain. I've put you in a trance.'

Liz raised her eyebrows, pursing her lips in mock concern. 'Well, that's a friendly way to act, I must say.'

'If it helps, I don't like the fact that I've done it.'

'Can't say I do much, but presumably I had no option.' Liz realised the house and garden were gone. They were standing in a huge room, with blank walls and a large door at one end. Liz decided it looked like a school science lab. There were Bunsen burners on the many benches and intricately built objects of tubes and focusing microscopes, thrown together like Salvador Dali's interpretation of something out of *Goodbye Mister Chips*.

'I recognise this. Why?'

'It's where we first met at UNIT's temporary headquarters in central London. Before we all moved to Priory Mews in Denham. I spoke to you in Delphon. Remember?' The Doctor was sitting cross-legged, floating about two feet off the floor, framed and silhouetted by the massive rectangular window behind him. Liz decided that the bright light from whatever was outside made the Doctor's indistinct form look angelic – there was a kind of golden aura around him.

'Ah. It's all coming back now. OK, so why the trance?'

The Doctor smiled. 'It's an old Tibetan trick. It slows your metabolic rate right down to the bare minimum. You're still breathing, your heart is still beating, but only just. And this discourse we're having is your brain, needing to keep busy, latching on to the telepathic connection I've tried to establish with you. Simple really.'

'Isn't it just. But why?'

'Ah, that's the tricky bit.' The Doctor floated towards her. 'I hope you can cope with this. No, I'm sure you can.' He smiled. 'You're a very strong young woman.'

Liz rolled her eyes. 'Yes, Doctor, but as scientist to scientist, let's dispense with the archaic flattery and talk sense. Please?'

'All right. Liz, you've been shot.'

'As in by a gun? As in bang?'

'As in bang.'

'So I'm not dead yet?'

The Doctor unfurled himself; planted his feet on the floor and crossed to the lab window. The room was starting to distort slightly. The window the Doctor was near became arched, and behind him a spiral staircase materialised. The whole room contracted, the cold grey walls of the London headquarters giving way to the dull hospital green of Priory Mews. 'Never liked that colour,' Liz muttered.

'When we get back, I'll get Lethbridge-Stewart to repaint it,' said the Doctor.

'Oh, so I am going to get back then?' Liz joined the Doctor at the window. Instead of the familiar Slough Canal, the outside was a massive starfield, planets and stars competing for her attention in the rich, textured dark background. 'My mother once told me that everyone has a star, Doctor. And when that person dies, their star vanishes from the sky.' She turned away, looking back into the laboratory, but sat on the windowsill. 'When my grandmother died, mother took me outside into the back garden. She pointed up at one of the stars, a faint one that was twinkling. "That's Nanna's star," she said. "It's marking her death with respect as we all should. In the morning the star will have gone, having collected Nanna and taken her to Heaven." And no matter how often I looked that next evening, I couldn't see that star any more. I think I still look for it today, if I'm out late. Or working here late. Not consciously, but when I look at the stars I think of Nanna and all the wonderful things she told me.' Liz touched the Doctor's sleeve, pulling him round to face her. 'You'd have liked her. She was your type.'

'Oh, and what type's that, Liz?'

Liz shrugged. 'Oh, I don't know. She knew lots of things and –' Liz smiled at him – 'when she didn't have the answer, she'd make one up that sounded exactly right.'

'Well, we'd have got on like a house on fire.' The Doctor crossed to one of the benches and stared at a piece of equipment. 'Funny thing, the subconscious. Here I am in your mind, your memories, and yet I'm holding my Triacteon Zeiton Regulator and it's fixed. Ever since I was exiled here, the TZR has needed repair, but I've never managed it. Something to do with the block the Time Lords put on me.' He looked up, smiling at her. 'Thank you, Doctor Shaw. When we get back, I now know how to repair it.'

Liz was not really listening. 'Is my star twinkling right now, Doctor?'

'Now, Liz, we are both scientists. We know what makes stars twinkle. We also both know that those sorts of questions cannot be simply answered. When I go back to the real world, it will be up to you to help get yourself through this. I can try and save your physical body, but your spirit needs to be strong too. Your body has gone through a massive trauma as a result of this wound. That shock has caused your subconscious to retreat to a level where we can communicate like this. You need to reintegrate yourself with your conscious mind in order to survive.'

'But do you think I will?'

The Doctor started to fade away. 'I don't know, Liz, but I certainly hope you do. We still need to get to know each other properly.' And he was gone. So was the UNIT laboratory, and Liz was back alone by the garden swing. Black clouds ranged across the sky. It was going to rain.

The Doctor's eyes snapped open, and Sula backed away, alarmed.

'What were you doing?' she asked tentatively.

The Doctor pushed himself up from his cross-legged position and walked across Baal's laboratory to where Liz was lying on a stone slab.

'Communicating. Telepathically.' He touched the slab. 'This is very warm.'

Sula pointed at some controls on the wall above the slab. 'The rock absorbs and distributes the planet's natural warmth. It is the same principle that heats the whole Shelter. Baal reasoned that Apes need a lot of warmth.'

'Then I must thank him. He's right, Liz needs to be kept warm.' He touched the dressing around her shoulder. It was made of the same stringy webbed twine as the clothes he had worn when travelling underwater. 'What a fascinating material.'

'One of our major discoveries.' Baal entered the lab from

the direction of Marc Marshall's cell. 'The Apes have yet to synthesise anything similar. It has staunched her bleeding and should help to heal the wound. It is semi-organic, this version carrying a form of antiseptic through its strands. We can adapt it to carry anything we need: heat, light, even antibiotics.'

The Doctor gently touched the material. It pulsated slightly. 'It's alive?'

Baal smiled. 'Sort of.' He gave the dressing a harder poke. It shivered slightly. 'Red blood. I had forgotten that your blood was that bright.' He looked at the Doctor. 'I believe she will live. No vital Ape organs were damaged. One lung has a slight tear along it, but it didn't break the whole tissue. She will be weak for a while. You and this Ape are fond of each other? You are bonded, perhaps?'

'We are friends. Nothing more.'

'Nevertheless, I can sense your pleasure at her survival. Apes give off very strong pheromones in such situations. As a scientist I am always eager to learn new things.'

The Doctor smiled. 'Your new-found compassion does you credit, Baal.'

Baal stepped back. 'Do not mistake scientific interest for compassion, Ape. My study of your companion is purely for the purposes of survival. Ours rather than hers. It suits our purpose to keep her alive.' He pointed back towards Marc Marshall's cell. 'His presence no longer suits us, however. If Auggi were to find him, it would be difficult to explain his condition. Tahni has agreed to take the two of you back to the mainland where she found you both. After that, he is your responsibility.' Baal waved a clawed hand over a sensor. 'And then you will return. Alone.'

'Why?'

Baal pointed at Liz. 'The one she arrived with, the other

female. She wounded Krugga and murdered Chukk. She also deliberately shot your friend with her projectile weapon. Crude it may be, but it is effective. This can only mean that someone knows we are here. Someone who wishes to stop my work. I cannot let that happen. Your return will ensure our safety.'

'How do you reason that? What makes you think I won't return with armed soldiers to wipe you all out?'

Baal laughed. 'You think I am a fool because I am rather single-minded in my attempts to save my generation, don't you, Ape? You're wrong. I listened to what you said about your role in Okdel's Shelter. Unlike my mother, I do not see war as the only answer. But if such strategies please her, and keep her away from my real work, I will not interfere. You said you tried to make peace and I believe you. Chukk believed you, for all the good it did him.' Baal opened Marc's cell. 'We are both scientists, Ape. We both long to increase our knowledge, to expand our horizons. I will protect your friend here; you will return to aid me with my researches. I have a list of things I need you to bring back. Tahni would not understand them by herself; or know where to get them from.' He passed the Doctor a small electronic data pad and ran a finger over a stud on it. A list appeared. 'Tahni will translate our script.'

The Doctor looked at Marc's quivering form. 'And what's to stop you doing this to Liz?'

'Your Liz is mature. This was a hatchling and its internal chemistry was still in a state of flux. That was what I needed to explore, to try and integrate with our physiognomy. Liz is useless to us as anything other than a hostage to ensure Tahni's safe return.'

With surprising gentleness, Baal reached down and scooped up Marc's prone body. 'I don't know if your science can help him, nor do I care particularly, but nevertheless I hope he survives. As a scientist, I would not wish to be thought of as a murderer.'

Sula walked in with some of the webbing. She wrapped it around Marc like a cocoon and Baal passed him to the Doctor.

'You know, Baal, you are a very good scientist. Remarkable in fact. But you will never be a great scientist, a true scientist, until you stop regarding everything you do as justified whatever the cost. A true scientist always remains, if you'll excuse the pun, humane.' He started walking into the main lab, looking towards Liz's unconscious body. 'Mankind's history is littered with the dead bodies of scientists who forgot, or ignored, their moral responsibilities. I hope I don't return to find you added to them.'

Tahni was in the doorway. 'This way, Ape. Auggi is in the Council Chamber asserting her authority. We must leave now.' She pulled him out of the laboratory and down a small tunnel. 'Our only means of escape is a battle cruiser. This way.'

The Doctor ran just behind her, trying not to bounce Marc too much. Once or twice, the boy stirred slightly but then relapsed into his coma.

'Just round this corner,' puffed Tahni, and ran straight into a recovered Krugga.

'What are you doing—' he began, but then saw the Doctor and Marc. 'No!'

Before he had time to stop her, Tahni's third eye glowed brilliant red and, already weakened from his injuries, Krugga dropped to his knees. His own eye flared red for a moment and the Doctor felt a stab of pain across his forehead, but it vanished almost instantly. For a brief second, Marc's body too convulsed.

Krugga fell forward onto his face and Tahni waved a hand over a door control. 'Why was he here, I wonder?' she muttered as she led the Doctor onto the battle cruiser.

'Is he dead?' The Doctor looked back at Krugga's still form as the hatchway slid closed.

'I don't know. He was already injured.' She suddenly swung round on the Doctor. 'And I don't care. He isn't one of us, isn't a hybrid. He isn't, or wasn't, going to die within the next few years because of other people's meddling.'

The Doctor raised an eyebrow at her vehemence. 'I thought you were all very proud to be hybrids.'

Tahni scoffed as she started up the cruiser's power. 'Yes, well, Baal and Auggi would like us all to be, but frankly a majority of us would rather they hadn't bothered having us. What's the point of living only a few years?'

'That rather depends what you do with them.' The Doctor sat in what he assumed was the navigator's position. The craft shot forward rather jerkily and he cast a look down at Marc's comatose body, huddled by the door. 'You'll have to forgive my lack of concern for your wellbeing, but if Marc there is the end result of your researches, then you deserve all you get. At least you'll have a life. You've destroyed his.'

Tahni slowly looked at the Doctor. 'Surely your science can repair him?'

'Repair him? I don't even know what Baal did to him. I assume it was some kind of DNA splitting but this planet hasn't developed sufficiently advanced methods to restore him.'

Tahm looked back at Marc. 'We only want to survive.'

The Doctor looked straight ahead. 'No one on Earth would criticise you for that. It's just your methods that need some restraint.'

The rest of the journey was made in silence.

The pale young man was in his office. Opposite him was Sir Marmaduke Harrington-Smythe. Near the door were Cellian and Ciara. There was a knock on the door.

'Come in.'

The door opened and Cellian stood slightly aside as a dark-haired woman walked in. Sir Marmaduke frowned. 'Wildeman? Cathryn Wildeman? What are you doing here?'

The American zoologist walked over to the pale young man, and stood slightly behind him. 'I work here, Sir Marmaduke. I have done for about three years. Even before I went to Cambridge.'

'I convinced Sir John to select her for your Glasshouse project, you see,' said the pale young man. 'Ms Wildeman has been exceptionally useful in feeding me tit-bits of information.' He smiled. 'Actually, that's not true. To be honest, she's given me every security code, every Top-Secret, D-Classified, UNIT-initialled piece of paper that she could lay her hands on. It was Cath who passed Ciara and Cellian much of the information that I required.'

Sir Marmaduke glared at the American woman. 'You betrayed me. What about the others?'

Cathryn Wildeman smiled an insincere smile, all teeth, with no honesty in her eyes. 'Oh, I betrayed them too.' She produced a small notepad from her pocket. 'Sir. You may be pleased to know that our agent following up the leaks from Whitehall has arrived on L'Ithe – a small Channel Island. The documentation provided by the leak led her and Doctor Shaw there a few hours ago. Her last report stated that if it was a Silurian base, she was going to seek entry, capture a specimen and return with it to the mainland. She suggested a rendezvous at Smallmarshes, since it's in a direct line with the island and too isolated to draw too much attention. We've not heard from her since.'

The pale young man nodded. 'Fine. Send a squad down to Sussex. They ought to be there in three hours or so. Use the stealth fighter – that ought to stop UNIT or anyone else tracking us.'

'One other thing, sir,' said Wildeman. 'The Glasshouse has been dealt with. We have the WPC here, along with Doctor Morley.'

'Any others?' he asked.

'Alas, sir, Griffin and Atkinson didn't survive the visit.'

The pale young man frowned momentarily. 'Did our man leave any evidence?'

Wildeman paused before speaking. 'A few bodies. Including Atkinson and Griffin, I'm afraid. Did he make a mistake?'

'Another one, yes.' The pale young man smiled. 'Still, killing people is what he's good at. For the most part.' He turned to Wildeman. 'I think we'll dispense with his services for a while. Contact him, pay him, thank him and say we'll be in touch next time he's in the country.'

'Yes, sir.'

Sir Marmaduke was appalled. They were discussing deaths, contract killers and future murders as if ordering a Chinese take-away. 'Do you people have any consciences at all?'

The pale young man looked at Wildeman in mock confusion. 'Do you understand what he's talking about? The man who set up the Glasshouse, the man who has gone to great lengths to lie, steal and cheat his way through life asks us if we have consciences?' He suddenly leant over his desk, staring straight into Sir Marmaduke's face. 'No, Sir Marmaduke. We don't possess a conscience of any type because we don't need one.'

Wildeman made her farewells and left. Ciara and Cellian followed, leaving the pale young man and Sir Marmaduke alone.

'The few things I still need, Sir Marmaduke, are UNIT's requisition codes, their secret military wavelengths and their communications passwords. You see, I have C19 where I want it, I now own and run the Glasshouse and so all I need for total control of this country's military espionage departments are those little things. And you are going to tell me.'

Sir Marmaduke started to sweat. 'I don't know anything about UNIT.'

'You are lying, Sir Marmaduke.' The pale young man crossed to stand beside his seated prisoner. He bent over, took Sir Marmaduke's left hand in his, and tapped gently on his little finger. Sir Marmaduke howled in pain.

'That's right. One little tap and I've broken it in two places. That's the kind of man I am. Or was. Or will be, even.' He tapped Sir Marmaduke's index finger, shattering the bone.

Tears were streaming down Sir Marmaduke's face.

'Can't take a little pain, eh, Marmie? But you're a big army man. Former instructor in the noble art of survival of the fittest.' He broke another finger. 'Who's the fittest here, you lump of lard? Me or you?'

Sir Marmaduke tried to speak, but all that emerged through the pain was a sort of strangled squeak.

The pale young man frowned. 'Sorry, old boy, didn't quite catch that, what? Try again, old sport.' He broke his trapped foe's thumb. 'Next it'll be the other hand. Then your feet. Your genitals. Your neck. Enough to destroy you, cripple you for life. But not enough to kill you. So why not save yourself all that, and tell me what I need to know?'

A trickle of blood threaded its way down Sir Manrmaduke's chin as he bit through his tongue. The pain was excruciating, but he no longer cared. He would endure anything rather than tell his tormentor what he wanted to know. Seizing on his new-found resolve, reserves of strength he had never known he possessed, he glared into his captor's eyes until, for the first time, an expression of uncertainty crossed the pale young man's face.

'Where am I?' Even as she spoke, Liz knew it was a redundant question. She was in a Silurian Shelter, deep beneath a small island.

She had seen the Doctor and then something had hit her. The Doctor said … no, the Doctor hadn't said anything. Yet she felt that they had talked. Impossible.

Something to do with stars… no, it must be in her imagination. So, what had hit her?

'A projectile, from this.' A Silurian faced her, wearing a mesh vest of some sort. It resembled the Silurians she had seen in Derbyshire, but there were subtle differences. Her scientific interest was piqued. Different genetic strains of the same species. As humans were black, white, yellow and so on; tall and short; fat and skinny, so the Reptiles must be equally varied. This one's eyes were far more fish-like, and instead of the wide ears, it had fins. The skin was a mottled green rather than the dark and olive hues she'd seen before.

And it was holding a pistol. Liz recognised its distinctive shape immediately. And then wondered why she hadn't before. 'That's a UNIT service pistol, supplied to C19-related personnel only. They tried to teach me to use one once, but I flunked out.' She looked straight at the Silurian. 'How did you get it?'

The Silurian put his (her? its?) head on one side, the flap over its mouth sucking in and out rhythmically. Liz realised it was wondering what to say. She decided to help out. 'It is Jana's. It was in her handbag, so how come you've got it?'

'Your companion had this. She used it on you. She is dead.' The Silurian turned away, dropping the pistol into a pocket in its stringy coverall.

'How? And why?'

'She killed our leader. The Council killed her, just after she shot you.' The Silurian looked back. 'Chukk was a good Earth Reptile. Even Baal thinks it sad that he died.'

'Who is Baal?'

'He saved your life. He is our scientist.'

Liz took this in. 'I am a scientist. Maybe we should talk. You are…?'

'Sula. Baal's sister. And he won't discuss science with you. Apes are not capable of being scientists. You do not have the brain capacity to learn enough. You have brains no bigger than ragga-nuts.'

'And that is very small indeed,' said a new voice.

'Baal I presume? My name is Liz Shaw and I'm a doctor. I gather I must thank you for saving my life.'

Baal shrugged. 'It was of no consequence. The Doctor wanted you to live, so you are now my hostage. It is of no relevance.'

'Nevertheless, I am grateful.' Liz pointed at the machine

in the far corner. 'That's a particle disseminator. For breaking down DNA and other genetic structures. Why do you have one?'

A look passed between Baal and Sula but, unfamiliar with their faces, Liz could not tell exactly what it meant.

Baal looked back at Liz. 'You are a scientist, then?'

'I always thought so, but then again if my brain is only the size of a ragga-nut, I suppose I can't be.'

Baal stared at her, then back at Sula, who shrugged.

Baal continued. 'I believe that Apes ought to be eradicated. You have overrun our plant, destroyed many of our Shelters. You have tried to destroy us.'

Liz pulled herself into a more comfortable sitting position on the slab. 'That's not true,' she said, hoping that it wasn't and that Baal couldn't prove her wrong. 'The only Shelter we've come across was in Derbyshire.'

Baal looked back at Sula again. 'Shelter 873?'

'Apparently,' Sula replied.

Baal waved his hand towards a screen in the wall next to the particle disseminator. It immediately glowed into life, showing a map which Liz recognised as Earth as it had been millions of years ago, one large land mass. Baal waved a claw over a stud and hundreds of red dots appeared.

'Your Shelters?'

Sula said they were, adding that many of them were known to have been destroyed when the great land masses separated. 'Some filled with water, drowning the non-aquatic Earth Reptiles. Others were crushed by tectonic movements. But many have been destroyed by the Apes testing their nuclear bombs in the oceans, or poisoned by you dumping your waste products into the seas or burying them in the deserts. One colony awoke about fifty years ago in the Antarctic regions. They left us communiqués saying that they had awoken and requesting other Shelters to get in touch as soon as they awoke. Their last message was about invading Apes, destroying their city.' Baal looked hard at Liz. 'That city was probably the last surviving piece of our above-ground architecture, and the Apes destroyed it. Your Doctor associate has been pledging the Apes' support for a unified Earth, where we would all live together. He is a fool. You know it and I now it. Apes will never share their planet any more than we will.'

Liz took a deep breath. 'No, you're right. Not yet they won't. But in the years to come they might. If you really want to work towards peace, then you need to plan ahead.'

Baal snorted. 'You mean stay hidden. Here. Until the Apes have evolved enough to lose their egos and accept co-habitation?'

'Yes.'

'Why should we? We have the means to wipe you all out.'

'No you haven't,' said Liz. 'Otherwise, you'd have done it. In fact, you know too well that your plague doesn't work. We discovered an antidote. You're bluffing with an empty hand, Baal.' She stared back at him. 'What are you really so scared of? I don't think it's we Apes, or you wouldn't trust the Doctor, or use me as a hostage.' She looked at Sula. 'Where is he, by the way?'

'Back on the mainland. With Tahni. You are to remain here—'

'As a hostage, yes, your brother said.' Liz staggered off the slab, and Sula helped her stand. 'Thank you,' said Liz. Now, Baal, Sula, if I'm your prisoner, I'd better work for my keep. What are you really doing in this lab that needs a particle disseminator? Something's wrong with your genetics, isn't it?'

Baal actually looked surprised. In fact, Liz decided, that look probably meant he was completely taken aback.

Sula stepped between them. 'Yes, Doctor Shaw. Baal, Tahni, myself and all the other hatchlings here are dying—'

Baal pushed her aside. 'Sula, no!'

But Sula turned back, her third eye glowing for a brief second, and Baal winced. 'No, Baal, I have had enough of our mother's pride and your inability to have your own thoughts that aren't hers. I am as much in trouble as you or the others. I choose to survive by trusting this Ape with the information.'

'Yes, but what information?' asked Liz.

Sula told her everything.

Auggi was addressing her new Council. Some of Chukk's major supporters had been removed from power and were now sulking in their quarters or in the Great Chapel. Auggi's supporters hung on her every word, however.

'Chukk is gone. With him, his soft ideas of how to deal with the Apes. I say we eradicate them. Totally destroy them. And—'

An elderly Sea Devil Warrior limped into the chamber. 'Leader,' he hissed. 'Leader, I was on duty in the monitoring section, watching the screens when—'

Auggi was livid at the intrusion. 'This had better be good, Naalix. I don't like being interrupted.'

'A Cruiser has been stolen. Krugga was attacked again. He said it was the Ape and—'

'The Doctor! I should have had him slaughtered.' She pointed towards the doors. 'Naalix, find me Baal. I want him here, no arguments.'

Naalix limped out. Auggi smiled at her Council. 'At last,' she said. 'At last I have the excuse that was needed. Prepare to eradicate that cruiser. Blow it out of the water.'

'No, Mother, you cannot!' Baal was in the right-hand tunnel entrance, Naalix hobbling behind him.

Auggi ignored him. 'Naalix, blast that cruiser out of the water. Every long-range torpedo we have.'

'Yes, Leader.' Naalix vanished, and Baal hurried forward.

'The Doctor is not alone on that cruiser, Mother. Tahni is with him.' He expected her to countermand her order. Stop the attack. Instead she just smiled. 'My daughter, captured by the evil Ape, sacrificing her life so that we may all live. How noble.'

Baal stepped back. 'She is your daughter, Auggi! My sister.'

Auggi glared at him, and Baal saw something in his mother's eyes that he had been too devoted to see previously, too blinded by admiration and the need to keep his own secrets from her.

'I don't care.' Auggi smiled. 'Blast that cruiser to atoms.'

And Baal finally realised what Chukk had always known. Why Chukk and the Triad had refused her original application for leadership after his father's failure to survive hibernation. Auggi wasn't just hungry for power, driven by obsession. She was completely mad.

'Mike! Look!'

Carol Bell pointed into the night sky, trying not to shiver despite her heavy parka anorak. Something had flown low overhead, momentarily blotting out the moon.

They were huddled down by the old cottage on the top of the Smallmarshes cliff-side, the one where the boy had vanished and the policewoman had been driven mad. It was cold, slightly damp and she wished she were back at UNIT HQ, running her efficient Communications Division, aided by Maisie Hawke and Larry Parkinson. She was not made for late-night surveillance, no matter how desperate the Brigadier was for extra troops. Mind you, the overtime would be useful.

Mike Yates tried to keep track of the low-flying object, but it was so dark that he could not see a thing. 'Wonder what that was.'

Bell gave in to her shiver. 'It wasn't animal, that I can tell you. The ground trembled very slightly as it went over. And my ears needed to pop.'

Yates looked at her. 'Are you sure?'

'Yes. Why?'

'You must have been directly below it. Maybe it landed on the beach.'

'What did?'

Mike put his finger to his lips. 'Don't ask too many questions. I only know about it because I stumbled on some meeting the Brig had with Major General Scobie a few weeks ago.'

'Can I ask just one question?'

Mike nodded. 'Make it one that requires a quick answer.'

'What the hell are you talking about?'

'A stealth plane. Low-level reconnaissance. Possible armament as well. Got nicked from Geneva about a month back. They blamed our Government for leaking its existence. Scobie was asked to shift the blame onto us.'

Bell could imagine the Brigadier's response. 'I bet the old man was livid.'

Mike smiled. 'Well, he wasn't best pleased. Gave Scobie an earful that John Benton and I could hear from the Mess.'

'So, who did nick it?'

Mike shrugged and started down the cliff path. 'Whoever it was just landed it down in that cove. Look.'

Bell peered over the cliff path's edge and saw a cove which, during a hot summer day, was probably swarming with bathers believing they'd found somewhere exclusive. It certainly had to be looked hard for. Sitting on the sand, like a huge shadow, was a triangular-shaped aeroplane. A small one, large enough for five or six crew only. Despite the bright moon and stars, no light reflected off it at all. It was like a huge triangle of black had been carved into the beach. They could not see how high or low it sat; it simply did not possess any points of reference for gauging such things.

Bell pointed to the left, further in towards the cliffs. She could see about six or seven black-clad guards, slightly more distinguishable than the craft in which they'd arrived. She shot a questioning look at Yates, but he shrugged.

'Never seen those uniforms before. The guns are standard UNIT issue, though.'

Bell nodded. 'Which means they're unique. Our SLRs have faster reload and less recoil than regular issue.'

'I thought I'd noticed a difference.'

'That's nothing, Mike. C19 are working on developing a sub-machine gun that fires armour-piercing explosives like bullets. You lot should have them in a few months.'

Mike Yates tapped his service revolver. 'I'm happy with this tonight. Less cumbersome. Are you armed?'

'Of course.'

'Prepared to use it?'

'Of course.'

'Ever used a gun out of the practice range at Guildford?'

'Of course not.' Bell smiled. 'But there's always the first time. There aren't many telephonists that get to shoot up the bad guys.'

Mike touched her arm. 'You'll be all right. Don't take any risks. Whoever these chaps are, they're not on our side, despite their armament. It's more important that at least one of us gets to report back to the old man, as you call him, than that we both be heroes. Is that understood, Corporal?'

Carol Bell stared at him, then at her gun. 'Yes, Sergeant. Sir.'

Yates grinned. 'Okey-dokey, you watch them, I'm going down.' And he slipped off into the darkness.

'She's firing on us!' Tahni was astonished. 'My own mother has launched torpedoes at me!'

The Doctor was staring at the same read-out as Tahni. 'I thought this was a battle cruiser. Can't you fire back?'

Tahni shook her head. 'No. This is a craft designed for short-range manoeuvres. The missiles we carry are good, but not at that distance.'

The Doctor waved his hand over the console, bringing up a picture of the torpedoes streaking towards their craft. 'Where are your short-range missiles?'

Tahni pointed to a control on her side of the cruiser. The Doctor gently eased her aside. 'Excuse me.' He sat at her console, and she sat at his.

'What are you doing, Ape?'

'Watch. And learn.' The torpedoes were almost upon them. The Doctor cast a quick look at Marc, unconscious in the corner, then back at Tahni.

'Hold very tight. This will hurt.'

The expression of puzzlement was still on her face

as the Doctor fired their short-range missiles. He waved his hand over the button again, and the cruiser bucked violently as the missiles exploded outside, neutralising the incoming torpedoes as well.

The Doctor held tightly to his seat, but Tahni was flung out of hers and over the back, where she thudded to the floor next to Marc. She was on her feet in seconds, however, as the Doctor wrestled with the controls.

'Clever, Ape.' She pushed him aside and sat in her seat, trying to calm the cruiser. A massive explosion wrecked a rear console, showering the Doctor and Marc in sparks. 'Outer hull breached,' Tahni hissed. 'We're going to be taking on water in seconds.'

'How far to the beach?'

'A few more seconds and we'll be at the underwater tunnel I created. It's airtight, but you might want to wear our clothing for warmth.'

'No time.' The Doctor pointed at the side of the cruiser where the console had exploded. A dribble of water was seeping through, setting off more minor bangs. 'Get away from those controls,' he yelled.

Tahni did not need to be told twice. She swivelled round and jumped towards the Doctor as both the pilot's and navigator's consoles erupted, shattering the view screens. 'We're moving blind,' she shrieked and an instant later the cruiser crashed into something hard.

'We'll have to swim for it,' the Doctor cried, grabbing Marc and throwing him over his shoulder. He pointed at an emergency red switch. 'Is that for the hatches?'

Tahni nodded. 'This will fill with water in seconds. You'll drown!'

The Doctor ignored her, hitting the hatch release. The catches on the hatch opposite exploded but the door flew inwards rather than out, almost hitting the Doctor and Marc. There was a small splash, and for a moment it seemed as if they were safe. Then a massive inrush of water filled the cabin, flushing the three bodies straight out.

The Doctor looked for the darkest patch above him, knowing that this usually indicated the safest place to surface. A few seconds later he and Marc broke the surface and the Doctor gasped for air. He turned his head. The beach was close and, lying Marc on his back, the Doctor dragged him, half-swimming, half-puffing towards the sand and pebbles. Just as they got there, the water behind erupted in a fountain of froth. The cruiser had exploded. 'Tahni?' called the Doctor. 'Tahni, where are you?'

'She's right here,' said a man's gruff voice.

The Doctor found himself staring down the muzzle of a high-velocity rifle. He looked to his left and realised that sitting on the beach was one of the Government's new, and highly secret, stealth aircraft. 'Interesting,' he murmured. 'I didn't think that had made it beyond the drawing-board yet.' Tahni was being held by four other men, a gun at her head. The Doctor caught her look, and saw her third eye begin to flare. Hoping that Reptiles could see better in the dark than humans, he mouthed a 'No' and was relieved to see the red glow fade.

Another soldier was hauling Marc over his shoulder. The man who had initially spoken waved his gun at the plane. 'Into the Blackbird, all of you.'

The Doctor, the man carrying Marc and those with Tahni all boarded the ramp. The leader looked around, then whistled.

The man who was obviously the group's look-out heard

the whistle. He was about to give one back when a large lump of rock caught him behind the ear. He dropped like the proverbial stone, but before he even hit the ground, he was yanked back into the darkness of a recess in the cliff.

Mike Yates unclipped the man's belt and used a knife to slice through his boot laces. Mike had already shed his own top clothes and was trying not to shiver as he unzipped the black coveralls. The whole procedure only took thirty seconds, but it was long enough for the leader to whistle again. Hurriedly, Mike zipped up the coverall on his own body and slipped on the damaged boots, hoping no one would look too closely at the laces. Pushing on the helmet and snapping down the visor to cover his face, he stumbled out of the recess, almost crashing into the group's leader.

Mike mumbled an apology as indistinctly as he could.

'Yeah, well, we'll discuss your look-out abilities back at the Vault,' said the leader, pushing him towards the plane.

Forty-five seconds later, the plane executed a perfect vertical lift-off and, watched by Corporal Bell, silently shot back into the sky and headed northwards.

Auggi and Krugga watched the cruiser explode into millions of pieces as their torpedoes hit.

'Excellent. The Apes cannot be warned by my treacherous daughter.' Auggi pointed to Baal. 'And you had better return to your laboratory. I thought you had the stomach for war, the love of it that you should have inherited from your father.'

Baal looked hard at her and Krugga and then stepped back to the right-hand tunnel. But instead of heading down it, he waited, listening to his mother's next order to her Council.

DOCTOR WHO

'The Apes are pathetic,' she was ranting. 'Chukk was wrong. The Triad are wrong. It is our job to start a war with these usurpers. We will attack now, while it is dark.' She raised her hands dramatically. 'Arm the battle cruisers. Activate the Myrka. We'll attack now, destroy every Ape we see and take over this land mass. Once that is ours, their world will soon fall.'

Baal hurried back to his laboratory, then hesitated in the doorway, watching Sula and the Liz-Ape using the computers. The Liz-Ape's arm was in a sling, but she was clearly quite efficient at what she did.

Had he got it all wrong? Was his mother's fierce upbringing responsible for blinding him to the truth? Sula and Liz were working together. To some extent he and the Doctor were working together. Chukk and the Doctor had certainly worked together.

Alarms rang throughout the Shelter. Young able-bodied Earth Reptiles of every sort threw themselves into one, two or three-person cruisers and headed for the mainland at maximum speed. Auggi and Krugga led the attacking fleet from the main cruiser, which also housed the fearsome Myrka.

Auggi watched as the coastline grew in the viewscreen. 'Within a few hours, this planet will be ours!'

264

SEVEN

The Brigadier was sitting at his desk when Sergeant Benton looked around the door. He was staring at a sheet of paper and Benton decided he looked so lost in thought that he'd better go out again and knock.

'Don't bother, Sergeant, I saw you. Come in.' The Brigadier waved him into a seat. Benton lowered himself down and looked across the desk. He had begun working with the Brigadier shortly after the business with the Great Intelligence in the London Underground. When the Brigadier had been promoted and had set up the basic structure of UNIT, Benton had been a private in the regular army. It had been Major-General Rutlidge, the Brigadier's original liaison with the army, who had put John Benton's name forward for the Brigadier's short-list of potential UNIT troops. Both he and Jack Tracy had experience of undercover work, and that seemed to appeal to Lethbridge-Stewart; enough for him to call both men in for a meeting, outlining UNIT'S future role in the defence of Britain. And the world, as it turned out. Both promoted to corporals, they had met Captain Turner and Sergeant Walters, the Brigadier's immediate staff. Maisie Hawkes and Carol Bell had been there from the start, too.

Benton thought briefly of those who had passed through UNIT's ranks. Jimmy Munro, now back with the regular army. Sam Hawkins and Sergeant 'Big' Hart, both victims of the Silurians. Countless squaddies, corporals and technical bods. And at the heart of it all, Brigadier Lethbridge-Stewart, a man Benton not only respected and admired as his leader, but liked enormously as a person. Benton would never be so gauche as to think of his commanding officer as a friend, but there was a mutual respect between them both that Benton enjoyed.

He was fiercely loyal to the Brigadier and knew that Lethbridge-Stewart was equally loyal in return. After all, the old man had pushed hard to convince Major-General Scobie, Billy Rutlidge's successor, to make Benton up to a sergeant. Slowly, the team that the Brigadier had always wanted had been formed. Apart from non-active corporals like Bell and Hawke, UNIT now had a handful of rotating corporals – Tom Osgood, Jack Tracy and Steve Champion, a couple of sergeants in himself and Mike Yates and even a major, Alex Cosworth, on attachment for six months from the regular army. Cosworth, however, was another non-active officer, brought in to help sort out the administrative side. Benton thought he was OK, a bit of a university snob who was pretty good at pushing pens, but likely to be useless in field action. The Brigadier presumably agreed since Cosworth had yet to leave the confines of the Admin block at the Guildford HQ.

Benton's reverie was halted as the Brigadier pushed the sheet of paper he had been reading in Benton's general direction. Taking the hint, the sergeant picked it up and glanced down it.

It was a personal letter, from Beech and Co, solicitors, of Putney. It detailed the claims of their client, one Fiona Lethbridge-Stewart, regarding her filing for divorce upon the grounds of irreconcilable marital breakdown.

Benton passed the letter back. 'I'm very sorry, sir.'

The Brigadier harrumphed. 'At least I get the car and

rights to see Kate. Very little else.'

'It's good that she's not contesting you seeing your daughter, though.'

'Hmmm. Only because she knows that I'm unlikely to be able to do so very often.' The Brigadier tapped at a framed photograph on his desk with his pen, knocking it onto its back.

Benton could see it showed all three Lethbridge-Stewarts gathered around a Christmas tree. He guessed it must be two years old, because he knew the Brigadier had been in Geneva all over last Christmas.

'Oh well, back to business. What can I do for you, Sergeant Benton?'

Benton stood up immediately to make his report. 'Corporal Bell has radioed in, sir.' He produced a full transcript of her report and handed it over.

The Brigadier scanned it with professional speed and then grimaced. 'I hope Yates doesn't do anything stupid.'

'No, sir. We don't want to lose our new captain, sir.'

The Brigadier looked up, raising his eyebrows questioningly.

Benton cleared his throat. 'Talk amongst the lads, sir. Bets are on that Mike gets his pips soon.'

'Really, Sergeant? And why do they think that?'

Benton opened his mouth to give an answer, and then realised he did not have one. 'Don't know, sir. Just idle chit-chat.'

The Brigadier stood up, straightening his uniform. He bent down, putting the solicitors' letter into a drawer. 'You've been with me since the beginning, John. Don't you think that you're in the running as well?'

Benton licked his lips. 'Permission to speak candidly, sir?'

'Of course.'

'It's not me, sir. I know that. You know that. Mike Yates knows that. He's an officer, sir. Like you, it's in the blood. The lads respect him, admire him if you like. So do I. Frankly, I couldn't give orders to someone like him any more than I could to you, sir.' Benton knew he was flushing slightly. 'Really, sir, I'd much prefer it if he was a captain. It would be good for morale, provide a chain of command and help things run more efficiently. Added to that, sir, I don't want that responsibility. I'm a soldier, not a politician. Mike's a better juggler of high-ups than me. I can deal with grunts on parade, but give me one of those bods from C19 or the Ministry, and I'm out of my depth.'

'Good grief, Sergeant.' The Brigadier smiled. 'I don't think I've ever heard you say so much.'

Benton could not help but smile back. 'Been practising this speech, sir.'

The Brigadier nodded. 'I'll take your thoughts on board, Sergeant, if I get the budget to fund a promotion.' Benton turned to go, but the Brigadier continued: 'Oh, and Sergeant Benton?'

'Sir?'

'Thank you for being candid.'

'Sir.'

'Now,' and the Brigadier was all business again. 'This report of Bell's. If it is the new C19 Blackbird she saw, she recommends getting Parkinson to trace it. According to her, we have its transponder codes fed in.'

'Already taken care of, sir. I'll go and ask Parkinson if he's got a destination yet.'

The Brigadier nodded. 'Thank you, Sergeant. Somehow I thought you might have done that already. Report back to me when you have a location. Then I've got a task for you.'

'Sir?'

The Brigadier pointed at the map of the south coast behind his desk, which Corporal Hawkes had transferred from the communications room. 'I'm going to take one squad to wherever the Blackbird is. I'll try and get the Doctor and Sergeant Yates back safely. However, according to Bell, there was a Silurian with the Doctor. That means that they are using Smallmarshes regularly. I want your squad to rendezvous with Bell and keep an eye out for the blighters. I don't care if you have to stay there for a night or a week, but until I can speak to the Doctor again, we don't know what the Silurians are planning. I want you there just in case they attack. We got caught out last time; I don't want it to happen again.'

'Very good, sir. I'll check up on Parkinson.' Benton saluted and headed back to the communications room, grateful that as a confirmed bachelor he would never have to go through a divorce.

The three-dimensional schematic hovered in front of her. Using her pad, Liz could select and illuminate whichever section of the Earth Reptile's physiology she required.

To her right hovered another hologram, this one a wire-frame of the same figure, picked out in green. Every so often, Liz made a slight adjustment to her readings and spoke a command into the pad. The schematic's internal organs would dilate, shrink or move slightly at her command, then she would place one hologram over the other and see if it required any adjustments to the basic body shape.

She had been working one-handed at this for some time now, ninety per cent of her concentration focused on the job at hand. The other ten per cent was thinking about Jana, and the bizarre set of circumstances that had led her here. Jana was clearly a trained assassin; her expert use of a C19-issue pistol left no doubt of that. The fact that she had so casually shot dead this Chukk person, and then taken a pot-shot at Liz herself, conclusively proved that she possessed little in the way of a conscience. Sadly she was dead, and the solution to the mystery of who had employed her would have to wait for another day.

Sula moved into the laboratory as quietly as possible, but Liz was aware of her. Something triggered some kind of warning in her mind, like the time she had seen the Silurian – no, Earth Reptile – in the barn at Squires' farm, or on top of L'Ithe when she and Jana had first arrived. She had learnt to suppress that feeling, the primeval fear of the race. Not just because it would be inappropriate, not to say awkward, if she got the heebie-jeebies every time she saw Sula or Baal, but because it was scientifically important to prove that those fears could be overcome. If mankind and the Earth Reptiles were one day to live in peace (God willing, let it be during her lifetime), then this race-memory thing was going to have to be squashed or people taught to overcome it.

Sula passed Liz a mug of liquid, taking the pad away and placing it on a tray she held. 'Liz, you must drink this. It acts as a support to the webbing we put on your wound. It backs up the antiseptic.'

Liz looked at the liquid. 'Lovely, but is it safe for mammals like me?'

Sula thought about this. 'I don't know. No mammals have ever been given any to my knowledge. Then again, no mammals had been treated with the webbing and that hasn't killed you.'

'I suppose not. Oh well, all in the name of science. Bottoms up!' And Liz swallowed the contents of the mug in one go. 'If I could have done that with a pint of Guinness,' she said, wiping her lips on her sleeve, 'I could have won a flyer at the Christmas bash.'

Sula just stared at her, obviously not understanding a word of it.

'Never mind,' said Liz. 'Just ignore me. I'm rambling.'

Sula took the mug and looked inside it. 'You were supposed to sip it gently over half an hour.'

Liz frowned. 'Oh well, I'm not dead.' She swapped the mug for the pad. 'Thanks.' Then she suddenly smiled at Sula. 'You and Baal seem to have accepted me as more than just an ignorant Ape all of a sudden. Why?'

Sula's skin seemed to grow a fraction darker, but she did not reply.

'I'm sorry,' said Liz. 'I didn't mean to embarrass you. I just genuinely wondered.'

Sula crossed to the particle disseminator, placed the tray on the floor and activated a viewscreen. On it was pictured a small ape-like mammal.

'Your ancestor,' she said simply.

Liz stared at it. Living history. Real prehistory rather than a jumble of artistic interpretations made up from fossils. 'My God, it's beautiful.'

'Really?'

Liz glanced at Sula and then back at the screen. 'Aesthetically, no. But scientifically, yes. We could learn so much from you. For hundreds of years we have wondered what the past was like. You were there. You can tell us.' Liz excitedly pointed at the image on the screen. 'Hell, you can show us. There are so many questions that could be answered if we all co-operated.'

'I don't know if the Triad would agree.'

'Sadly, those in power never do. I doubt many of our world leaders would leap at the opportunity either. It's up to ordinary people like you or me to show them how necessary co-operation is.'

'For so long my mother and others like her have taught us, almost bred into us, a total loathing for Apes. You have over-run our world, destroyed so much of its natural beauty. We were taught to destroy you.'

Liz nodded. 'But you see it now, don't you? You see how you and I are working together, co-operating.' Liz pointed at the mug on the tray. 'You say you didn't know if that would work on me. That it might kill me, even. Well, that's the joy of what we're doing: learning together. From what I've gathered from Baal's notes, you haven't been able to sort out your genetic problems, so you kidnapped a human boy and experimented upon him, right?'

'Yes.' Sula look ashamed.

'But it went wrong, and that's no one's fault. You don't understand our physical make-up any more than I understand yours. Only through co-operation will we get to an answer. The Doctor would have helped you.'

'But can you find the answer?' asked a male voice behind them. Both Liz and Sula turned and watched as Baal walked across the room, his eyes looking at the floor rather than them.

Sula was immediately concerned. 'Baal? What's happened?'

He sighed deeply and took her face in his hands. 'Our mother ordered the cruiser containing Tahni and the Doctor to be destroyed.'

'Her own daughter?' Liz was appalled, not just for Tahni's sake, but the Doctor's as well.

'My mother is, well, beyond reason. You must have heard the alarm chimes. She has taken the fleet to attack the Apes.'

Sula looked shocked. 'But why? What will that achieve?'

Baal shook his head slowly. 'Remember, our father was an elite, a Sea Devil Warrior. They bonded because she admired their ways. She sees extermination of the Apes as the only way forward, even if accomplishing that costs her own life.'

'Who has gone with her?' Liz asked quietly.

Baal shrugged. 'Her followers. Many of our people, more than half I imagine. Few of our generation, though – most of the hybrids know better. We had planned our research to find a cure together.' He sat on a seat next to the map screen. 'If we are the only ones to survive this Shelter, we need to find a cure.'

Liz knew she ought to find a way to warn the human authorities of the impending attack. She also knew that, whatever their current doubts, Baal and Sula would never consent to this betrayal of their people. If she wanted their trust, she would have to earn it. 'Then let me help you,' she said. 'I'm a scientist, my field is chemistry, and I'm a human doctor. No one here is better qualified at least. What have you got to lose? You know your biology, I know mine. Between us, we ought to be able to find a cure for this problem.'

Baal and Sula stared at each other. Eventually, Sula touched his arm.

'Baal, our mother is wrong. What she has done to Tahni is unjustifiable. What we did to that Ape hatchling was unjustifiable. None of those things can be reversed, but we can go forward. Learn from our errors. Liz can help us. Please, let us all be equals now or we'll never leave this

Shelter for fear of what we are and what will happen to us.'

Baal stared straight ahead. 'The Doctor asked me if I believed that what I was trying to do justified the way in which I did it.'

'The ends never justifies the means. It's an established science principle. One by which most respectable scientists live,' Liz said.

Baal looked her in the eye. 'Even if it means that ultimately you fail? Even if it condemns you to death because you weren't prepared to take risks?'

'Many of our scientists have argued that,' Liz said. 'It's a question of individual morality. Whether you can live with yourself regardless of the good or bad consequences. Science, Baal, isn't just a job, a vocation. It's a commitment to other people rather than just yourself Other people can live or die by your decisions, your successes or failures, more so than in any other profession.'

Baal walked towards her, holding out both hands. Liz grasped them.

'Together,' he said. 'Please join us and help us find a cure for our illness. Then, I promise, we will find a way to all live together on the surface.'

Liz let his hands go, and watched as he and Sula began discussing rearranging the laboratory. She was dimly aware of their conversations as they worked out ways of adapting their machinery and ways of working to fit in with her.

This is it, she thought. This is what it's all about. What UNIT, the Doctor and the Brigadier are all about. My place isn't with the Doctor, running around helping him repair his TARDIS. My place is working here for a while, helping to mend these people and fostering some kind of relationship between them and us.

Her eye was caught by a white light blinking on and off on one of the panels. Like a star twinkling. She found herself smiling. OK, Nanna, this is it. I want to be here, I want to do this, I want to use my training, my knowledge to help these people. And I'm going to.

The Doctor was getting the guided tour. Along with the entire squad of black-clad guards from the beach, he was being escorted through corridors and laboratories, aircraft hangars and stadium-sized monitoring stations. The Vault was almost a small town buried beneath the Cheviot Hills.

He presumed this was the full VIP treatment, although the place that the pale young man who was showing him around clearly did not receive many visitors. And the Doctor wondered how many of those who entered ever left again.

'Frankly, Doctor,' his host was saying, 'without your contribution, I doubt the Vault would be half as successful as it is. I mean, look. Here we have Cyber-Guns, Nestene energy units, phials of the Silurian plague. You might even recognise that over there. One of our first trophies.'

The Doctor looked in the direction to which the pale young man had pointed. Inside a barred cage was the lower half of a cream-coloured Dalek, stained with green and pitted with bullet holes. The Doctor was sure he'd never seen a Dalek like that, least of all in the twentieth century.

'How fascinating. Now, I've enjoyed our guided tour. When do I get to see how Marc is doing? And where have you taken Tahni?'

The pale young man ignored him. 'And then over here,' he said as he led the Doctor through a steel door and into a room illuminated by a blue light, 'is our cryogenics section. There might be some people here you recognise.' He smiled benignly. 'Let's take a look, shall we?' He punched some buttons on the wall-mounted console. A partition slid back and then up on a hinge, revealing what appeared to be a mortuary. Embedded in one wall were forty drawers each large enough to contain a body. 'Who's this?' said the pale young man. At the press of another switch, a drawer slid silently out of the wall; inside it was a glass coffin, frosted over. The pale young man peered at the name plaque, then rubbed it with his sleeve. 'Oh, George Ratcliffe. Right-wing leader of a post-war pro-segregation group. Know him?'

The Doctor just stared back. 'Is there any point to this?'

'How about this one?' Another frosted coffin slid out. 'Melvin Krimpton. I'm sure you knew him.' He waved his arm at the remaining drawers. 'In fact, I'd put a penny to a pound that you knew the vast majority of these people, and were present in whatever face you wore at the time during the circumstances that led to their deaths. Up there is one Stephen Weams, over there is George Hibbert and right back here is Mark Gregory, a scientist of my acquaintance. Did you ever meet him? I'm not sure, but does it matter? The fact is, Doctor, that all these people died at the hands of something beyond the purview of normal police or military jurisdiction. Their bodies are kept here for research, to aid the future.' He paused, then laughed. 'I wonder what his parents put in young Stephen Weams' grave? What was faked up to keep even the families of those who died unaware of the Great Intelligence's true evil?'

'Why?'

'Because, Doctor, all this needs to be collected, sifted

and sorted. And because with the technology here, this country can be powerful. Imagine if we sent an army of Autons into Northern Ireland. Imagine if we'd helped the Yanks in Vietnam using a War Machine or two. And if this Government doesn't want to stain its lily-white hands, the next one will. Or the one after that. And if the price is right, they can have whatever they want. And, before you ask, it's all legitimate. I work for C19. I work for Sir John Sudbury, your bridge partner. Not that he's aware of any of this, any more than he was aware of what was going on at the Glasshouse. British politicians and civil servants make excellent ostriches, burying their heads and not seeing what they find distasteful.'

The Doctor stroked the back of his neck. 'Are you saying that Sudbury, Scobie and even Lethbridge-Stewart knew about this place?'

'Good grief, no. No one knows, except those that work for me. And who are they? Well, that's my secret, but rest assured, they have infiltrated every walk of life. Politicians, actors, newspaper journalists, shopkeepers and dustmen. People keeping an eye or an ear out, just to keep me happy.' The pale young man replaced the last coffin.

The Doctor glanced around him. There were three doors from the cryogenic chamber, including the one they had come through. There were two guards holding him while the leader stood a little behind; all three were armed. He had no way of knowing whether the pale young man carried a gun, but he placed a silent bet with himself that he did. Never mind.

'Why did you want the Silurian girl?'

The pale young man smiled. 'She is a bonus. We were aware that someone here was feeding information back to Whitehall, possibly to someone within C19 itself. That person contacted an investigative journalist famous in Holland, who could work under cover here. She began using this stolen information which enabled her to piece together what we already knew – that L'Ithe contained something worth investigating. Deciding to let this charade continue, we substituted the journalist with one of our own and, along with your Miss Shaw, they found the Silurian base for us. I've always wanted a Reptile; their genetic structure is so unique.' He leant back against the wall, as if he and the Doctor were discussing an old movie rather than a terrible plan to pervert human science. 'Imagine a breed of super-soldiers, Doctor. Capable of withstanding the extremes of the Antarctic and the Sahara. Able to breathe underwater and on land. The Silurian evolution is far superior to ours. Now that my people have had a chance to experiment on that poor boy you brought with you, I can see how it might be achieved. An army of eugenic fighters, Doctor. We'd rule this whole planet. Westminster would be the heart of the Western world, and eventually the Eastern, too. What do you say?'

The Doctor looked straight at him. 'Just this. Hai!' He flicked both his arms up and then back, catching his guards under their chins, and then slamming his flattened hand against the backs of their necks. Both guards skidded across the floor, dazed. The guard leader went for his rifle but a high kick from the Doctor sent it spinning into the far corner. A second kick took him in the solar plexus and left him rolling on the floor, gasping for air.

The pale young man shoved his hand inside his jacket but before he could bring his gun up to bear, a rifle shot rang out, sending the gun spinning across the floor. The pale young man grabbed at his stinging wrist and looked down at one of the guards the Doctor had sent sprawling.

He was up on one knee, his rifle aimed squarely at his employer's chest. He tossed his head back, and his helmet flew off.

'Sergeant Yates!' The Doctor hurried over to him. 'My dear Mike, I'm terribly sorry to have hit you so hard.'

A little hoarsely, Yates muttered that it didn't hurt. He rose slowly, still covering the pale young man with his rifle.

The guard captain also staggered to his feet, stumbling over to his boss, followed by the third guard.

'You were infiltrated, Leader,' said the pale young man. 'Presumably at Smallmarshes.'

'Correct.' Yates's voice was getting stronger now.

Suddenly the pale young man lashed out with his fist, striking the guard leader's head.

Mike winced, expecting to see the guard fall back down, possibly losing a couple of teeth. Instead, his head was torn from his shoulders with a horrible ripping sound, sending blood and tissue everywhere. The head bounced a couple of times, before coming to rest by the door. A second later, the body hit the floor.

Without hesitation, Mike fired eight bullets into the pale young man's chest, but again the expected failed to occur. The man just smiled, and looked at his shredded suit, a line of smoking bullet holes dotting his chest.

'Cybernetics. He's been augmented by Cyber-technology!' The Doctor pulled Mike away. 'Run!'

Yates didn't need telling twice, and followed the Doctor through the door behind them. He turned briefly to put a bullet into the electronic keypad on the other side. 'That'll either stop them, or make it easier for them. I wonder which.'

The door didn't open, but a massive rip suddenly split

it diagonally, and a suited arm thrust its way through the breach, feeling for the keypad.

The Doctor frowned. 'There's your answer, Sergeant, but I don't think it's going to keep them long. We ought to split up. Can you find us some transport?'

'I can probably find the Blackbird again.'

'Excellent. Get it ready. I need to find Marc and Tahni and get them away. Give me half an hour. If I'm not there, go and get Lethbridge-Stewart, Sir John Sudbury, Scobie and the whole United Nations if necessary. This place needs to be shut down.'

'Right-ho, Doctor. Good luck.' Mike slung his rifle over his shoulder and ran to the left, down a corridor.

The Doctor wondered which way to go. As the door opposite was ripped cleanly off its hinges, and hurled ten feet towards him, his decision was made for him. He ran in the opposite direction.

The pale young man and the surviving guard stood framed in the doorway. 'Kill him! Shoot him down.'

Sergeant Benton and his armed party, now in frill uniform, were waiting on the beach, watching the sea. Corporal Bell was there as well, as were a couple of local police officers including Sergeant Bob Lines.

One of the soldiers, Private Millar was operating a powerful sonar.

'Still approaching, sir. About eight craft plus something I can't identify. ETA approximately three minutes.'

Benton turned to Lines. 'How is the evacuation going?'

'Complete, Sergeant Benton. Just myself, WPC Haggard and PC Attrill are left here.' Lines turned to the WPC. 'Pat, any news from Hastings?'

'No, Sarge, but we've set up road blocks everywhere.

Nothing larger than a field mouse could get into Smallmarshes.'

'Good girl.'

Attrill walked over. 'Sarge?'

'Harry?'

'I know this seems strange, but the street lights are going out every so often. Electricity at the station is going on and off.'

'Probably something to do with this lot,' said Private Farley. He was pointing out to sea. Breaking the waves were a series of almost featureless egg-shaped capsules.

Each had just two tiny indentations at the front which suggested that they carried torpedoes of some sort.

'Right men, get prep—' Benton never finished. Breaking the water between the capsules was a massive horse-shaped green creature, covered in scales. Sharp fins ran down from its crested head to its long tail.

'It's a dinosaur,' muttered Private Johnson.

'It's bloody Nessie,' said Corporal Champion, priming his machine gun. The other soldiers followed suit.

'You three, get back to the station,' said Benton to the police officers. 'Corporal Bell, go with them. Contact HQ if you can and request back-up.'

'Aye, sir.' Bell led the police officers away.

Farley was the first to open fire, seconds after the previously seamless roofs of the capsules slid open, revealing three Silurians in each. He saw their third eyes glowing red and Private Beaton, nearest to them, dropped his rifle and fell dead. Farley's first burst took two Silurians full in the face and they dropped lifelessly into the water, but the others ploughed on relentlessly.

Benton did not hesitate. 'Fall back, near the cliff-side cottage,' he yelled. Without waiting for further instructions, the soldiers retreated, firing. Another Silurian died, but two of Benton's platoon were killed in return.

Benton unclipped a grenade and Millar beside him did the same. Benton's aim was off, and his grenade exploded harmlessly near the massive bulk of the huge green sea creature. Millar's, however, landed right inside one of the capsules and exploded immediately, sending two Silurians into the air, their bodies alight. A chain reaction started, and two more capsules exploded, presumably killing their occupants.

Benton and Millar scrambled up the cliff to the cottage, but neither could see the other men.

'We can't be all that's left, sir,' Millar said, dropping his sonar tracking pack.

'No, we're not. The others are with Farley over there. Look.'

Farley was on the higher ground further from the cliff. He waved frantically to them.

'What's going on?' Millar wondered.

Benton turned and saw the sea creature behind them, just disappearing around the back wall of the cottage.

'Stay quiet, Millar.'

Millar flattened himself against the wall, while Benton stepped slightly forward. At that moment, the sea creature's head peered around the wall on its long neck, and for a second Benton saw a spark of intelligence in its eyes. It was sizing them up, he realised, working out where they had gone.

Benton turned back to Millar as the sea creature lifted a front flipper and touched the corner of the cottage. A massive blue flash caused Benton to cover his eyes and, as it faded, he saw Millar, still gripping the wall. His eyes were gone, his skin blistered and puckered. Smoke emerged from his empty eye sockets and mouth, before he pitched forward onto his face.

Benton fired his revolver pointlessly a couple of times before scrambling up the hill above the cliff.

'I can't see a bloody thing through this smoke,' he muttered as Farley helped him up the last few feet.

'We lost Beaton, Ashton and Mitchell, sir, as well as Millar. And I've not seen either Corporal Champion or Private Salt.'

Benton watched as one of his men carefully picked off another Silurian. 'We're going to need to stop that creature before anything else runs into it, Private. You get the flares, light some and see if you can guide Champion and Salt towards us. I'm going to get the heavy artillery out.'

He dashed back to one of the UNIT Landrovers and hoisted a bazooka out of the back. He flicked the catch, loaded it and put two more shells under his arm. He then headed back towards the cliff top in time to see Farley lighting a flare and hurling it into the fog.

The flare landed at the feet of the sea creature, and it backed off slightly. Suddenly, emerging from the smoke, he could see Champion and Salt running towards him. Champion saw the creature, but Salt was not so lucky, running straight into its tail and then frying as thousands of volts spasmed through his body.

Benton fired the bazooka, but it exploded harmlessly beside the creature. As Farley hauled Champion up, Benton fired again. Farley too lobbed another flare into the murk. Again, the creature ignored the blast, but moved away from the flare. Benton suddenly dropped the bazooka and snatched the bag of flares from Farley.

'How many?'

'Er, about twenty, sir.'

Benton placed the bazooka missile in the bag and then shoved a grenade in as well, yanking out the pin. He drew back his arm and hurled the bag towards the sea creature. It landed between its legs and then exploded, setting off the biggest fireworks display Smallmarshes was ever likely to see.

The blast wiped out a few Silurians, but it was not that which stopped the sea creature. It was the sudden blinding flash of twenty flares all detonating at once.

The UNIT troops covered their eyes in anticipation, but still saw the huge white flash through their hands. The effect on those on the beach was devastating. The few surviving Silurians dropped to their knees, temporarily blinded. The sea creature itself gave a huge roar and then collapsed dead, crushing a hapless Silurian who had staggered into its path.

The UNIT troops began to move onto the beach to round up their prisoners. Suddenly, Champion yelled a warning as a Silurian at least three times bulkier than the others reared up before Benton.

For a moment, the sergeant hesitated, and Farley saved his life by emptying a clip of bullets into its back. Despite its horrific injuries, the huge Silurian still managed to turn, trying to use its third eye. For a second, it looked as if it would succeed, but its injuries were too severe and it fell, rolling away onto a clump of rocks, where it finally lay still, staring up at the sky with sightless eyes.

Auggi watched her people being massacred on a viewscreen within the safety of her cruiser. Beside her lay two dead Earth Reptiles who had dared to suggest that all three of them join the attack. No, she had decided, that was Krugga's job.

Now she realised that Chukk had been right; the Apes were stronger than she had thought. It was down to Baal now. To develop a better strain of the virus and help her unleash it upon them.

She used the scanner to contact Baal in his laboratory. Seconds later his face appeared on the screen.

'Mother! What are you doing?'

'The Apes have wiped out my fleet, my son. It is up to us now to destroy them once and for all.'

Baal shook his head. 'No, Mother, you are wrong. We will aid the Apes, the humans, and they will aid us. Observe.' He moved out of her line of sight and Auggi saw Sula and the Doctor's Ape-woman friend working together, the image of the hybrid wire-frame hovering around them.

'You… you have told her of our secret? Our shame?'

Baal moved back into sight. 'No shame, Mother. It is our birthright, and we must work together to cure it.'

'But the Apes have killed your friends.'

'No, they have been killed by you. You led them on a foolhardy mission. This planet is no longer ours. We have to share it if we are to survive. We are like a tiny voice in a crowd of millions. If we have nothing positive to say, then we have no right to wake up the other Shelters.'

Auggi stared at her son. She stared at the two dead hybrids at her feet. She then glanced at another screen, showing the Ape warriors sifting through the carnage. 'I am betrayed on all sides,' she said, and cut the transmission.

She programmed in a new course, away from both the coast and from her Shelter. She would go to a place where no one would embarrass her further, and where she could plan her revenge against the Apes in safety.

The battle cruiser sped away through the waves.

Mike Yates threw himself through the door of Blackbird control, much to the astonishment of the two people inside, a black-clad armed guard and a white-coated young female technician.

The guard frowned. 'What's going on?'

'There's been a breakout. That Doctor from UNIT, he's causing trouble.'

The technician stared at the guard. 'See, Lawson, I told you the boss would want to know.' She looked back at Yates, pointing at her radar screen. 'UNIT helicopters, about three of them, surrounding us. They know we're here, somehow.'

Yates brought up his rifle. 'Probably homed in on me,' he said and clubbed the guard into unconsciousness. He trained the rifle on the now terrified technician. 'Where's the Blackbird?'

The technician pointed through a smoked-glass window, and Yates could just make out a dark outline. 'Open the hangar doors. Now!'

The technician pressed a switch and Yates heard a clang as the double doors directly above the Blackbird started to part. Sunlight streamed in.

The technician took advantage of his distraction, whipping out a sidearm, but the movement caught Yates's eye just in time. He feinted to one side and they fired simultaneously.

Yates fell back as the bullet ripped through his shoulder and out the other side. Blood trickled from the wound but, miraculously, it seemed to have missed any main arteries. His bullet found its mark, straight through the technician's heart, and the white-coated woman died soundlessly.

He looked back through the glass and could see one of the Brigadier's helicopters coming through the gap, UNIT soldiers leaping out, armed and ready.

He lifted the technician's chair, smashed it through the glass, and yelled, 'It's Greyhound Two. Don't fire!'

By now two of the helicopters had landed, one on each side of the Blackbird. Yates saw Tom Osgood open the hatch of the Blackbird and dive in, probably intending to disable it. Then he saw the even more welcome sight of the Brigadier, pistol in hand. 'That's Yates up there. Someone go and help him down here.'

Mike Yates let himself relax. The cavalry had arrived.

In his plush office the pale young man was shouting at Ciara and Cellian.

'Get him. Kill him. The Doctor must die, and I don't care who gets in your way. Everyone here is expendable.'

Ciara and Cellian nodded and left him. After they had gone, he stabbed at a button on his desk. A picture opposite slid away, revealing a screen. Bailey's face appeared on it.

'Where are you, Bailey?'

'In the east labs. Why?'

'Problems. Clear everything out to the safety zone. I'll meet you there in a couple of days.'

'All right, sir.'

'Oh, Bailey?'

'Sir?'

'Make sure you take the Stalker. One day it's going to be used to get the Doctor.'

'Yes, sir.' The screen faded.

The pale young man stared across the room at Sir

Marmaduke Harrington-Smythe's dead body. 'Fat lot of good you were. A real waste of time.'

He pressed another button on his desk. 'Sorry, boss.' He straightened his tie, pushed his chair under his desk and opened the wall safe by Sir Marmaduke's body. Inside were microfiches, microfilms and video cassettes. Beside them were sheaves and sheaves of papers, all marked Confidential or Top Secret: Eyes Only, Department of Science and Technology, or Ministry of Defence. All bore the C19 crest and motto: *Quis Custodiet Ipsos Costodes* – 'Who guards the guards themselves?' He picked them up and deposited them on his desk.

'Yes, who indeed?' He returned to the safe and pocketed the microfiches and films. He looked at the cassettes, then back at his watch. 'Ah well, I'll try and find some copies in Sir John's offices one day,' he muttered and threw them onto the desk.

With a last look around, he exited his office, checking the door was firmly shut. He counted off another ten seconds and moved forward, allowing a metal shutter to slam down behind him. Then he heard a muffled bang and a roar from within the office as it was reduced to fine ash.

'Cobalt. Always said you couldn't better Cyber-technology.'

The Doctor had battled his way past more than a few guards by the time he found the laboratory he was hunting for.

He pushed the doors open, knocking the surprised guard to one side.

'Hai!' The Doctor delivered a throat jab, and the man dropped unconscious.

He stared ahead of him. The room was massive, like a

football pitch, but the high walls were covered in monitors, computer banks and switches for every kind of machine. To the left was a bed, on which lay Marc Marshall. Bending over him was a man in a white coat.

In the centre of the room was a chair, rather like a dentist's. Strapped firmly into it was Tahni, struggling as best she could, her third eye covered by a metal strap. A young, dark-haired woman, also in a white coat, bent over her, fixing electrodes to the Earth Reptile's breasts.

On another bed on the opposite side of the room sat a young blonde woman, scribbling frantically on the wall. She kept casting frightened looks back at Tahni and drew as if her life depended on the completion of her master work.

The female scientist looked up. 'The Doctor, I presume?' she said with a distinct American accent.

The man also stopped and looked over. 'From UNIT?'

'Yes. Move away from those people, if you don't mind.' He aimed one of the guns he'd stolen from a guard earlier.

The man complied, but the woman ignored the Doctor's threat. Instead she looked back at the man. 'Get on with the boy, Peter, there's a good chap. The Doctor has morals about using guns on us mere humans.'

The man called Peter ignored her, and instead undid the straps holding Marc down. 'I'm Peter Morley, from Cambridge. I'm a xenobiologist and I'm being forced to work here against my will.'

The woman looked up. 'God, Peter, you are a prat.' She took out a pistol and aimed it at Tahni's head. 'Retreat, Doctor, or your lizard girlfriend gets a fourth eye.' She smiled. 'Oh, I do love Raymond Chandler films.'

She was still smiling when the far door burst open and a massive pulse of energy blasted her literally in two.

Tahni instinctively flinched, and even the woman on the other bed dropped her pencil.

Morley ran to the Doctor's side. 'It's the Irish Twins. Ciara and Cellian. What are they doing here?'

The Doctor stared at the newcomers. They both held their right arms outstretched, palms flat. The fingers had dropped away on a hinge, revealing a stubby muzzle emerging from just under the thumb.

'We were one of the Vault's earliest experiments, Doctor,' said Ciara calmly.

'You're not Autons, not in the truest sense, surely?'

'No, not at all,' said Ciara. 'We're humans, but the Vault replaced our blood with the Nestene fluids from the tank at AutoPlastics. These little additions –' she nodded towards her arm – 'were our commander's little touch. The fluids provide the energy for the weaponry. Ingenious, don't you think?'

'You were the forefront of his little hybrid army then,' the Doctor said. 'The ultimate killing machines. Humans with alien technology grafted on.'

'We were his main inspiration. With our armaments and that thing's genes, he would have made an invincible army.'

Understandably angry at being referred to as 'that thing', Tahni began to struggle. Ignoring her, the Irish Twins walked around her until they were face to face with Morley and the Doctor.

'Resistance is useless,' said Cellian.

Morley gaped. 'You can speak! You've never spoken before.'

'Never had anything worthwhile to say.' Cellian aimed his energy weapon at the quaking scientist.

'Not much worthwhile now, either,' muttered the

Doctor.

Unseen by the Nestene-adapted twins, Marc Marshall had dropped off his bed and was pulling himself painfully across the floor, his progress hampered by his painfully distended skin. He had reached Tahni, and was trying to undo her restraints when the woman on the other bed began screeching, like a terrified chimpanzee.

Cellian calmly swung around, blasting her apart with an energy bolt. Ciara was about to do the same to Marc and Tahni when the door through which they had come was blown off its hinges. Through the resulting gap rushed the Brigadier followed by about thirty UNIT troops.

The Irish Twins threw glances at each other and then barged between the Doctor and Morley, running out through the door by which the Doctor entered.

Leaving the soldiers to follow them, the Doctor rushed to Marc and Tahni, while Morley went to the woman on the bed.

The Brigadier stared down at the Silurian. 'Good to see you again, Doctor.'

'Brigadier, you must warn your men, those two they're chasing are effectively Autons.'

'Right you are, Doctor.' He whipped out his walkie-talkie. 'Greyhound Leader to all Traps. Male and female you are pursuing are highly dangerous. Auton facsimiles. Approach with caution. Use explosives if necessary.' He looked back at the Doctor. 'How are your patients?'

Tahni stared back at him. 'I am fine thank you, furry Ape. But the hatchling is dead.'

'The strain was too much for his young heart, I'm afraid.' The Doctor closed Marc's staring eyes. 'He tried his best. Brave to the end.'

Tahni placed a clawed hand on the Doctor's shoulder.

'I am sorry, Doctor. Baal will be too, I know. He has much to learn.'

Morley walked over. 'WPC Redworth is dead. Cellian didn't leave much of her.'

The Doctor looked at the Brigadier. 'Lethbridge-Stewart, I think you need to get old Scobie, Sir John Sudbury and your Prime Minister up to see the abhorrence that is the Vault.'

'Yes, Doctor. A good idea.' He turned to go. 'By the way, where is Miss Shaw?'

Three days later, Liz and the Doctor were going over some photographs in their laboratory at UNIT HQ.

'That's Krugga,' said the Doctor. 'Poor chap. But what on Earth is that?'

Liz looked at the photo, which showed a massive sea creature. She touched it with the hand that wasn't still in a sling. 'If I didn't know better, I'd say it was the Loch Ness Monster, but I think it's a Myrka.'

Sergeant Benton placed a cup of cocoa on the bench for each of them. 'Yeah, bloody great thing killed a few of the lads. We killed it with the flares. Bright light just seemed to burn its brain out.'

'Do you have to be so graphic, Sergeant?' asked Liz.

The Doctor touched Liz's hand. 'How are things on L'Ithe this morning?'

Liz sat on a stool, her good hand in her lap. She smiled tightly. 'Baal and Tahni have taken control. We've returned Sergeant Benton's prisoners, under the terms of the Geneva Convention, and everything seems calm. They've asked me to work with them, to try and find a cure for their problems. I said I would think about it.'

'Oh but Liz, you must,' said the Doctor. 'Think about

what you could learn. Think about the thrill of discovering a whole new science. Earth Reptile science. A marvellous opportunity. Oh, Liz, we could do so much for them.'

'We?'

The Doctor coughed. 'Well, obviously, it would be your project.'

She laughed. 'Yes, of course it would be. For a couple of days.' She sighed suddenly. 'I'll have to think about it.'

Before the Doctor could reply, the doors opened and the Brigadier walked in, followed by Yates, his arm also in a sling.

'This lab looks more like a field hospital every day,' the Doctor said. 'What do you want, Brigadier? We are busy in here.'

'Yes, hot cocoa all round, is it? Well, just time to pass on some reports.' He cleared his throat. 'Firstly, as you know, we've made official contact with this Baal character and his associates. Diplomatic overtures are being made and I gather Miss Shaw has been asked to be involved.'

Liz nodded. 'I think we need to discuss that later, Brigadier.'

'Fair enough. Sir John Sudbury has been up to that Vault place. It seems that we hardly saw any of it when we were up there. Whatever was there, if anything, has gone. However, your cryogenic bit has certainly been gutted. We lost track of those semi-Auton types, and Sir John recognised his secretarial aide from your description, Doctor, but has not had sight nor sound of him since.'

Liz snorted. 'Oh great, so the bad guys won.'

'Not exactly, my dear,' said the Doctor. 'They lost, but they do live to fight another day. As, it would seem, does Auggi.' He tapped the photos. 'I've been looking for her here, but unless she's in little pieces—'

'Look who's being gory now,' murmured Benton.

'If I may continue, sergeant. She's either in pieces or escaped. I know which I'd put my money on.'

The Brigadier sighed. 'Well, one bit of good news. C19 has taken over direct running of the Glasshouse now, and will appoint an Executive Director very soon. Hand-picked by Sir John, so there shouldn't be any more funny business from there at least. Going to a new, secret location, too.'

The Doctor nodded. 'Well, we can all rest easy in our beds, then. I mean, Sir John presumably hand-picked his secretarial aide, who ended up being half cybernetic, creating hybrid Autons and goodness only knows what else from our previous battle spoils.'

'Yes. Well.' The Brigadier looked at Mike Yates. 'Oh, yes, and say hello to my new Number Two, Captain Mike Yates.'

'So, Sir John coughed up the cash then.' Benton smiled, shaking Mike's left hand vigorously. 'Good on you, sir. Captain!'

Mike Yates grinned, especially when Liz kissed him. 'Congratulations, Mike.'

'Absolutely, Mike. I'm delighted.' The Doctor also shook his hand. 'Now, if you're all going to have a party, do it elsewhere. Miss Shaw and I have a lot of work to do.'

The Brigadier ushered Yates and Benton out.

'Oh, Alistair,' the Doctor said quietly.

'Doctor?'

'I am truly sorry about Fiona and Kate. I hope you find some amicable way to get on with your respective lives without too much pain.'

The Brigadier stared at the Doctor, trying not to let any emotion show. 'Well, one of those things, Doctor. Thank you anyway, I appreciate it.' He left.

The Doctor stopped shuffling the photographs and stared into space. 'Poor Alistair.'

Liz kissed him on the cheek. 'Sometimes, Doctor, you can be a good person.'

Regent's Park was serene, surprisingly empty of people considering the heat wave, and those that were around tended to be sunbathing rather than noisily playing football or rounders on the great expanses of greenery.

The Doctor and Liz Shaw had walked for quite some while now, discussing the weather, the pros and cons of the Zoo and whether the Park itself ought to fall under the auspices of the rapacious Westminster Council or the more liberal Camden.

The drive there in Bessie had been something of a nerve-wracking experience for Liz; she couldn't bear the traffic in London at the best of times, and it was far worse sitting next to the Doctor as he jumped red lights, cut other drivers up and generally behaved in a way that Sir Robert Marks would have had kittens about. They had narrowly missed scattering a group of tourists gathered around Nelson's Column and had honked loudly at a couple of young men in sheepskin jackets and Lautrec-style fedoras, one of whom Liz was positive was David Hockney. The Doctor had yelled something about how one day Trafalgar Square would be largely pedestrianised and therefore he was making the most of it, but Liz was not too sure how serious he was. Every so often, he would reveal a bit of foreknowledge, then wrap it in a swaddling of exaggerations until you could not trust anything he had said.

They had sped up St Martin's Lane, across St Giles

Circus and cut into Tottenham Court Road. Liz had pointed out that this was hardly the most direct route to the park, but the Doctor replied that he enjoyed having company in Bessie and was making the most of it. Liz found herself incapable of ruining his pleasure. And yet there had been something in the way he had said that... a sadness? A resignation?

Could he have guessed? No. No, he was not that sensitive to other people's feelings, surely? And yet it might explain his eagerness to take her to London in the first place. Why he let her choose the Park and arrange the picnic.

And why he had even contributed a rather glorious bottle of Bulls Blood from something called the TARDIS vineyard. Another exaggeration, of course.

Or was it? Having finished the picnic, they had set off on a walking tour of Regent's Park, avoiding the Zoo, not just because of Liz's disapproval of it, but because it reminded the Doctor too much of what he had just witnessed in Northumberland.

Conversation inevitably turned to their lives, their pasts and, hopefully, futures. As they talked, Liz began to see a warmth, a compassion emerge from the Doctor's usual veneer of sarcasm and cynicism. She suddenly realised how little she knew him.

For the last eight months, ever since that bizarre visit to the Cottage Hospital in Essex where the Brigadier had seen an unfamiliar face on someone who recognised him immediately, Liz had got to know the Doctor as a colleague, trusted and respected, but that was all. She could not have put her hand on her heart and said she actually liked the man. Time Lord. Whatever. They just happened to work in the same room in the same building. But now, as they wandered through London's most regal park, and he pointed at flowers, trees, shrubs and woodland animals, noting each one's name and history with a frightening encyclopaedic knowledge and enthusiasm, Liz realised she felt a real regret.

'I wish we had been friends. Real friends. The sort of people who, oh I don't now, had dinner. Played Scrabble. Went to the pictures.' Liz had stopped, thinking the Doctor would think her foolish.

'Had been?' he had said after a few seconds. 'I take it that I've guessed correctly. You're going?'

Until then, Liz had not honestly been sure. Her logical side said she had to get away from UNIT before it stifled her, both mentally and in terms of motivation for her work. Yet, as he said those few words, Liz was overcome with a feeling of nostalgia. Of wanting to see those other worlds, other places he spoke of so often. She wanted to shake hands with an Alpha Centaurian table-tennis player. To play hide and seek with a Refusian, or say hello to a Delphon with her eyebrows (and she had even caught herself practising in the mirror one morning).

'Yes,' she heard herself say. Then, more strongly, 'Yes, I am.' Why did she want to cry suddenly? Why was she upset? He infuriated her, made her own hard-fought and hard-earned knowledge seem so inadequate. There were times she wanted to shove his teeth down his throat, wrap a Bunsen burner lead round his neck or just take Mike Yates's service revolver and put a bullet through his alien temple. But as she looked into his blue eyes, with their unique mixture of childish enthusiasm and centuries-old wisdom, she knew her own eyes were welling up. 'I'm really sorry, Doctor, but I have to… '

'Why?'

'Because… because. Just because.' She was aware her

voice was rising. 'Because of you. Of me. Of the Brigadier. Of everything. A teenaged male has just died at the hands of the people who have been paying my salary for nearly a year.'

'Oh. Is that all?'

Liz froze. That was it. That was the excuse. He had lit the fuse, touched the red button, blown out the… well, whatever, he'd gone too far. Liz did not keep down either the volume or the bitterness.

'All? Is that all? You heartless… *alien*, Doctor. He was a kid. Just a kid and that… that creep at C19 was responsible for his death. And all you can say is "is that all?"'

She was sobbing now, her yells emerging as a hoarse whisper rather than the outraged screeches she heard in her head.

'At last. At last, I'm seeing the real Elizabeth Shaw. It's taken until now, but she's there.'

Liz slowed her breathing, holding back her tears. 'What, what do you mean?'

The Doctor took her shoulders, ignoring her attempts to shake him off. Eventually she gave in.

And he smiled. The most radiant – no, beautiful – smile she had ever seen him wear. 'You, Liz. Not the detached scientist. Not the calm, collected and efficient UNIT Doctor Shaw. You referred to Marc as a "teenaged male". You talked in professional terms. Upset you may have been, but you were still holding back. Then you finally called him a kid. You even swore. I've not heard that before.' He sank down to the grass, gently pulling her with him, and she sat, cross-legged, opposite him. He began plucking odd blades of grass, as if embarrassed.

And if he wasn't, she certainly was.

'I realised not that long ago that I didn't know very much

about you, Liz. As you say, it's been all work and no play. That's my fault. And if you're going back to Cambridge, then the opportunities to mend that breach are going to be few and far between. But for what it is worth, I value you. Your judgements, your ideas and your ethics. You've been my calm in a storm. My white when I've been black. I don't think either of us realised how much I've relied on you over the last eight months. Eight months, two weeks and four days to be exact.' He held out his hand. In it was a necklace made of grass, intricately interwoven. Sturdy but fragile-looking. 'What will you do?'

Liz swallowed as she gently took the proffered necklace. 'I'm going to spend some time with Jeff Johnson. He's got a place in Cambridge, somewhere to stop over until I find my own place. I've been asked to return to my old college, to restart some of the projects I abandoned when the Brigadier hijacked me.' She shrugged. 'I'm going to apply for a grant to research genetic disorders. I have agreed to help Baal and Sula find a way to cure their condition and extend their life-spans. And even if I can't help them directly, we know there are more Shelters out there. More Silurians, Earth Reptiles, whatever, who need help adjusting to our climate. Our pollution. Our diseases. And I feel that what we learnt from Marc Marshall, from what happened to him, could be invaluable in helping our own children with polio, cancer, leprosy, whatever.' She looked the Doctor straight in the eye, and his smile broadened. 'I suppose what I'm saying is that I'm going home. To do something. To achieve what I can't achieve as your assistant. You don't need me to pass you test tubes, and tell you how brilliant you are.' She smiled back. 'We both know that already.'

He nodded. 'Do you want a lift back to your flat?'

Liz looked around her. People were still sunbathing. A few were walking. A couple of children ran by and one careered into her, fell on its face and began to cry. She stood up, picked the little girl up and smiled as she passed her back to her distraught mother.

'Heaven help us, maybe I'll get married and have children.' She looked down at the Doctor, who had remained seated, but he didn't catch her eye. He was watching a caterpillar crawl over the back of his hand, twisting his wrist slowly so it always had more ground to cover. 'No, thanks, Doctor. I'll take the Tube.'

'Goodbye, Liz,' he said, still not looking at her.

She was going to cry again. Real tears now, not rage, frustration or anger. Not tears of bitterness. Something far better. Far more important.

'Goodbye, Doctor. Will… will I see you tomorrow if I come by to get my things?'

The Doctor was still staring at his caterpillar. 'No,' he said quietly. 'I'll explain to the Brigadier later today. I'm off to help sort out the Cheviots with our newly promoted Captain Yates.'

Liz pulled her handbag tightly over her shoulder and shrugged. 'Well, then I… well…'

'Goodbye, Liz.' The Doctor finally looked up. 'We will meet again, I promise you.'

'We'll catch that film, eh?' she said brightly.

The Doctor returned to the caterpillar. 'Who knows?'

With a last look at the top of his head, Liz straightened up and walked away, towards Regent's Park underground station.

The sun was shining brighter than she could ever remember as she approached the road. She allowed herself one final look back, one final image to be placed in her gallery of memories.

The Doctor, lying outstretched, his hand moving as he continued to play with his caterpillar.

'God bless you, Doctor. I'm really going to miss you.'

And she crossed the road, determinedly walking towards her future.

Also available in the Doctor Who *Monster Collection:*

PRISONER OF THE DALEKS
TREVOR BAXENDALE
ISBN 978 1 849 90755 2

The Daleks are advancing, their empire constantly expanding.
The battles rage on across countless solar systems – and the
Doctor finds himself stranded on board a starship near the
frontline with a group of ruthless bounty hunters. Earth
Command will pay these hunters for every Dalek they kill,
every eyestalk they bring back as proof.

With the Doctor's help, the bounty hunters achieve the
ultimate prize: a Dalek prisoner – intact, powerless, and
ready for interrogation. But with the Daleks, nothing is what
it seems, and no one is safe. Before long the tables will be
turned, and how will the Doctor survive when he becomes
a prisoner of the Daleks?

An adventure featuring the Tenth Doctor, as played by David Tennant

Also available in the Doctor Who *Monster Collection:*

Touched by an Angel
Jonathan Morris
ISBN 978 1 849 90756 9

'The past is like a foreign country. Nice to visit, but you
really wouldn't want to live there.'

In 2003, Rebecca Whitaker died in a road accident. Her
husband Mark is still grieving. He receives a battered
envelope, posted eight years earlier, containing a set of
instructions with a simple message: 'You can save her.'

As Mark is given the chance to save Rebecca, it's up to the
Doctor, Amy and Rory to save the whole world. Because this
time the Weeping Angels are using history itself as a weapon.

*An adventure featuring the Eleventh Doctor, as played by Matt Smith,
and his companions Amy and Rory*

Also available in the Doctor Who *Monster Collection:*

Illegal Alien
Mike Tucker and Robert Perry
ISBN 978 1 849 90757 6

The Blitz is at its height. As the Luftwaffe bomb London, Cody McBride, ex-pat American private eye, sees a sinister silver sphere crash-land. He glimpses something emerging from within. The military dismiss his account of events – the sphere must be a new German secret weapon that has malfunctioned in some way. What else could it be?

Arriving amid the chaos, the Doctor and Ace embark on a trail that brings them face to face with hidden Nazi agents, and encounter some very old enemies…

An adventure featuring the Seventh Doctor, as played by Sylvester McCoy, and his companion Ace

Also available in the Doctor Who *Monster Collection:*

SHAKEDOWN
TERRANCE DICKS
ISBN 978 1 849 90766 8

For thousands of years the Sontarans and the Rutans have
fought a brutal war across the galaxy. Now the Sontarans have
a secret plan to destroy the Rutan race – a secret plan
the Doctor is racing against time to uncover.

Only one Rutan spy knows the Sontarans' plan. As he is
chased through the galaxy in a desperate bid for his life,
he reaches the planet Sentarion – where Professor Bernice
Summerfield's research into the history of the Sontaran-Rutan
war is turning into an explosive reality…

An adventure featuring the Seventh Doctor,
as played by Sylvester McCoy

Also available in the Doctor Who *Monster Collection:*

STING OF THE ZYGONS
STEPHEN COLE
ISBN 978 1 849 90754 5

The TARDIS lands the Doctor and Martha in the Lake
District in 1909, where a small village has been terrorised
by a giant, scaly monster. The search is on for the elusive
'Beast of Westmorland', and explorers, naturalists and
hunters from across the country are descending on the
fells. King Edward VII himself is on his way to join the
search, with a knighthood for whoever finds the Beast.

But there is a more sinister presence at work in the Lakes
than a mere monster on the rampage, and the Doctor is
soon embroiled in the plans of an old and terrifying enemy.
And as the hunters become the hunted, a desperate battle of
wits begins – with the future of the entire world at stake…

*An adventure featuring the Tenth Doctor, as played by David Tennant,
and his companion Martha*

Also available in the Doctor Who *Monster Collection:*

CORPSE MARKER
CHRIS BOUCHER
ISBN 978 1 849 90759 0

The Doctor and Leela arrive on the planet Kaldor, where
they find a society dependent on benign and obedient
robots. But they have faced these robots before, on a huge
Sandminer in the Kaldor desert, and know they are not
always harmless servants…

The only other people who know the truth are the three
survivors from that Sandminer – and now they are being
picked off one by one. The twisted genius behind that
massacre is dead, but someone is developing a new, deadlier
breed of robots. This time, unless the Doctor and Leela can
stop them, they really will destroy the world…

*An adventure featuring the Fourth Doctor, as played by Tom Baker,
and his companion Leela*

Also available in the Doctor Who *Monster Collection:*

THE SANDS OF TIME
JUSTIN RICHARDS
ISBN 978 1 849 90767 5

The Doctor is in Victorian London with Nyssa and Tegan – a city shrouded in mystery. When Nyssa is kidnapped in the British Museum, the Doctor and Tegan have to unlock the answers to a series of ancient questions.

Their quest leads them across continents and time as an ancient Egyptian prophecy threatens future England. To save Nyssa, the Doctor must foil the plans of the mysterious Sadan Rassul. But as mummies stalk the night, an ancient terror stirs in its tomb.

An adventure featuring the Fifth Doctor, as played by Peter Davison, and his companions Nyssa and Tegan